A BODY ON THE HILL

A BODY ON THE HILL
A Mitch O'Reilly Mystery

Brad Shreve

BEESON
PRESS

ISBN: 978-0-578-70450-0

Published by Beeson Press

Edited by Dee Masters

Cover design by UmeWorks, LLC - *umeworks.com*

Visit *bradsheve.com*

For Eros,
who never ceases to be my inspiration.

Acknowledgements

Many thanks to the following for their
contributions to this book:
Denise Shiozawa, Dee Masters, Nuna Bosler,
Gary Hart, and J.Y. Olmos, author

A BODY ON THE HILL

One

The butler, who introduced himself as Paul, closed the front door and escorted me to the Mooney mansion's foyer, which would more accurately be defined as a lobby. We stopped next to a monumental gray statue of a smiling man, wearing a toga, lifting a woman in the air. She was wide-eyed and laughing. It was the only gleeful thing I'd seen in the complex.

Paul said, "Mr. Mooney is on the phone at the moment. He asked me to have you wait in the sitting room."

As we walked across the marble floor his slacks made a swishing sound. They were bunched at the ankles above his black loafers and hung a bit beneath his shoe. It seemed odd for a man who was flawlessly dressed in every other way.

The cushion on the gold neoclassical chaise in the sitting room was soft on my ass, but the straight hard back made it impossible to get comfortable. The curled arm dug into my side, but at least allowed me to lean some. Paul offered me a glass of water from the marble wet bar, which I accepted. He then excused himself. The sound of his shuffling pants cuff waned as he drifted down the hall.

The wisps of air as I turned the pages of a coffee table book were the only sounds that could be heard in the eerie silence of the cavernous mansion. It was titled *T.J. Mooney: A Legend in Films*. One full, stylized photo covered each page, illustrating his fifty-year career as a director and producer. I wondered what type of man would keep a book about themselves in their foyer. With little thought, the answer became obvious—a man like T.J. Mooney.

After twenty minutes I assumed I'd been forgotten. I stood to find Paul when a boisterous voice echoed from the grand hallway. "Have a seat, Mitch. You're late."

I sat, but rose again with my arm extended when he approached.

"I said to have a seat."

"Sorry for being late, Mr. Mooney," I said. "I'd hoped since you were on the phone that it wasn't an inconvenience."

"Everyone calls me T.J. I didn't say it was an inconvenience, but that doesn't make it acceptable," He tugged at the neck of his pine-colored turtleneck sweater. "I expect the people who work for me to be professional and dependable." The expensive sweater was designed to cling to a fit body, and only served to emphasize his belly.

I'd made a commitment to my PTSD support group that I would maintain my composure and refrain from pissing people off. It was apparent the upcoming conversation was not going to make it easy to keep that promise.

I said, "Again, my apologies, T.J., but I wasn't aware I work for you."

"That's why you're here and what we're going to discuss. I need to hire a private investigator, and I hear you're the man I need to speak with." He stepped up to the wet bar. "I see Paul gave you water. I'm having a gin and tonic. Would you like something stronger?"

"No, I'm good."

He gave me a quizzical look. "Are you an alcoholic?"

"Your reputation for being blunt is accurate. No, not an alcoholic. Cutting back is all."

"There's a difference between bluntness and matter-of-fact. Let's get straight to it." T.J. sat on a white, speckled wingback chair and placed his drink on a round, gilded side table. He huffed two times as he struggled to cross his knees. "I'm concerned about my son Austin, and I'm looking to hire you to follow him. When can you start?"

"Tailing people is my specialty. Tell me something about him. What are your concerns, and what do you want me to look for?"

T.J. sighed and shuffled in his chair. "I love my son. He's always been a good boy and a fine young man, but now I'm concerned about him. He even lives in some seedy squalor rather than here in this beautiful home. My goal is to learn more about him, his life, his friends, his work. I want to know as much as I can. I have concerns about him and the life he's chosen."

"Tell me more about the life he's chosen." I gulped down half of my water.

"He is pursuing a career in the business—an actor, for God's sake. I thought I taught him better than that. He's resourceful, self-confident, and intelligent. Reminds me of myself, and I respect that, but it does make me uneasy. He may be smart, but he's naïve, and I don't think he understands that bad decisions can follow him forever. Hollywood can be unforgiving."

"There's a lot of private investigators in this city. Why me?"

"I believe you know Warren Barone. You worked with him on a case recently."

I sat up straight on the lounge. "Yes, we have a brief history."

"He and I go way back. We're just acquaintances really, but his ex-partner and I, God rest his soul, worked together on several projects. I bumped into Warren at a show at the Mark Taper last week, and you came up during our discussion. He's living it up these days."

"He did just inherit a load of money, so that's no surprise, though it was my understanding he was leaving LA."

"I don't know about that, but he highly recommends you." T.J. pointed his finger at me. "He says you're the man for the job. He added that you're a smartass, but you also saved his life."

"He's right on both counts."

"While I'm hesitant hiring a man known for being mouthy, I do respect that Warren is still alive because of you."

"I'm surprised and honored he referred me. Tell me more about your son."

T.J. stood at the bar and made another drink. "Are you sure you wouldn't like something?"

I raised my water glass. "Nature's champagne is okay with me."

He sniffed and sat back down in his chair.

"My office can send you any details we have," he said. "You should know he uses Bouchard, his mother's last name."

"I'd like to hear more about Austin before we come to an agreement."

"I didn't expect you to want to know everything now. As I said, my assistant will send over plenty that will get you started, but for now, I can tell you he lives in Koreatown with a slew of roommates and has a good-for-nothing boyfriend."

I wondered why the son of one of the richest men in Hollywood would choose to live in an area of town far sketchier than what his dad could provide.

"Oh, and Austin is gay," T.J. continued. "He spends a great deal of time in West Hollywood. You would know that, of course."

"Of course. As all gay men do." He grimaced when he caught me rolling my eyes. "Where does he work?"

"I hear he landed a promising role, though this is new news. He's a lot like me, which gives me little doubt he'll become a huge success. That is where I think I've had the greatest influence—his drive and ability to become a master at what he does."

"I respect what you've made for yourself. *Jekyll* is one of my favorite movies."

"It was one of my earliest films, and I believe my greatest achievement so far. The critics loved it, but it did mediocre in sales. Too heady for the general populace is what the studio said."

"That's why I love it," I said. "No one else has gotten into the deep psychological turmoil of Dr. Jekyll and Mr. Hyde before."

"Or since. It was brilliant. A cult classic today, but it wasn't until six years later that I became a household name. Hollywood considered me a fool for thinking the public would see a dramatic film about lawn sports, but the studio heads stopped laughing when *Croquet Crackerjack* became one of the top grossing films in 1976."

"Yes, I'm familiar with it." I refrained from telling him I thought it was shit. "Sorry I got us off the rails. We were talking about Austin's work."

"I hope it's true he has this great gig because it would get him out of what he's doing now." T.J. shrugged and sighed. "He's a waiter of all things. How cliché is that for an actor? It's at some club on the Sunset Strip—a gem of some kind. Turquoise? Extremely popular, I understand. The *in* place, though we know that changes each week in this town."

"I think you mean Topaz, and yes, it's the hot spot now. LA's most beautiful people line down the street to get in. Typical thing for that neck of the woods. What are your expectations as far as time? I do have a store I run and other clients."

"Times are not important. In fact, I'd rather not lock you in that way. I'd prefer you view him in a variety of hours and days. Let's stick with number of hours in a week to allow you to follow his whereabouts at different times. As far as those other clients go—discard them." He waved a dismissive hand. "I'll make it worth your while."

"That's mighty generous. It won't be cheap."

"You don't believe that's an issue, do you? However, I'm no fool. I pay for quality service, but I won't be taken advantage of."

I crossed my arms. "Point taken."

The butler entered the sitting room and placed a tray on a center table. "My apologies for interrupting, gentlemen. It appears it will be a late dinner for both of you, so I brought something to tide you over."

T.J. looked at the mix of sliced fresh vegetables and yogurt drinks. "My God, I hate this stuff, Paul."

"I'm aware of that, sir. As you know, you insisted the staff provide you with healthier foods, and we are to ignore your protests."

"It doesn't mean I like it. Not one damn bit."

Paul nodded to each of us, shuffled through the foyer and down the hall with the sound of his overlong pant cuffs brushing the floor. T.J. stood and raised a finger. "One moment, Mitch."

When he entered the hall, T.J. called Paul's name. Although loud, I couldn't hear most of the conversation, but enough to understand Paul was in trouble.

"It's unacceptable," T.J. grumbled. A few seconds later, I heard, "As much as I like you, there—" *Indiscernible grumbling.* "I expect no less from you—" *More fuzzy words.* "Change your pants immediately and—" *Final bit of grumbling.*

T.J. came back, grabbed a carrot, and dropped in his chair. He eyed the vegetable and tossed it back on the tray. "Where were we?"

I pointed down the hall where he had hammered Paul. "You have high expectations, don't you?" Leaving out I thought he was an asshole.

He glared across the glass as he sipped his yogurt drink. "I didn't get where I am today by tolerating substandard performance. I hope you remember that, Mitch."

"Crystal clear." I reached to grab a baby tomato, but accidentally pinched a piece of kale. T.J.'s eyes were glued on my every move. I had no choice but to take the foul stuff and put it in my mouth.

"I think that's enough talk for now. My office will have all the information you need, as well as our cost proposal, delivered to your store in the morning. When will you be able to start?"

"Assuming we seal our agreement in the morning, I should be able to start tomorrow night."

"That would please me very much. I find you more agreeable than Warren Barone implied."

"We're just getting started, but I am trying to behave."

Two

When I pulled up to my store, Eye Spy Supplies, Frank was sleeping in my vestibule as he does every night. Until the previous week, he had a girlfriend who he had met at a bus stop, but she was gone one morning after deciding the weather would be better in San Diego. Being despondent, more than usual, he had two empty bottles of cheap wine lying by his head.

I gave him a shake. "Good morning, Frank. It's time for me to open the store."

It took a little more prodding before I could get him to stir.

"Huh," he said. "Is it 10:00 already?"

"Afraid so, my friend. Time to head out, so I can open up."

Frank sat up on his sleeping bag, placed his hands on his raised knees and sighed. "I sure do miss her."

"I know, and I'm sorry."

"Sure, you're sorry. I've been a lonely man since." He stood, pulled his greasy army jacket to stretch out the wrinkles, and scratched his head. "What was her name?"

"You only ever called her 'she' or 'her.'"

"Well, whatever it is, I'm a lonely man again."

Frank had served in the Iraq War around 2003, ten years before I fought in Afghanistan. I was able to piece together his age as around forty-five, though he looked at least fifteen years older. I gave him a bag of new socks I bought at Target. He nodded a thank you and took off down the street with his shopping cart.

Being a slow morning, I was washing the 1970s paneling on the wall behind my counters, when the bell on the door jingled, and my first customer of the day walked in. He was a stocky, broad-shouldered Asian man who stood about five and a half feet tall. He looked to be about fifty.

"I'm looking for a camera for my body," he said. "I need it to take videos."

"A body spy cam? Anywhere on your body you want to wear it?"

"I'm not sure." He stroked his dark, long mustache. "I didn't consider that."

I waved him to follow me as I walked to the middle of the glass display case where I keep my spy cams.

"There are cameras here in eyeglasses, mock cell phones, watches. What are you wanting to tape?"

His face went blank. Typical of customers who don't want to share their secrets. I had learned a lot about people in the two years since I opened the store. Before then I worked for Regency Investigative Services, the largest detective agency in California, but my only job was to shadow people usually suspected of cheating by jealous spouses. Following targets in my car and snapping pictures when interesting things happened was rarely interesting. I thought I knew people then, but running the store and talking face to face with all types was a far better education.

Mr. Spycam stood speechless, staring at the ceiling, and stroking his chin. His dark hair split in the middle and his sturdy frame beneath a high end, bright blue suit coat, made him look like a prohibition mobster.

I broke the silence. "I think the watches are great because they have a more realistic look and feel to them, especially since it appears you don't wear glasses. However, the glasses give you greater flexibility of taping if you plan to move around. With the watch, sometimes people wonder why you're standing or walking with your wrist in the air."

I chuckled, while he stayed sober.

"I want to tape things to my side while I'm standing. Do you have anything that looks to the side?"

I reached into the glass case and pulled out fake earbuds. "These sound like what you're looking for. You plug the end of the cable in your phone and pop these earbuds where they belong. The camera points straight out. It's not a real working earbud, but that's the beauty of it because you can wear the camera in either ear depending on which direction you want to tape."

"May I put them on?"

"Sure." I took the buds out of the box and put them in his hand. I figured I could wash them off with a little alcohol if he didn't buy them. He stuck them in his ears and walked to a side wall, faced it, and stared. A buddy of mine Harold entered, sporting a huge grin. He gave me a firm handshake.

"Good morning, Mitchell."

"Yeah, yeah," I grumbled, "You know I hate being called Mitchell."

Harold said, "There you go with that attitude."

I raised a hand to him. "Hang on while I help this guy. Go take a seat in the backroom if you want."

Harold left the storefront while Mr. Spycam continued facing the wall. He cocked his head to one side, then cocked it to the other. Occasionally he'd step a few feet away, walk back to the wall and cock his head more.

"May I try the watch?" He asked. "I think it'll work better for what I need."

"What did you say you need them for?" I was making another attempt to satisfy my curiosity.

He ignored my question, dropped the earbuds on the counter, put on the watch, and walked back to within inches of the wall. He stood motionless, but from time to time he'd look at the watch and raise and lower it a bit. I had nearly given up figuring out what he was doing then noticed that most of the time he clasped his hands at his crotch. I scrutinized his moves as he would back away from the wall, step back up to it again, put his hands at his crotch, then would let one dangle and move it up and down. It dawned on me what his plans were, and I allowed his absurdity to continue for several minutes until he came back to the counter.

"I'll take this," he said. "How much did you say they cost?"

"I didn't say, and I'm not going to. You need to go."

"But I'd like to buy the watch."

"And I'm not selling it to you." I snatched the watch off the counter and threw it underneath in the case. "I don't give a damn about people's kinks or fetishes, but I have limits on what's acceptable."

He quivered and his eyes darted side to side. "What are you talking about?"

"What people do sexually is no business of mine as long as it's consensual. Secretly taping guys cocks while they're taking a piss is not consensual, you sick bastard."

"What makes you think I—"

"You plan to use those at urinals. Can you give me a better explanation why you would stare at a wall holding a camera like that?"

"Uh, um… um. I won't post them on the internet or anything."

I paused, smiled, and placed my hands on the countertop. "Oh, you're not? I'm sorry. I misunderstood. That's different."

"It is?"

"Hell, no it's not." I pointed to the door. "Turn your ass around and get the hell out of my store."

The man scurried across the floor, but I stopped him when he placed his hand on the knob.

"Hold it!" I yelled. His shoulders tensed as he looked back at me. "If I'm ever in a public bathroom and I see your face, I swear to God I'll—"

He was halfway across the parking lot before I could finish my sentence. I tossed the earbuds on to the back counter and fumed into the storeroom.

One corner of the back room makes up my office where Harold was sitting at my large, gray, steel, government surplus desk. He had maneuvered the mounds of paperwork enough to use the keyboard to surf the net. I picked a box off my battered turquoise couch, tossed it to the side, plopped down and put my feet up.

Harold spun the desk chair to look at me. "Did I hear you toss a customer out and lose a sale?"

"Not something you'll see very often. It takes a lot to make me turn down money."

"I'm impressed. It's good to know you have scruples." He nodded toward the door. "I noticed your landlord filled the potholes in the parking lot."

"Yeah, Jeff pours gravel in them about every six months. God forbid he actually use asphalt."

Harold waved a finger. "There's that attitude again. You'll have a smooth drive across them for the next few days at least."

"You may be my mentor, but you need to get over this shit about my attitude."

"Mentor? I'm your friend."

"And right now, not a very good one."

Harold Beavers and I met a few months earlier when I began attending a PTSD support group at the VA hospital, while my sister ran the store on Saturdays. He was an accountant, owned a ranch house in the valley, and had three kids, who he had custody of every other weekend. He was a good dad, but I sometimes wondered why no one ever called Child Protective Services on him. With his shaggy uncombed red hair, scraggly beard, and ratty stained jersey shirts, he looked like a killer on the run. We were from different worlds, but he took me under his wing at my first meeting, and we'd been friends ever since.

He leaned forward and slapped his hands on his knees. "How about we stick with baby steps? We'll stay out of your head and not work on improving your attitude for now. Let's focus on curbing your tendency to piss people off."

"Fuck off." I sat upright. "Last night I talked to T.J. Mooney, right in his very own home without riling him once, and he's a major asshole."

"T.J. Mooney? As in the producer, T.J. Mooney?"

"Yep, he's the one. You can believe everything you've ever read about him. Arrogant bastard with an ego that stretches from here to Anaheim." I gave a polishing motion with my fingernails across my shirt. "The movie mogul himself has hired me for a job. A good paying one, too."

"It's good you're a hardworking man," Harold replied. "Malcolm Gladwell once said, 'If you work hard enough and assert yourself, and use your mind and imagination, you can shape the world to your desires.'"

"If you knew my desires, you wouldn't want me to shape the world that way." I shuffled to the coffee pot and put in a filter. "Who's Malcolm Gladman?"

"It's Gladwell. Not Gladman. He's a journalist, a writer. Typically, psychology and social issues stuff. He's a fascinating man."

"I'll take your word for it."

"I believe Gladwell is Canadian. I'm not sure, though. I suppose it doesn't matter."

I mumbled, "No. Please find out. I must know."

Ignoring his glare, I continued, "What brings you over?"

He said, "See, you say you did great with T.J. Mooney, but now you're coming at me with that smart-ass attitude again. We have a lot of work to do. Anyway, I'm so proud. Imagine you sat in a room with a man like that, and he hired you, anyway." He laughed.

I tossed a throw pillow, which flew past his head, bounced off the wall and landed on top of the desk, spilling a pile of papers to the floor.

"Leave them there," I said. "That happens all the time. I'll clean it up later."

Harold sneered as he looked around the room, eyeing the scattered boxes, cleaning supplies on the floor, and the overflowing trash bins. "You know, your office here reflects you. Maybe straightening this room can be a step in straightening your life."

"Stick to accounting. You're a lousy psychiatrist."

"How are the dreams going?"

"Nothing's changed. I'm still having the nightmares as much as I used to, but the group has helped. I'm learning to accept they're a given. What I'm struggling with now are old memories coming to the surface during the day, and it impacts what I'm doing. I'm having flashbacks."

"Memories of Jackson?"

Jackson was my fiancé, killed by sniper fire while stationed together during the war in Afghanistan in 2013. It'd been five years since, but he rarely left my mind. Each night I had different dreams of the horrific things I experienced there, and no matter what I dreamed about, Jackson would show up in them one way or another. The situations were different, but I always woke in terror after seeing him die a violent death. A death that occurred while I was in the hospital and was not there to watch.

"No, Jackson and I were together during my second tour. These memories are from when my outfit was ambushed during my first tour in 2010."

"Repressed memories that you want to talk about?"

"No, not repressed. They've been there, but I bury them whenever they surface. It's getting harder now, but I don't want to talk about it."

"Fair enough." He stood, scooped up some papers off the floor and put them on the desk. "I have two tickets to the Dodgers game Thursday night. Interested?"

While in college, I had become a major Dodgers' fan and went to as many games as possible on my meager budget. I'd lost interest during and after the war, but Harold was a bigger fan than I was. Our friendship sparked my interest in the game and the team again.

"Very interested in going," I said, "but I have to pass. I've got plans."

"A date with the boyfriend?"

"We've only been dating three months. Trent is not a boyfriend. We're having dinner with my sister, Josie, to meet her new boyfriend."

"How long have they been dating?"

"About three months."

"She started dating him at the same time you started dating Trent, and they're boyfriend and girlfriend, but Trent—"

"We're both busy at work. We hardly see each other these days."

"That's a shame," he said. "but 'If you make friends with yourself, you will never be alone.'"

"Oh, dear God." I face palmed. "Who said that?"

"A man named Maxwell Maltz. Look him up."

"You betcha. I'll get right on it."

I got off the couch and walked to the storefront. "What are you doing here at this time of day anyway?"

"I've got one client that works on this side of town. I'm meeting him for lunch." He looked at his watch. "Speaking of which, I need to go." I followed him out and stood on the sidewalk while he walked to his car. "Don't forget," he said before climbing in. "Keep talking nice."

I went back in and made a bowl of ramen. I ate while standing at the cash register, eyeing the dreary shopping plaza with disdain, resenting being stuck there another day. I worked for Regency Investigative Services long enough to earn my PI license but left detective work and opened the store instead. My plan failed miserably. I didn't make enough from the store to stop being a private investigator, and I didn't make enough as an investigator to close the store. Having no choice but to keep snooping on the side, I wound up running two low-income business operations and allowed little free time for myself.

The strip mall where I opened Eye Spy Supplies, was over forty years old and looked like they hadn't laid a paint brush or fixed a crack since. There were seven storefronts, but the only businesses open were my place, The Master Lock and Key Shop, and Evelyn's Alterations. As if things weren't slow enough in the plaza, Evelyn only worked four hours a day.

The plaza sat on Carvajal Street, a quarter mile from Hollywood Forever Cemetery, and two blocks off Santa Monica Boulevard. It was the same Boulevard that ran through West Hollywood, Beverly Hills and straight out near the beach in Santa Monica, but those cities were a far cry from my end of town. Not far from Paramount Studios, the neighborhood had grown tired, and rough, with some respectable pockets sprinkled here and there. My place was on one of the rougher blocks. Recent growth in the area meant I'd eventually be priced off the street. I hoped that would happen either after I closed the store, or when I'd be bringing in a steady enough income to move.

I was scarfing some ramen noodles when a package was delivered by courier from T.J. Mooney's assistant. I ruffled through the contents and spread them across a counter. The first thing I looked at was the fee proposal, and before I bothered eyeing the rest, I emailed that I accepted the job. As for the information, there wasn't much except Austin Bouchard's home address, his phone number, and that he worked at Topaz, which I already knew. He had a boyfriend named Hector, but there was no last name. Austin was twenty-three, grew up mostly in Palm Springs and excelled in high school and college. There were no arrest records of any kind. I had expected more, then the obvious occurred to me. That's why T.J. hired me. He wanted to know more.

Besides some home photos, there was a studio head shot of Austin. His light toned face, fresh and rectangular, rounded and softened at his chin. He had bluish-green eyes and light golden-brown hair that was stylishly shaggy in the front and then swept back. His broad smile was confident, yet tight-lipped, as if he was holding back a laugh. In the days of early television, Austin would have been typecast as the clean-cut wholesome boy next door that any mother would love.

After phoning to put some cases on hold from my regular clients, I started digging online. There was little information about him other than being T.J.'s son. The only thing scandalous I found were reports of him being caught kissing a conservative congressman's son on the hill near the Hollywood Sign. From the entertainment rags to the New York Times, it was a hot news item for about three days in 2013.

I prepared to start my new case that night. I needed to know where to begin, so I called the club where my target worked to see if he'd be there.

"Hello, Topaz," An enthusiastic woman answered the phone. "How may I help you?"

"Hi," I replied. "Is Austin Bouchard working tonight?"

"I'm sorry, but we're not allowed to give work schedules. Anything else I can help you with?"

"No." I hung up. It was the expected response. For employee's safety, it's standard policy at most businesses to not give out schedules. You never know if they have a crazy spouse or boyfriend trying to track them down. But worth a try.

I killed thirty minutes cleaning the microwave in my office before calling the club again.

"Hello, this is Topaz," a different, not as enthusiastic, woman answered. "What can I help you with?"

"Hi," I said. "This is Zane. I need to talk to Austin. Can you put him on?"

"Austin's not here."

"Damn. I'm supposed to pick him up when he gets off tonight, but he didn't tell me when. Do you know?"

"You should probably call Austin," she said with a sarcastic tone. "He ain't working tonight."

"Thanks." I hung up.

I didn't know where to find him, but I knew where not to begin.

Three

After closing shop, I jumped right on the Mooney case. With Austin Bouchard's clean-cut history, I was curious what concerned T.J. Mooney enough for him to hire me. My gut told me there was more to the story, but it being my first night following him, I didn't give it much thought. My focus was to find him and learn his routine. That is what I was hired to do, and not bother with the whys.

With the information packet T.J.'s assistant sent me, I found Austin's tired apartment building where he lived with two roommates in Koreatown, the most densely populated district in the city. While initially, mostly Koreans occupied the area because of segregation laws in the 1930s, it was small until an immigration boom in the '60s and '70s. The district remained the hub of the Korean community, but over time became one-half Latino and only one-third Korean. As for the rest, many of them were millennials of various ethnicities, who sought cheap housing in areas not as depressed as nearby MacArthur Park.

About a mile from Koreatown's main hub of shopping, restaurants and karaoke bars, the apartment flanked San Marino Street. I found a white Toyota Corolla with

Austin's license plate number near the intersection of
Westmoreland Avenue. The streets were lined with parked
cars, leaving me no choice other than to abandon my
vehicle three blocks away. My parking spot was far beyond
the range of the Hearken-Royale listening device I had
brought. Not that it'd help anyway without knowing where
to focus on Austin. There was no need to carry it with me
when I walked to his building. It's hard to remain
inconspicuous while holding a gun like device with a large
cone at the end.

I was able to use my least complicated locksmith tools
to get through the rickety front door of the building to find
Austin and friend's mailbox which said they lived in
apartment 302. A quick, risky run up the staircase led me to
their door, so I knew where their place was located. I
hustled back down the stairs and across the street before
they could spot me. I hung outside the building, trying not
to look like a stalker. I was a stalker, but a paid one.

The old, four-story building was red brick except for the
front of the first floor which was clad with a molded
concrete finish. A barber shop occupied the left side of the
nondescript front entrance. On the other side a store was
identified by a sign with Korean lettering. The best I could
tell, it was some kind of thrift shop. Lights were on in

Austin's apartment, two floors above the barber shop. It had three front facing windows covered with blinds that hung crooked. There was no movement inside. Just three lit windows staring into the night.

Staying in the car during surveillance was always preferable to trying to look inconspicuous in public places. There wasn't much to make myself look busy. There were no businesses on that block except for the two in the apartment building, and they were closed. Since the best way to stay inconspicuous is to be conspicuous, I lit a cigarette, leaned against a fence, and stared at my cell phone. At times it seemed as if the cigarette smoker portrayal was the most difficult part of my job. I detest the damn things.

After twenty minutes, I needed a break from the smokes, so I took a stroll from the corner at Westmoreland Street a block down and back again. My traipsing ended when two men climbed out one of the apartment's windows onto the fire escape, which hung in the center of the building directly above the entrance. Despite the distance and the shadows, I recognized Austin from his photographs. He was about six feet tall, appeared fit, yet not overly developed. The friend with him had a shorter, stocky, muscular build and had bleached blond surfer-boy hair that held a windblown look. They tossed a couple of pillows to sit on and popped some beers.

I crossed the street and sat on the front steps directly below them. Again, no master disguises are all that necessary. I wore an LA Dodgers' hat and kept my head down and pretended to text. It doesn't get more innocuous than that. Listening to them above, I learned Surfer-boy was a roommate and friend named Cody. Their other roommate, Devin, stayed inside to watch a movie.

The two dished and laughed about the latest episode of *Queer Eye*. The conversation strayed to the hotness level of the actors in the Marvel Avenger's movies. Chris Hemsworth and Chris Evans tied with ten points each but were rated high for different reasons that I couldn't make out.

"Wasn't Chadwick Boseman perfect as Black Panther?" Austin asked.

"Oh my God!" Cody replied. "The movie was awesome except he had too much clothing on. The shirtless scenes were way too short."

Austin snickered. "Have you seen him on any of the talk shows? He's totally different. His hair is longer, spiked a bit. He has bright eyes and the goofiest smile that's so damn cute."

"Really? He has a goofy smile? Did he ever smile in the movie?"

"I don't know, but he's so hot. Not the same hot as his portrayal of the fierce Panther, but still hot. It's like you could have a three-way with just you and his split personas."

The two men continued to gossip and laugh, and I had to force myself to listen as my interest was fading until I heard Judy Garland's name come up. Being thirty years old, men my age rarely talked about her. It was surprising to hear her discussed by two guys seven years younger than me. A minute into their discussion I understood.

"What do you mean?" Austin exclaimed. "How can you be an actor and not know Judy Garland?"

"No, you idiot." Cody replied. "I know who the hell she is, but I don't get what it is with these old queens and her. Why is a girl in a checkered dress singing in a barnyard such a big deal?"

Austin said, "That wasn't Judy in the barnyard. That was a part she played. I talked to Wally about her once. You know, the hairstylist. He says she was idolized because they admired how she overcame adversity, but that doesn't make sense. I'm sorry she had a rough life and all, but she nearly drank herself to death and died of a drug overdose."

"You hear the same thing about Whitney Houston. Her life was tragic, but she didn't come out on top."

"Neither of them had anything on—"

"Audrey Hepburn," Cody cut in. "Here we go again."

"Oh, come on. Audrey was beautiful, sophisticated, and chic. She is who we should all aspire to be. Before she died, she did all kinds of charitable work, stayed beautiful, and she didn't self-implode."

Cody said, "But did she overcome adversity? Wasn't she born of aristocracy?"

"God, no! Well, not really. Yes, her parents were noble, but her father deserted her in the 1930s, and Word War II devastated her and her mom. They survived by eating tulip bulbs. People think she was a duchess or something because she had such grace. Now that's overcoming adversity, my friend."

Austin continued idolizing Hepburn until 8:15 p.m. when he and Cody agreed it was time to head out and climbed back in the window. They didn't say where they were going; I sprinted to my car and pulled into a red zone near Westmoreland Avenue. It was a short wait before they came out. Austin looked sharp in jeans and a gray, collarless bomber jacket covering a white t-shirt. Cody wore a more casual outfit of pink chino pants and a pastel green shirt with *I'm Shy* in bold letters. I grabbed my camera and zoomed in on the smaller words below that completed the sentence, *but I have a big dick.*

White cars, like Austin's, are easy to lose. I purposely bought a silver Honda Accord because of its characterless appearance, but it was still important not to get too close. Tailing people is not like in the movies. If you stay only a car length behind your target, they'll figure out they're being followed. Fortunately, he turned onto Olympic Boulevard, which was busy enough to stay under cover, but not so busy I'd lose them.

There was no challenge keeping up with the two men. Austin never went over the speed limit, didn't weave through traffic, and used his blinker well in advance when he changed lanes. I had a good idea we were heading to West Hollywood - WeHo. He confirmed my hunch when we turned onto San Vicente Boulevard.

It was Tuesday, and even on weekdays the nightlife didn't begin until after 10:00 p.m., which made it easy for us to find street parking. I pulled in a half block behind them. They walked to the front of The Abbey Food & Bar, or what those in the know refer to simply as The Abbey.

Rated by social sites as the best gay bar in the United States, it had been one of WeHo's prime spots to see and be seen for almost thirty years. It was a regular hangout of mine while I was in college. Being there brought back a lot of good memories of a time that seemed so long ago.

A man, who appeared to be about their age, came out and waved them inside. About six-six, he stood above the other two, and was significantly thinner. Stylishly unkempt, black hair parted in the middle topped his oval face. Despite the several days of scruff, he had a seductive look to him.

The founders of the hot spot, renovated an old stone masonry, added stained glass and some pews, and gave The Abbey a WeHo style spiritual experience. Some tables were inside, but most patrons chose the extensive outdoor dining patio for maximum exposure. I was in West Hollywood Park, next door, and stepped out to the curb in time to see the three men seated at a coveted spot near the sidewalk. It allowed them to check out the passersby and gave me a clear shot of their goings on.

Like in Koreatown, I was left exposed and in need to keep undercover, so I grabbed some garbage bags that I keep on hand in the trunk of my car and wrapped a couple over myself. I wore a grubby John Deere hat and sat crossed legged on the parking lot across the street from the bar. It's hard for me to stay humble, so it's my least favorite disguise. After being a private eye for four years, I should have been used to the feeling, but I could feel myself blush whenever some good Samaritan would hand me a buck or two.

As was typical, what should have been a thirty to forty-minute meal lasted well over ninety minutes. The three of them were regularly interrupted with the socialization that was a normal part of The Abbey dining experience. Austin could only get a few bites in between each new well-wisher offering broad smiles, and firm embraces and laughs. Cody and the tall one had their fair share of attention, but Austin was like a magnet to every guy, and girl, passing by. It appeared everyone in Austin's circle was Hollywood gorgeous.

Once again, boredom set in until Cody stretched out his arms and knocked a tray out of a server's hands. I heard the sound of them hitting the patio until I was no longer in WeHo. I had been transported to Afghanistan. I was firing rounds with a small cluster of local women behind me, as I tried to get them out of harm's way. I screamed when a bullet struck one's head. Despite opening my eyes and finding I was still in the USA, my screaming continued,

much to the discomfort of those passing by. I drifted from a
feeling of not being a part of the world and back in
Afghanistan over and over again until I got my head
straight. My body still trembled. My head hurt, my stomach
twirled, and my hands shook violently. I needed something
to drink. A bottle of water would do, but there were no
convenience stores in the area, and the only close options to
grab a bite to eat were the two restaurants directly behind
me. I could risk losing Austin by going to either.

I shed the plastic bags and tucked the hat in a bush. I
planned to recover it later. I had no choice but to make a
risky, yet strategic move. I waited until Austin and his
friends were served another round of beers, then charged to
The Abbey, and squeezed my way in to order a drink to go.

I was placing my order when a man next to me, who was
giggling hysterically, bumped me off my feet. I stumbled
backwards and into the arms of Austin Bouchard.

"Be careful, honey," he said with a toothy grin while
looking down at me.

Having never gotten myself in such a spot, I was unsure
what to say. I braced a hand on Austin's shoulder and
pulled myself upright. While I tugged on my polo to
straighten it out, surfer boy Cody came forward and
adjusted my collar.

Austin cocked his head and smiled. "At risk of sounding like a come on, I don't think we've met before." He held out his hand. "I'm Austin."

"Hi," I stuttered. Not wanting to say my name was Mitch, I had to come up with something off the top of my head. "I'm Mitchell."

I felt like a fool.

"This is Cody," he gestured to the windswept hottie panting at me like a puppy.

"And, he's Zach." The tall one gave a thin smile, squinted his olive-green eyes, and gave a firm grasp when we shook hands. Less casual than his friends, he wore black slacks and a white button-down shirt with the sleeves rolled up to his elbows.

Cody gently placed a hand on my back. "Where you from, Mitchell?"

"Not near here. I don't get to WeHo as much as I used to."

"We're going dancing at Euphoria," Cody said while linking his arm with mine. "Why don't you join us?"

Zach looked down and shook his head, while Austin chuckled at Cody's lack of inhibition.

"I'd love to, but I'm meeting up with someone soon. I'm sure it's my loss."

"No," Cody said. "I believe it's mine."

"Never mind him," Austin interjected. "Cody can't resist a pretty face."

"I don't get called pretty much."

"Pretty is not the right word," Zach spoke for the first time in a monotone voice. "I'd definitely say ruggedly handsome, though. More Lands' End than J. Crew."

"Thanks, guys," I backed off, squeezing through the crowd to the exit. "It was great meeting you."

Once on the sidewalk, I took a few breaths and debated whether to continue to follow or call it a night. Not known for making the best decisions, I stepped back to West Hollywood Park until they came out and headed toward WeHo's main strip, Santa Monica Boulevard. Austin and his friends crossed the Boulevard to the busier side of the street, while I tailed a few steps behind on the other. They were pulling out their ID's to show the doorman at the dance club when an unruly drunk started toward them.

"Fuck you, fucker!" he bellowed. "Fuck all of you."

All the foot traffic halted as the disheveled man swayed up the sidewalk. He was Latino with short, ragged black hair. His sweaty bangs clung to his forehead. Like most of the pedestrians, he was in his early twenties, but stood out because of his dirty jeans and ripped yellow t-shirt.

"I'm talking to you, you sonofabitch." Everyone looked around to figure out who he was referring to. I deduced his target when Cody and Zach spread their arms out and stood between Austin and the drunk.

When he reached the three, he swung his arms wildly in what looked like a pitiful attempt to hit Austin. The lush screamed when the doorman at the club reached from behind and put the guy in a choke hold, but the violence didn't end. The drunk man used the momentum of the hold to raise his legs and kick both his feet squarely into Zach's stomach. Zach fell forward to the sidewalk and his head hit the concrete.

At that point, the doorman spun the drunk around and body slammed him on to the pavement. There were whoops and hoots from the crowd, cheering the hero, while Cody and Austin helped Zach get to his feet.

With one arm pinned across the drunk's neck, the doorman waved his other one at the three of them, yelling for them to move on. Amid the chaos, I made a quick jaywalk across the street to get closer to the trio so as not to lose them.

Cody asked, "Do you guys want to go home?"

Zach, still clutching his belly, shook his head. Austin whined, "No. We need to find somewhere to chill. How about—"

"Mitch O'Reilly!" A man blurted, sticking his face only inches from mine.

I cocked my head to look over his shoulder, and in a near simultaneous motion, he moved his head in my way. "You remember me, don't you?"

The guy stood my height, had a bald head and a long brown beard to the middle of his chest. He was a muscle bear, and if the circumstances were different, he would have had my full attention.

"Yeah, sure," I said as I stepped aside trying to keep my eyes on the trio moving through the crowd. "We'll get together and talk soon."

I stepped forward, and he grabbed my arm. "You little shit." He grinned. "You don't remember me, do you? I'm Dave. We met on studs4studs.com last year and hooked up a couple of times." I tried to pull away, and he grabbed my arm tighter and pulled me back. "My place is right around the corner. Have time for some fun?"

"Look, Dean—"

"It's Dave."

"Yeah, yeah. I remember you Dave. I'm sure it'd be a good time, but I can't."

"You seeing someone?"

I lost sight of Austin and friends in the crowd. I tried to whip around Dave again only to have him step right into me. "Is he your boyfriend?"

"No, not a boyfriend," I pushed him aside and sped past yelling behind, "Just someone I'm seeing."

Once I broke free of burly Dave, I hustled to the spot where I had last seen the three, but they were gone. I paced up and down the street for twenty minutes, focusing my attention on the quieter bars, but the guys were nowhere in sight. Frustration consumed me until I ran the amount of time worked through my head. I'd had Austin in sight for well over three hours and had a lot of notes to make. That seemed a good start for the first night.

Feeling famished, I pulled into a Taco Bell drive-thru, on the way to my home in Silver Lake. While waiting behind an excessive line of cars, I played the evening over in my mind, noting that other than the brief fight, it was uneventful. I was going to have to look deeper into who the drunk was, though.

I was pleased that this well-paid case looked like it would be a piece of cake.

Four

Closing Eye Spy Supplies early was a rare event. Financially, I couldn't risk the loss of a single sale, but feeling cocky with the impending check I'd receive from T.J. Mooney, I gave myself a break for a day. The previous evening, I tailed Austin Bouchard for the second time. There wasn't much to it since he only left his apartment twice after his WeHo excursion with friends. Tuesday night he had a jovial dinner with a friend I hadn't seen before. Wednesday, he went grocery shopping. Thursday night would be the third night in a row, but I had dinner plans beforehand, which I scheduled early to give myself time for the investigation. I pulled down the store's security gate and locked the door at 5:00 p.m., an hour earlier than my posted closing time.

While Jewish enclaves had spread throughout LA, especially to the San Fernando Valley, the Fairfax district south of West Hollywood was still considered the hub of the Jewish Community. The unassuming Fairfax Avenue shopping district, popular for its kosher restaurants and delis, was also home to the Olexi Greek Restaurant, known for its outstanding food and entertainment since 1949. Contrary to the building's drab exterior was the inviting entrance with double cobalt doors edged with intricate, old world gold molding.

Upon seeing me, the restaurant's owner threw her arms in the air and exclaimed, "Kalós órises." For a petite woman who was near seventy, she had quite the hold when she embraced and nearly forced the air out of my lungs.

"Kalispér. Ti kánis?"

"Sorry, Aunt Ada," I shrugged. "I'm still learning."

"I asked how you are, but don't you mind." She flit the back of her hand off my chest. "You look good as always. Follow me. Trent's been waiting for you."

Trent Nakos was Ada's nephew who I met when his attorney hired me for an investigation. He had managed a bathhouse at the time, and we'd been dating since the case had closed over three months prior. Even after several months he captivated me each time I saw him. His broad smile rarely left his round face, and his amber eyes opened wide and glimmered when he saw me approach the booth where he sat. He stood and wrapped his powerful olive-skinned arms around me.

"I've missed you." He stepped back and held a hand on each of my shoulders. "It's been over two weeks, I think."

"It's been awhile." After glancing around the room to ensure we weren't the center of attention, I gave a quick peck on his lips before sliding into the booth. His new beard matched the color of his spiky auburn hair. "Your beard's looking good. I like it."

"It's coming in better than I thought," he said as he stroked it. "As long as I keep it trimmed. I like the scruff you've grown out. Your longer hair, too."

"Just a little longer. I always kept the buzz cut because I've been worried that as stark black as my hair is, that the added stubble would make my pale Irish skin look bright white."

"Nah, you're as sexy as ever."

Despite Trent's attempts at making his aunt paint the restaurant, the walls, the booths, the tablecloths, and napkins were all the same, but different shades of blue, they had been for decades. Even each of the belly dancers in the center of the room wore costumes in different shades of blue.

"How'd you finagle getting off on a Thursday night? Isn't this your regular shift?"

"Business doesn't pick up here until 7:00 or 7:30. Slave-driver Aunt Ada has taken my shackles off long enough to allow me to spend an hour or so with you."

"I heard that," Ada said, laughing as she passed. "My sweet loving nephew is so ungrateful."

I leaned forward so Ada wouldn't hear if she walked back. "Have things gotten any better? You haven't been happy since you've been working here."

"I feel bad when we talk about it because she was a big help by getting me out of the old job, but I made it clear that this wasn't a full-time gig. I stressed over and over that my focus was on my writing, and this job was for bare necessities only. She swore she understood, but it's obvious to me, and the rest of the staff, that she's trying to groom me to run the place. Just because I'm the last in line in the family shouldn't obligate me to inherit the restaurant. Being a part time supervisor is hard enough."

Trent was a struggling science fiction writer. Though several of his short stories had been published in anthologies, he had no luck getting a book deal. Paying taxes and upkeep on his parents' house that he inherited made his financial situation almost as shaky as mine. Ever the optimist, he considered any job a part time gig to allow him to pursue his writing career.

"I wish I had advice about Ada, but she's as bullheaded as they come. You're looking damn good, though."

And he did. As usual, he wore a shirt at least one size too small so that it clung to his body, emphasizing every contour. His pecs, which were pumped in his normal state, were looking explosive.

Trent said, "Since I've started working out with your sister, I've been bulking up a lot more. I'm trying to hit that sweet spot just before the overly bodybuilder level. Right now, I think I'm leaning too much on the big side."

"You're looking mega buff, but who's complaining. I knew you helped Josie at the gym, but I didn't know it was a regular thing."

"Oh yeah, we get together at least three times a week."

Ada interrupted, "Oh my, Trent you need to talk with the staff later. You two have been waiting too long." She set an ouzo in front of each of us. "Enjoy these while you wait for Josie to come."

She put her hand on Trent's shoulder, gave me a smile, then scurried off to greet customers who came in.

"I'm happy with how things are going with you," Trent said. "You seem much happier. I think the group therapy is helping. Have they put you on any medication?"

"The last time we talked I said I was only thinking about meds. I told the doctor no. I don't see how chemicals swirling in my brain can help me get my head together."

He reached over and took my hands in his. "I'd like us to get together this week. I'm not working Sunday or

Monday, and since your store is closed those days, I was
thinking we could get away."

I said, "We'll see, but I have a new case that may take a
lot of my time." I leaned into whisper. "Don't tell anyone—
"

"I never do."

I continued, "T.J. Mooney just hired me to work a case
for him."

"The T.J. Mooney?"

"That's the one. With that starting, I can't make any
firm commitments, but we should be able to have lunch or
something." He bit his lower lip and looked away. "Look,
Trent. I'm sorry I've been busy. With work, the meetings
and spending time with Harold, I don't have much time on
my hands. Not enough to give you the time you deserve."

"You've been spending more time with Harold than
me." He bowed his head. "I think that's a good thing,
though. I know he's helping with your PTSD. You're
quieter these days and seem more balanced. How are you
really feeling?"

"I'm okay. Just working through some shit."

"I hear from you so little; is everything okay between
us?"

"Of course, I don't know why you—"

"Trent!" My twin sister Josie's' voice squealed from behind. Before Trent had a chance to scoot out from the booth, she leaned down, hugged him, and gave a peck on his cheek.

She said, "Hi, Lil' Bro," and leaned and gave me the best hug possible from across a table.

Trent laughed. "It's fun seeing you at night. We don't get out for dinner much."

Standing quietly, next to Josie, stood a man I presumed was her new boyfriend. He wore a dark suit jacket and slacks, white shirt, and a red tie. Behind his black rimmed eyeglasses, his pupils darted at me, then to Trent and then away. He went through that process several times.

"Guys, I'm sure you've guessed this is Stu," Josie said with a hand flat against his chest. "I'm excited you all finally get to meet."

Before Stu could speak, she jumped into the booth next to Trent and scooted her butt to get him to slide down. Grabbing his hand, she pulled Stu next to her.

I said, "You're looking great, Josie. Trent, your training has done her good."

She gave one of her rare giggles. "I know, thanks. I was getting so big, and then your man entered my life and look at me now. I never would have believed anyone could make training so fun. We laugh the whole time and get dirty looks from all over the gym."

My twin sister, older by only a few minutes, did look beautiful. She took more after our Mexican mother and had flawless light bronze skin.

"I may be a good influence," Trent said. "But she's really bad. She has us going out to breakfast almost every morning. I'm lucky I'm not as big as a house." He rubbed his hard stomach.

There was a lull in the conversation, which Stu took the opportunity to seize. "I'm happy to meet you gentlemen." He gave Trent and me a limp-wristed shake.

"I was beginning to think you were a figment of Josie's imagination," I said. "Where have you been hiding?"

Stu chuckled. "It's not her fault" He wrapped an arm around her and awkwardly squeezed her. "Since taking this new job, I'm working an incredible number of hours, plus I live down in Torrance, so when I get free time, it's a good jaunt up this way. It took me over an hour to get here just now. You always hear about LA traffic, but until I arrived, I never dreamed it could be as bad as it is. We complained about our commute time in Baltimore, but it was like a step across the street compared to here."

Josie said, "He travels a lot too, which I don't like at all."

Josie and Stu looked at each other and gave exaggerated frowns.

Trent asked, "What brought you to LA?"

"He got a great promotion," Josie interjected. "He's an efficiency manager for Terra Disposal Services."

Stu scooted upright and clasped his hands on the table. "Terra is one of the fastest growing waste management companies in the nation. That's why I took the chance moving here on what I hope will be an opportunity for growth."

He looked at our hollow stares and chuckled. "Oh, I see it in your faces. How dull can you get, right?" He paused for a response that he did not get. "It's far more interesting than you may think. I mean, finding the means to increase the speed of curbside pickup by three seconds per household hardly seems like much of an accomplishment, but when I crunch those numbers and see the grand total, I've saved the company annually, well..." He smacked his fist on the table, "...it's exhilarating."

I nodded my head. "It certainly sounds more fun than one human could possibly stand." My sister glared.

A waiter came and gave a fresh round of ouzo for everyone and put appetizers on our table. We had spanakopita and baked feta.

"Are you ordering dinner?" Our waiter said. "Or, has Ada planned your meal"

Trent laughed. "When was the last time Ada ever let us order anything on our own?"

The waiter smiled and walked back to the kitchen.

I said, "Other than the traffic, Stu, are you getting a feel for the land?"

He nodded. "I have. I've always found Los Angeles fascinating. It's far more beautiful and cleaner than I expected. Have you seen pictures of the smog in the 1950s? You could cut it with a knife. There were only two million people then and now it's grown to eight million. Despite that, some days are crystal clear."

"I've seen the old photos," I said. "But I didn't know it had grown that much."

"Yes, California is leading the country in clean air. Did you know that twelve percent of the U.S. population lives in this state, yet it emits only 6.9% of the country's greenhouse gases?"

I gave a shit eating grin, "That's amazing. I didn't know that."

"Now I think you're mocking me. I'm used to that. If I had a dollar for every time someone called me a boring nerd, I'd have a mean daily income of $5.64 with a standard deviation of $1.25."

Trent howled.

Stu looked smug and smiled. "It's good to see that someone gets the joke. Many times, that goes right over people's heads."

Trent stalled, "That was really a joke? I thought you were being funny by pretending it was funny."

"Yes, it's a joke. I heard it at the last Doctor Who convention."

"Doctor Who?" Trent straightened up and beamed. "Now you're speaking my language. How long have you been a Doctor Who fan?"

"As long as I can remember. I was addicted from the first episode I saw."

"Which was that?"

"'Terror of the Vervoids' with Colin Baker. The best Doctor Who, of course."

"Colin Baker? No one thinks Colin Baker was the best, and definitely not 'Terror of the Vervoids.'"

Stu became defensive. "I didn't say 'Terror of the Vervoids' was the best, though I think it doesn't deserve the derision it receives. Colin Baker is grossly underrated. I presume you think David Tennant was best."

"Yes. He gets a lot of credit and is regularly rated as the best because he was the best."

Stu put a hand to his mouth and gave an exaggerated yawn.

Josie looked to me and said, "Do you have any idea what the hell they're talking about?"

"I haven't got a clue," I replied.

"Stu let me out," Josie pressed her body against his.

He stood for her to get out while continuing to talk to Trent. "I don't know if 'The Seeds of Doom' was the best episode, but I will agree it ranks near the top."

Josie and I each grabbed our ouzo's, put some spanakopita on a plate and slid into the next booth over.

She said, "I don't think they realize we left."

"I think it's a good thing that Stu's not gay, or I'd never see Trent again."

Josie reached across the table and clasped my hands. "With you at the support group while I'm working your store on Saturdays, I hardly see you anymore. I miss you, Lil' Bro. How have you been?"

"Good and bad. The good is that the group is going great—if a support group can be great. I told you about that guy, Harold. He's been helping me a lot. The nightmares are still there, but I'm learning to cope. The guys say they may never go away which is not what I wanted to hear." I paused. "The bad is I'm having flashbacks again—during the day, for fucks sake. Repeating the war in my dreams was bad enough. Now they—BAM! Walking down the street, or helping a customer, whatever and whenever."

"I remember them when you lived with me. What triggers them?"

"I'm beginning to learn all that. Let's not talk about it now. Let's catch up. Now that Trent is supervising here, I don't see him either. When he and I started dating, things were going well, but now I don't know if it will work."

Josie worked for my former employer, Regency, and helped me get the job and earn my private investigator license. Being back from the war, depressed and unemployed, her getting me that job was a blessing and a curse. Having been an MP in the military earned me extra credits to get my license. But that's what got me in the business I was dying to get out of.

She said, "You need to give it time with Trent. You two haven't been boyfriends for long."

I gritted my teeth to the point it felt like they were going to rupture. "We are not boyfriends."

She stuck her tongue out at me. "Whatever you say. Call it what you want, but you guys have a good thing going, and it'd be tragic if you don't make it work."

I remained silent to ensure Trent and Stu weren't listening.

"I couldn't agree more," I overheard Trent say. "It's a crime that Marvel has done nothing with Moon Knight. Why they haven't given him a movie or TV show is beyond me."

Josie stared into my eyes. "You're going to lose him, you know?"

"What do you mean?" I balked. "The guy is crazy about me."

Josie groaned, "You know I see him nearly every day. He's one of the most fun people I ever met. A lot like you before you joined the Army. You two should be perfect for each other and believe me, he feels a lot from you these days. He's feeling a lot of love and a lot of hurt and rejection. You have the poor man confused."

"In what way?"

"He loves you, and it's obvious you love him. You just need to say the words."

Before I could respond, Ada and two waiters sat large plates of dinner items in front of Stu and Trent.

"Get over here now," she scolded Josie and me. "Don't keep gossiping over there while your food gets cold."

We joined the other two, and the rest of dinner was a combination of Trent geeking out with Stu and laughing and telling funny stories with Josie. My plates were empty long before the others.

There were distinct districts in little West Hollywood that made it easy to forget you were in the same city of less than 40,000 people. Most known throughout the country was the LGBTQ community, which ran along and around Santa Monica Boulevard. Starting near the edge of the Russian neighborhoods, it ran straight to where WeHo ended at Beverly Hills.

Arguably the most famous West Hollywood district, that most people didn't know was part of the modest city, is The Sunset Strip. Once leaving Hollywood, which was as seedy as glamorous, Sunset Boulevard ran due West for about two miles through a series of strip malls, motels, and fast-food joints that could be Anytown USA. When the street hits the city limits of WeHo, it becomes "The Strip." Unlike the image Hollywood had successfully portrayed, most Californians were as plump and frumpy as the rest of the country except that section of Sunset. Some believed the law restricted the area to only the blond, the beautiful, and the botoxed.

During the 1920s, long before West Hollywood incorporated, the less than two mile stretch between Los Angeles and Beverly Hills was out of reach or ignored by city police. It became LA County's mecca for casinos, bawdy, yet extravagant nightclubs, and a place for mobsters and the Hollywood elite to cut loose and live in the nearly lawless community. By the 1960s and 70s, more locals and tourists came in, and music establishments such as Whiskey a Go Go and The Roxy opened. Those popular concert venues continued to exist alongside sophisticated restaurants and chic bars, where the city's most dazzling lined the sidewalks waiting to be let inside.

Topaz, near the Beverly Hills city limits, was one of the newer additions to The Strip. Offering clientele both a large musical venue and a more refined restaurant and bar, the mixed business was a gamble that paid off, making it The Strip's hottest new spot.

It took several calls to the club before I learned Austin Bouchard was scheduled to start his server job at 8:00 p.m. This gave me plenty of time to run by his Koreatown apartment after leaving Olexi Restaurant. I got there as his roommate Cody Dakota left the building wearing his red paisley bartender vest, apparently starting an earlier shift at Topaz. Thirty minutes later, Austin came out donned in his black slacks, gray shirt, and muted yellow tie waiter uniform.

As always, he drove the proper speed and obeyed all traffic rules, making him easy to follow. When we reached the club, he pulled into a gated drive which led to an employee only parking area in the back. There were several valet options nearby, which I had a strong aversion to. Fortunately, there was one spot left in a tiny paid lot next door that gave me a clear view of Austin's car.

For hours I entertained myself by listening to news reports and a podcast that features an unsolved crime each week. Despite not being much of a reader, I tried getting into one of Trent's favorite classic science fiction novels. Although the futuristic story of a cruel alien race dominating Earth piqued my interest, I tossed the book aside. I couldn't overlook the author had become a scheming religious quack before reaching the age of fifty.

Near midnight, I debated whether to go home or wander inside the club to get a feel for Austin's job duties, plus satisfy my natural curiosity about the atmosphere. If I hadn't bumped face to face with him three days earlier, I would have entered without hesitation. Given the circumstances, I felt it best to let more time pass before risking him seeing me again. I resigned myself to sit back and listen to an internet radio station out of London that boasts playing the hottest "gay music" twenty-four hours a day.

It had been an exhausting week, and within an hour I fought to keep my eyelids open. I'd gathered enough information on Austin for the week to make T.J. happy, so I started the car to go home, but didn't trust I could stay awake at the wheel. Instead, I leaned the seat back for a brief nap.

Pounding on my windshield roused me from a deep slumber.

"Hey, you!" the voice yelled. I was unable to focus through my bleary eyes. "Wake up. The lot's closed. You need to go."

It was 3:45 a.m.

When my head and vision cleared, I saw Austin's white Toyota sitting alone in the club parking lot. I rolled down my window to talk to the stocky man wearing a yellow vest who had knocked me out of my slumber.

"I'm waiting for a friend," I mumbled. "He's inside Topaz."

"No one's in there," the attendant growled. "They locked that place, and all left thirty-minutes ago."

"He must still be inside. That's his car there."

"May be his car, but he's gone. Go check The Viper Room or somewhere that's open twenty-four hours. Go wherever you want, but you can't stay here."

Bouchard could have been anywhere. There were numerous late-night clubs and restaurants within walking distance, or he could have ridden somewhere farther with friends. Wandering around the Sunset Strip looking for him would have been as fruitless as randomly searching for him had been a few days earlier. Besides, I had a store to open in just over six hours.

I went to Trent's home, which was a five-minute drive from Topaz with plans to surprise him. As I neared the curb in front of his adobe style house, I pulled away and went to my place instead. I would only get a few hours of sleep before heading to work, and I couldn't afford to spend much of that staying up with him.

Though normally an early riser, I slept over my 9:00 a.m. alarm. A call at 10:50 made me realize I was late opening my store. I would have ignored the call, but my reflexes got the best of me. It was Detective Matias Castro of the LAPD, Hollywood Division.

Five

"Austin Bouchard is dead,"

I looked at the phone and put it back to my ear. "Dead? What do you mean he's dead?"

Detective Castro said, "I don't know how to define dead other than dead—as in not amongst the living, Mr. O'Reilly."

"How?" I barked into the phone. "What happened?"

"Based on the marks, it looks like a blow to the head. I'm told you've been following him this week and would like you to answer some questions. I need you to meet me at the Hollywood station."

"The station? Why?"

"I want you to verify the victim is the one you've been following."

"It was Austin Bouchard. Isn't that all you need to know?"

"You may have been one of the last ones to see him alive. I've got questions. Lots of them."

Traffic being a bitch, as usual, I took side streets to get to the station on Wilcox Avenue. It didn't help.

"It took you long enough to get here, O'Reilly," the detective said as I sat at the front of his desk.

"Rush hour."

He scowled. "It's always rush hour in this city." He threw a manila folder in front of me. "Take a look."

I opened the folder and shuddered. I've seen so many dead bodies in my life I'd think it wouldn't affect me. But I've seen too many. Paperclipped at the top of the file was a picture of Austin Bouchard's face. Half his face was as handsome as ever and looked surprisingly peaceful. The other half was sloped down toward the metal table he laid on.

"That's Bouchard. The guy I've been following."

The detective pulled the photo away to expose another photo of a body wrapped in plastic lying in dirt surrounded by scrub brushes.

"That's the way he was found this morning around 5:00. A park ranger spotted it while patrolling along the Rattler trail. Looks like he was beaten with some type of rod to his head. Probably a tire iron or something like that."

"Rattler trail? Where's that?"

"On the side of Mount Lee, where the Hollywood Sign is. It was found next to a bench in the rough a few hundred yards under the sign. Forensics says it looks like the body was sat on the bench looking toward the city but fell over at some point. Left him on the ground looking like a pig in a blanket."

"You're a sensitive man."

He scowled again. "When was the last time you saw this kid?"

"Last night at Topaz. Around 8:00."

"I'm told he left that club. Were you following him?"

"Yes, up to a point."

"What point?"

"I followed him to the club and saw him go in but never saw him leave."

"What time did you leave?"

"I was there until 4:00 this morning. After he went in the club, I was tired, so I took a nap."

"Took a nap? What kind of PI are you? Sounds like a lazy ass one to me."

"That's what they call me – lazy ass. I always sleep during my stakeouts." He stared at me blank faced. "Look, my job was done for the night, and I was too tired to drive home. When I woke up, Austin's car was still there, but the place was locked up. I saw the guy go in, but that was it."

"You weren't suspicious when you saw his car?"

"A little, but he could have gone anywhere with friends. It wasn't my responsibility to keep tabs on him every minute."

"You worked that bathhouse job three months ago, right?"

"I solved that job three months ago."

"That was Detective Dirk Turner's case. He said you were a sharp guy. Here I thought he was pretty smart himself." He rubbed his chin.

"You didn't bring me here to insult me. What else you want?"

"What was Bouchard wearing the last time you saw him?"

"He wore a gray shirt and a yellow tie. He was dressed for work."

"He didn't work last night, and he wasn't wearing a gray shirt this morning. He was in a powder blue shirt with a copy of the Hollywood Sign imprinted on it."

"Set below the sign with it on his shirt too. Sounds like someone was sending a message."

"Doesn't seem like a coincidence."

"Can you track the shirt down?"

"We'll try, but it's one of those damn things that's sold in every souvenir store and hotel gift shop in town."

"How did you know I was following him?" I asked.

"When we notified the family, Austin's half-sister Erin Mooney identified the body and said her father hired you. You were working for T.J. Mooney? That's a step up for you."

"He was referred to me. I'm working for the muckety-muck these days."

"Why did Mr. Mooney hire you? What was the objective?"

"Not much of one. Said Austin might get involved in some wrongdoing and wanted me to track where he went, who he was with, and report on it. Find out what he does. Make sure he's not in trouble. That's all."

"You didn't ask for more details?"

"I didn't get that out of him. What he's paying was enough for me to get started. He didn't want Austin followed on specific days or times. He wanted me to follow Austin randomly at my convenience. It was the easiest case I ever had. The guy mostly stayed home and chilled with friends except for going out a little each day. Monday, he went to the bars. Tuesday, he had dinner with a friend. Wednesday, he shopped at Trader Joe's, and we know what happened Thursday."

Detective Castro sat silently and stroked his bushy mustache. His brown skin was bright red on top of his bald head. I presumed from standing on the hill in the bright sunlight all morning.

"You'd think if the killer or killers were sending a message, they would have set the body up at the Hollywood Sign. Guess it'd be a helluva climb."

"And damned near impossible," the detective said. "Security was beefed up around the sign after it was rebuilt. The new security cameras and motion sensors rid the area of teen parties and general nuisance until New Year's Eve of last year. That's when that idiot artist worked his way around the system at night and changed the sign to *HOLLYWEED*."

I chuckled. "The city was surprised to wake up to that in the morning. I nearly bust a nut laughing so hard."

"We didn't think it was funny. He made us look like fools. After that, the city got pissed enough to add more cameras and sensors and even helicopter patrols. We should have had more pointing further down the hill."

"I wonder what message they were trying to send."

"Whatever the reason they did it, it was worth it to them," the detective said. "My guess is they're trying to send a message too, but you never know. Remember that guy, Campos-Martinez seven years ago?"

"I was stationed overseas in 2011."

"The guy killed his boyfriend and left his head and some body parts up here. We never found out why he did it. He never said. Some people are plain crazy. Now that your job is over, I need you to back off and let us do our job."

"The following him part is over, but the family will want me to stay on to find out why he was murdered."

"The way his sister talked, I wouldn't bank on it. You're not high on their popularity list."

"What do you mean? I wasn't hired to tail the guy twenty-four hours a day."

Detective Castro said, "Don't bet on T.J. Mooney seeing you as innocent as you do."

"Speaking of Mooney, I should go see him now. Are you done with me?"

"Not for a while, Mr. O'Reilly." Detective Matias Castro pointed his finger at me. "You're staying right there. I want a play by play of that boy's entire week."

"I'd like to go to the site on Mount Lee when we're done."

"The trail is closed until forensics is done. You're going to have to bide your time."

Six

When I buzzed at the gate of the Mooney's Bel Air mansion, an older woman's voice came across the speaker.

"Who's calling?" she said in a cockney accent.

"Mitch O'Reilly. I'm here to meet with T.J."

She mumbled followed by a pause. "One moment."

I waited at the gate over five minutes and was reaching to buzz again when Ms. Cockney came back on the speaker. "Hold on while I let you in."

Paul, the butler, or house manager as he prefers, opened the door before I reached the stoop.

I said, "Hello again, Paul."

Never turning to look at me, he closed the door, walked through the marble foyer and down the grand hallway. "They're waiting for you in the family room."

I had been unable to prepare for that moment. Detective Castro made it clear that the family blamed me for Austin's death. No matter how illogical that was, I blamed myself, too. I feared what I was walking into.

We neared the end of the hall when Paul looked at me for the first time since my arrival. "I hope you're wearing a protective vest." He motioned his hand toward the wide-open entry to the room.

The design seemed formal and cold for a family gathering place, which was fitting since chills ran across my skin. A floor to ceiling Corinthian column stood on each side of the entry arch. Straight ahead T.J. Mooney sat on a light gold couch with arms that curved outward. His legs were crossed, and his eyes focused dead on me. To Mooney's left, a man my age and height, with sandy-brown hair, stood with a cocktail glass in his hand. In front of the man, a woman sat on a chair that matched the couch, and was angled toward T.J. She looked to be in her early thirties as well. She leaned forward, so she could see me as I entered. The room had as much appeal as a stalk of celery.

I hesitated in uncomfortable silence before stepping forward and sitting in the chair across from the woman.

"Do you not wait to be addressed before sitting down in someone's home?" T.J. sniffed.

I stood. "Sorry."

"These are my children." He gestured toward the man standing. "This is Jared. You may have heard of him. He's prominent in the tennis field."

It wasn't a friend of Austin's that had the fun filled dinner I had watched several days earlier. It was his half-brother. Jared was handsome like Austin but with a longer face and a slight curl in his hair. He wore black, skintight jeans on his long legs and a white polo. He raised his drink slightly and nodded his head.

I faltered, "I, um, don't follow tennis."

"I'm not surprised," Jared said with disdain.

A sneer briefly touched T.J.'s mouth then he nodded to the woman in the chair. "This is my daughter, Erin. She's a successful businesswoman which makes me certain you haven't heard of her."

I ran my palms down the side of my pants, hoping no one noticed. "I can't say that I have."

She gave no response.

"Are you going to sit down or not?" T.J. grumbled.

"Uh…" I sat back in the chair crossing my legs in one direction, then switching to the other. The three stared in silence. The only sound was footsteps as Jared walked to the couch and sat next to T.J.

"If this feels awkward," Jared said, "it's because we're waiting to hear what you have to say to my father."

I leaned forward. "I'm sorry for your loss."

Erin said scornfully, "I'm sure you are." Despite having golden eyes that were bright and wide, and giving a soft smile, there was tension around her mouth. Her light pink, oval-shaped face looked much like her half-brother Austin. Brunette hair ran straight and cropped at the neck cut even with the stiff collar of her starched royal blue business jacket that she wore over a soft-yellow blouse.

Jared lifted off the couch as he leaned forward to place his drink on the enormous coffee table, which sat too far away. Everything about this place encouraged discomfort.

Erin adjusted in her seat and brushed her skirt. "You should be sorry, Mr. O'Reilly. Or, may I call you Mitch?"

"Mitch is fine, Erin, and—"

"I prefer that you not refer to me by my first name."

"I'm sorry, Ms. Mooney. I was going to repeat my condolences."

T.J. grumbled, "You're sorry because you fucked up. That's why you're sorry."

"I don't understand. How did I fu... what do you mean?"

"You were watching over my brother. That's what you did," Erin chided. "Do you not understand that? Why should we have to spell it out for you?"

T.J. said, "You're incompetent and my son is dead because of it."

"There's nothing incompetent about doing my job as told, Mr. Mooney."

"I told you before, I am to be addressed as T.J."

"Yes, T.J. I'm confused how this can be my fault. I couldn't look over him twenty-four hours a day. That wasn't our agreement."

Jared asked, "Were you watching him last night?"

"Yes, I followed him from his apartment to his job. There wasn't anything more to see."

Erin Mooney sniggered. "Nothing more to see? Do you know what I saw this morning? My day started with looking down at my dead brother's face. That's what I got to see."

"I understand—"

"No, I don't think you understand," T.J. said. "You were hired to follow Austin, to know his whereabouts and—"

I held up my hands. "Whoa. Sorry to cut you off T.J., but what do you want from me?"

Jared stood, "This hardly seems the time to argue with my father."

"I don't mean to argue," I countered. "I'm confused is all."

I was confused because I expected to take heat for Austin's death, but I never expected T.J. to ignore the details of our original agreement. T.J. nodded to Erin who folded her hands on her lap. "We're not trying to be difficult," she said. "We are, for a lack of a better word, disappointed. My father gave you a job, and your incompetence led to my brother's death. It pains me, and my family, to know you could have prevented this."

"I wasn't hired to protect Austin," I countered. "Your father hired me only to follow him for a certain number of hours each week. Our agreement was not for twenty-four-hour surveillance." I looked at T.J. "Isn't that right?"

He shifted in his seat and belted out a few huffs. "I would expect he would have been safe under your watch."

I turned to Erin. "Look, T.J. hired me to follow Austin, and that's what I did. I was done for the night when he vanished." I didn't tell them I was sleeping in the parking lot. "As I said several times, I'm deeply sorry for your loss, and I can only imagine what it must be like to lose a son, but I don't get why you're blaming me for his death."

Erin frowned and looked at T.J. "Father is this true?"

T.J. looked to her and then to me. He growled, "You were hired to ensure Austin didn't get in trouble. That would be laughable now if it weren't so tragic."

I said, "T.J. I'm not going to frustrate you further. I will say that I'm sorry that despite our agreement, you still hold me responsible. I hope someday you will think it through and understand my position."

"You need to leave my house and do it now."

"I had hoped I could help to find your son's killer," I pleaded.

"Ha!" T.J. exclaimed as he pointed for me to leave the room.

I sulked down the hall. When I neared the foyer, Erin's heels clicked and grew louder as she approached me from behind.

"Mitch, please stop," she said.

I halted, turned around and glared.

She bowed her head, stretched her neck, and then stood straight. "I believe you," she said. "My father is distraught and did not fully explain why he hired you."

"He lied."

She stepped back. "What a cruel thing to say. He omitted."

"That's convenient." I lowered my head. "Look, I've given this a helluva lot of thought and still don't understand why your father hired me. Your brother acted like an altar boy. I saw nothing that would make me believe anything like this could happen, but I was obviously wrong. What did your father know?"

"I can't conceive of my father knowing Austin was in such serious danger that he wouldn't do more than hire you. It's clear there was a misunderstanding between you two. We never know what's on my father's mind about Austin. He had little to do with my father, and I believe that's affecting him deeply."

Erin stood tall with her head held high. Her voice was stern and direct, yet I detected a slight nervous stammer, perhaps her embarrassment for having been unreasonable when putting me on the spot.

"Do you know how your brother may have been in serious danger?"

"I didn't know that he was." She paused. "You may deserve an apology for how you were treated by my father, but his pride will prevent that, and it's not my place to give it to you."

"Okay then..."

"If you've noted Austin's actions for the days you followed him, I'd like the report emailed to me as soon as possible." She handed me her business card. "I'll also ensure you are paid for your time."

"Thank you. I'll get those files to you as soon as possible."

"I'd be appreciative." She stepped further away. "I must insist you go and not come back. It'd be best for both you and my father."

"I agree."

"I hope to get your report in the morning. Paul will show you out." She turned and started down the hall.

Paul had been standing by the front door. He opened it when I approached.

"Nice knowing you, Paul."

Without a word, he closed it behind me.

◆ ◆ ◆

"Rémy! Come back here, Rémy!" A woman called from somewhere in the yard.

The view from the rear windows overlooked the Mooney's extensive estate, but the front drive and yard was modest in comparison. Yet, I searched around my car and the fountain and couldn't see where the voice was coming from.

"Get back here right now, young man. You're in big trouble."

I didn't care to waste time dealing with some woman disciplining her kid. I climbed into my Honda and was shutting the door when I spotted a tall, thin woman digging into the bushes. She wore sandals and a casual dress, which made for a good guess she wasn't gardening. Was her child trapped in the bushes? I crossed to see if I could give her a hand. A deep brown skinned gardener wearing a tawny-colored uniform rushed up.

"Rémy, don't do this," the woman pleaded.

When the gardener and I were within five feet of her, a four-legged white puff ball yipped, and scurried out of the shrubs and across the driveway to the other side of the yard. In disgust, I turned toward my car when the woman touched my elbow.

"I'm so sorry. He's normally a good dog. Would you please help me?" She pulled her long, curly, ash-blond hair from her face.

She looked familiar, though I couldn't place her. Her wide, puffy lips stood out, but turned down. Her eyes were swollen and red.

"Sure," I said. "His names Rémy, right? He's fast."

"He's always so good, but he hates coming here. I think he knows I do, too." Her lips pouted and her forehead wrinkled.

The gardener jumped forward and landed flat on his belly, missing the furry creature by a few inches. I bolted and zigzagged through the grass with the dog until he reached a corner of the exterior block wall. I expected a growl, but he cowered and shook, refusing to look at me.

"Rémy, oh Rémy. Stay there, baby."

She scooped the pup in her arms and stroked him. I couldn't believe the wide-eyed, panting, relaxed animal in her hands was the one we'd been chasing.

"Thanks for your help," she said, waving to the gardener as he walked away. She looked to me and flashed a wide pursed-lips smile. "Thank you, too."

I snapped my fingers. "You're Dominique, aren't you? The Sunny Meadows Shampoo lady?"

She lowered her head and her eyes turned down. "Yes, I'm Dominique." She shook my hand. "Dominique Bouchard."

"Bouchard? I'm sorry. You're related to Austin Bouchard?"

She pulled a tissue from her small purse to wipe the tears careening down her cheeks. "His mother."

"I—"

She shook her head. "Don't worry. It's a common mistake." She blew her nose and stood straight. "People who only know Austin through his father are surprised by the age difference between T.J. and me."

"I also didn't know your last name is Bouchard."

"I understand, you only know me as Dominique. When I became a model, I did the Madonna and Cher thing and stopped using my last name. I felt very chic."

She stood tall, and the sun shining through her billowy dress revealed a fit, curvy body. Her silken, porcelain skin made her look to be in her early forties, but further inspection of her thin crow's feet revealed she was likely a decade older.

She took a small mirror from her purse, pulled her long, wispy sandy blond bangs from her face, and wiped the mascara from her cheeks. "Did you know Austin, or are you a friend of T.J.'s?"

"Uh, neither." I kicked at the grass. "I was working for T.J. I'm a private investigator."

"What on earth does T.J. need a detective for?" She raised her hand to her mouth. "He had you following my son, didn't he? He's been trying to keep tabs on Austin, and he hired you."

"I really can't say, Ms. Bouchard," I replied. "I said more than I should have." I started toward my car. "You keep your hands on Rémy, okay?"

"I'm a terrible person bringing him here where he hates it so much, but I couldn't imagine being without him right now." As I walked away she called, "Sir, hold on for just one moment, please."

I halted while she rushed to me.

"Do you have a business card handy? May I please have one?"

I felt uncomfortable yet saw no reason she couldn't have a card. I dug one out of my wallet and handed it over.

"Thank you." She looked at the card. "Mr. O'Reilly."

"Thank you, Ms. Bouchard. Again, my condolences."

She bowed her head into Rémy's fur, then raised her chin, and strode confidently to the front door.

I climbed into my car for the second time. Someone called my name.

"Hello, Mitch! Mitch O'Reilly! Hold on."

It was Jared Mooney strutting along a stone pathway from the side of the mansion.

"Mr. Mooney," I said. "I know you're upset, but I don't see that we—"

"Call me Jared." He smiled. "I'm not as uptight as my sister."

"Jared, I don't know what you have further to say to me, but I don't think you can make me feel any worse. I am not responsible for your brother's death, but knowing that doesn't make me feel any better about the situation."

He grinned and tapped my shoulder with his fist. "I was a hard-ass back there because my father implied you were responsible. It's also hard to be disagreeable with my father, as you already know. He is a legend, and I respect him, but his problem is that he knows he's a legend and uses it to do and act as he pleases."

I muttered, "This is quite the turnaround."

It was a turnaround, and a suspicious one. Sure, he was kissing Daddy's ass back in the house, but the sudden buddy-buddy attitude didn't ring true. I know a phony when I meet one, but I figured playing pals was the right move.

He said, "That's because I loved my brother, and I want to help in any way if I can."

Why the sudden change? I did consider how quiet he was through most of the conversation with his family, so maybe he was being upfront now. Perhaps he was legitimately intimidated by T.J. Perhaps he was full of shit.

"You had dinner with your brother on Tuesday night."

"You followed us to Providence." He nudged me with his elbow. "You little sneak."

"Just doing my job."

"It was his favorite restaurant, so I'd treat him when we got together. I wish I knew that was the last time I'd see him. He wanted to talk to me about the big role he got that had my father so excited."

We both leaned our backs against the side of my car and folded our arms. I took advantage of our relaxed conversation to start questioning nonchalantly.

"What do you think happened to your brother?" I asked gently.

"As long as you followed him, you know he was beloved by all, except that drunken, drugged up meth addict boyfriend of his. He's the one you need to be looking at."

"You and your brother were close?"

"Not as close as either of us liked. I was six years old when he was born." He laughed. "You can imagine how much I hated that little rug-rat stealing all my attention, but he was fun to have around, too. When Dominique divorced my father, Austin was only thirteen, and I was already at Stanford. It was after that we became closer. I would be here during summer vacations. He would be too, even though it was for Father's visitation rights and Father was always away on location. We bonded a little for a couple of years while I gave him some tennis lessons, but once I graduated, we lost touch."

"You didn't really know him then."

"Not really. We tried over the past two years, but he was working and auditioning and I'm always on tour. We had a friendly relationship and would go out to dinner when we could, but never as close as either of us would have liked, as I said. It rips me apart I'll never have that chance. There was a—uh, oh. This isn't good."

Paul was coming toward us across the driveway.

Jared asked, "What can I do for you, my good man?"

"It's your father," Paul replied. "He would like to speak with you immediately."

He stepped away from my car and turned his head toward me. "I'm fairly certain my dear old dad spotted us talking." He laughed. "You're a troublemaker, Mitch."

Jared walked toward the house while Paul stayed and clasped his wrists at his waist. He said, "You may go now, Mr. O'Reilly."

"I take it that's not a request."

"You are a good detective," he quipped. "You're quite perceptive."

Paul walked back to the front door and stood there until he saw me pulling out of the front gate.

Seven

"All the guys asked about you at the PTSD meeting today," Harold Beavers said over the phone. "Why didn't you say you weren't coming?"

"I got busy," I snapped. "Is there a requirement I go every week? Is that a rule?"

"No, but—"

A combination of anger and frustration had me treating Harold in a way he didn't deserve. Dredging up all the shit from the war was cathartic at first but had reached the point of being unbearable. I had come to believe it was best to leave things buried.

I sighed. "I'm sorry. I'm tied up at the store today. Josie couldn't work for me. I have a business to run."

"When you didn't show up at Denny's, I called at least three times. By the time my Lumberjack Slam breakfast came out, I had to take it to eat at the meeting. Not picking up my calls wasn't cool."

"I'm sorry, all right? I've got to go."

"Hold on!" He yelled. I took my thumb off the disconnect button. "You don't sound well. If something is wrong, you'll tell me, right?"

"Things are fine." I hung up and felt immediate guilt.

Josie, who was working her normal Saturday shift for me, sat on the stool behind the cash register waving a finger. "I can't believe you lied to Harold like that. Now I'll have to lie too if he asks about you working today?"

I was smug. "As if lying to cover your ass is new for you."

Josie briefly giggled. "Seriously, though. What's up?"

Knowing she'd follow, I walked back to my office and fell onto the couch. She sat on the arm next to me and rubbed my shoulders.

"You know what?" she said. "You look and act like the guy who came back to me five years ago. I want the brother I had before you went to war."

When Josie and I first moved to LA to attend UCLA, we were the best of friends who never stopped partying. Despite her late-night living, she was able to attend classes and make respectable grades. I did the same for the first year of school, but during my second I got into drugs, the bathhouse scene, and floating from one trick to another. Knowing expulsion was imminent, I joined the army, which sent me to Afghanistan twice. When I returned, I existed while living on the couch at Josie and her ex-husband Cal's condominium. I returned to my old decadent scene until they both had enough of it and demanded I get a job or get out. Josie getting me a job with Regency Investigative Services is what got me to clean up my act and stay off the streets.

I confessed, "Since I started going to the support meetings, it seemed like things were getting better. Now it's all gone to shit. Some poor sap died yesterday because of me."

She stood. "Died? Who died?"

"Someone murdered Austin Bouchard. He was T.J. Mooney's son. And, you know the model, Dominique? The one who does those shampoo commercials? She was his mother. T.J. hired me to watch over Austin. That's what I was doing after we all had dinner Thursday night. You know Topaz on The Strip?"

"Topaz!" Josie clasped her hands.

"Why bother to ask?" I rolled my eyes. "Of course, you know it. That's where that guy worked. I tailed him, I lost him, and first thing in the morning a Detective Matias Castro calls to tell me the guy was found dead below the Hollywood Sign."

"The body on the hill? That's the case you're talking about? It's all over the news."

'You know about it?"

"Not really. I heard the name Austin something-or-other and had never heard of him. I tuned it out. How cool is it you're working with a police detective again?"

I got off the couch, poured some coffee and walked out to the sales floor. I leaned against a display case and took a sip. "The detective and I aren't working together, and that's not the point. Someone murdered the guy while I was tailing him. T.J. threw me out of his house because of it."

She bounced. "What's his place like? I bet it's big and beautiful."

I cast an eye at her.

"Okay, so not important. Why'd you agree to follow him? How did you expect to run this store?"

"It wasn't a twenty-four hour a day job. It was flexible. I watched him when I could and was to report what he was doing." I placed a finger against my lips and held up a hand to her. "Before you say it, I know he wasn't my full responsibility, and that I shouldn't feel guilt over him being dead, but I do. You want to know why? Because my entire investigation was sloppy. It started as a low-key case, and I still fucked it up. He and his friends were at the Abbey in WeHo, and I bumped into him while I was tailing him. I literally fell right into his arms."

"How did that happen?" She cackled. "Instant love?"
She lowered her head. "Sorry, nervous laughter."

"It's not funny. I was across the street watching them on
the patio. You know, doing my homeless man wearing
garbage bags thing. Then I lost it when I had a flashback." I
was tapping my foot and the coffee sloshed around in the
cup from my trembling hand.

She placed a palm over her mouth. "Oh shit, Lil' Bro.
I'm sorry I laughed. But I don't get the connection between
that and you falling into his arms."

"After the flashback, I went into the Abbey for some
water or something and bumped into him. That's it."

"That couldn't be helped. You've not been yourself
since you started having the flashbacks again. I think it's
because you aren't getting help."

"I was going to meetings and now I've lost my touch,
and people are getting killed. I don't think I should do this
anymore."

I threw the coffee mug through the door into my office
where it shattered against a box. Josie jumped and had tears
in her eyes. "Holy shit. Relax Lil' Bro. You don't want to
hear this now, but going to the meetings is the problem
because that's all you're doing. Sitting around listening to

everyone's war stories without seeing a psychiatrist or any
other treatment."

"You sound like Harold." I pounded my fist on the glass
case. "I tried, and it ain't working. That's it."

"Three months ago, you had a case that got you in the
news. You've got people's attention. You're making a
name for yourself."

"That was my first big case, and I haven't had another
like it since. I went right back to following cheating
spouses."

"But you solved it. You caught the killer. You're
ignoring you were hired by T.J. Mooney. If that's not a step
up...I don't know what's happening, but I don't like the
Mitch I'm looking at. I don't like this Mitch at all. You're
acting like the guy who lived on my couch for months, and
I'm not letting you go through that again. Signs of the older
you who loved life were coming back. You're my best
friend. Trent is madly in love with you, yet you neglect
him. Sometimes you act like he's not even there."

"But—"

"No 'buts.' He wanted something more serious than you
could give him, so he compromised. He backed down and
agreed you two would date, and you had so much life in
your eyes. You light up when you see him, but that twinkle

dies out shortly after. You try to pretend you don't love him." She stood and put her hands on her hips. "Do you know why he loves you?"

"He's an idiot?"

She was right. When Trent and I began dating, he wanted something more serious. He was emphatic he wanted more than just a date now and then, but I couldn't offer it to him. Not then. I needed the freedom to be me and not be tied down. I told him then that I needed to focus on my PTSD, and he not only accepted, but embraced the idea. Yet, three months later I was in a situation where I was being bullied into being more than I said I could offer to begin with.

Josie said, "Somehow, he sees the man inside you I once knew. You were always a smart-ass, but not like you are now. You—"

"Hey, I've been trying extra hard to be nice these days."

"Thanks to Harold, but I see when you're fighting it and having to bite your tongue, and you didn't bite it hard enough when you were talking to Stu at the restaurant."

Time to deflect and bring up my sister's new nerdy boyfriend. "Speaking of Stu…"

"We're talking about you and Trent, not Stu. He tells me over and over again how hard you two laugh sometimes.

How good it feels to curl up to you. He knows you have a fun side, and he wants to grab onto it and hold it and hug it tight. That brings up the real reason he stays with you. He doesn't just love you—he needs you." Josie's lips turned down and her eyes welled up. "I want my happy brother again."

"I don't want to be needed," I muttered.

"He can't help that because he's a fixer. That's the way a lot of guys are. They want to fix people. I have never had more attention than when I divorced Cal. The fixers could spot my wounded soul from a thousand yards. They'd say shit like, 'I want to take away your pain,' or 'I can make you smile again." It made me want to puke. I didn't want fixed, I wanted to be a person who didn't need fixing."

"Trent has never said anything like that."

"That's where you're screwing up because you don't know how good you've got it. He's a fixer, but he's not a nut-job. He wants to help you but isn't willing to give up himself in the process. That's healthy. But, no matter how much he's got it together, he's still a fixer. You will lose him if you keep treating him the way you do."

I locked my fingers behind my neck and pulled my head down. The sound of my breath filled the room. In my gut I didn't want to lose Trent, but a part of me felt like he was doing nothing more than adding more stress and obligation to my life.

Josie said, "Something else is wrong. What is it?"

"That flashback at the Abbey wasn't a fluke. They're getting worse. I'm still having the nightmares, but these are during the day. I'll be wide awake doing my thing. and they hit me out of nowhere. The day flashes are from my first tour in Kabul. That was where I was in an ambush and watched my friend George Suzuki picked away by snipers. I keep seeing it happen over and over. It doesn't stop."

"It doesn't sound like skipping your support group meeting this morning was a good idea. You look exhausted. Go lay down in the back, and we'll go out after closing."

I complied and was drifting off when the bell on the front door jingled.

I let Josie handle whoever the customer was that came in the door. I was drifting off to sleep again when she ran in and shook me so hard I nearly fell off the couch.

"Guess who's here, Lil' Bro. It's Dominique, the Sunny Meadows shampoo lady."

I bolted upright in my seat and leaned forward to see Dominique waiting by the cash register. "What's she doing here?"

"Maybe you should ask her."

Not expecting to work that morning, I wore faded jeans with some rips at the knees and a Dodgers T-shirt. I combed my hair with my fingers and entered the front of the store. She wore a tailored half-sleeve mint dress. A large matching handbag hung over her shoulder. A wiggling black nose stuck out of the bag.

Knowing she had talked with T.J. right after we met, I prepared myself for the worst. "Dominique. You're a surprise. I see you didn't lose Rémy again."

She responded dryly, "You're funny, Mitch—may I call you Mitch? I'd like to talk about Austin if you have time."

"All the time in the world. Come back to my office."

She followed me, and I directed her to sit on the couch. I paid no mind to her reaction as she eyed the storeroom, which was in its typical disarray of scattered boxes and cleaning supplies shoved in a corner. I'd gotten used to the disgusted look people gave when they stepped in. I had forgotten about the coffee I tossed earlier, so I grabbed a rag and started mopping up the mess. "Just a moment." I chuckled nervously. "I tripped earlier with a cup in my hand."

"That must have been a nasty fall. That spill is six feet high." She brushed off a seat cushion with her hand and sat. She lifted her walking cotton ball out of her purse to place Rémy next to her. She glared at the cushion, hesitated, and placed the dog on her lap. I offered her a cup of coffee which she refused, poured some for myself and sat at my desk.

"How may I help you?"

"I want to hire you."

"For what?" I was excited. I wanted to investigate Austin's murder, but forced a calm, professional tone.

Tears welled in her eyes. She dug in her handbag, under the dog, and pulled out a tissue. "I want you to find who murdered my son."

"Did you talk to T.J.? He won't like that idea much."

"We talked. It was a long discussion about Austin, the murder, and you. He told me you came highly recommended. I believe with that glowing recommendation, and you having followed Austin during his last week, you're the right man to find out what happened." She hugged Rémy and sobbed. "I never dreamed this could happen to Austin. He was loving. He

was also a brilliant actor and now the world will never
know." She clutched the tissue in her fist. "You must find
the person who killed him."

"T.J. might be a problem. He doesn't think highly of me
these days."

"Don't worry about T.J. He agrees with me." She
sniffed into her tissue. "What happened wasn't your fault.
He'll never admit to it because he never admits to any
mistakes or errors in judgment, but he knows that's true.
That man has never given an apology in his life. You met
him. So, as surprised as you are, yes, I want you to begin
the investigation into Austin's murder immediately. I'll pay
whatever rate you charged T.J."

While T.J. paid me a ridiculous amount, I considered
explaining to Dominique that a murder investigation was
difficult. It should be more expensive than a simple job of
tailing someone. Before I could speak, I let my damn
scruples get in the way. The fees were more than plenty,
and for whatever reason, I liked her.

I tapped a few keys on my computer. "I'm printing out
contracts now. While we wait. Let's get started with some
general questions because I didn't get much from T.J. Tell
me what I need to know about Austin."

"Oh, that's so open."

"What was his relationship with you and his father? Tell me about the divorce."

"T.J. and I divorced ten years ago, when Austin was only thirteen. T.J. was never mean to his children. In fact, he loves them dearly, but he wasn't around. He has more money than the Catholic church, yet he never cut back on his work. I know it's what he loved to do. It's what he was born to do, but you would have thought he would have given them more of his time. He should have given *me* more of his time. He loved Austin, but showered his other two children, Jared and Erin, with more attention until after the divorce. Once Austin and I moved to Palm Springs, you would have thought I snatched the boy out of T.J.'s arms when he was a baby. He was hot and cold, though. He'd be off in New Zealand or somewhere filming, and then when he'd come back, he'd want to be father-of-the-year with Austin."

"How often did Austin stay with T.J.?"

"His father had custody of him every summer and occasional holidays. Austin would stay at the Bel Air estate every year regardless of whether his father was there. I tried insisting he stay in Palm Springs unless T.J. was in town, but he was defiant. He enjoyed being there in the summer months and had no real trouble with Jared or Erin."

"No real trouble, sounds like code for not so good."

"Never really a problem with Erin. She's eight years older and was attending Columbia University by the time he was nine. Jared was six years older, which was a millennium at their younger ages, but Jared took Austin under his wing the last year before the divorce. Austin was eleven. Jared would give him tennis lessons and such. They were never close friends but were close for a brief time before Jared left for college. He went to Stanford which has a marvelous tennis program." She pulled her cell phone from her purse and looked at the time. "As important as this questioning is, I need to leave soon. I'm meeting T.J. to complete the arrangements for Austin's service."

"One more question, because it's something I find curious. The first night I met T.J., he said Austin had a boyfriend, but over the past week I never saw him with anyone who looked that close. Never heard one mentioned either."

"Poor Hector. They were on the outs again. There should never have been an in. I have tried to help that boy so many times. A delightful young man with severe problems that broke Austin's heart and mine. There is so

much to tell about them, and I will, but I don't have the
time right now."

Dominique stood and picked up her pooch. "Come on,
Rémy let's get you back in the bag. We're running late."
She pulled the contract off the printer. "May I bring these
with me when I meet you again?"

"Of course."

I followed Dominique to the parking lot and held the
door to her candy-apple-red Mercedes. "Before you go," I
said. "I need some direction. Where do you think is the best
place to start my investigation?"

"I meant to tell you. If you can go to Austin's apartment
now, it would be a good time. His roommates Cody and
Devin are helping to get his things together for me. I'll be
there as soon as T.J. and I are done at the cathedral."

"Thanks, Dominique." I closed her car door. "I'll head
over there now."

Eight

"Mitchell?" Cody answered wide-eyed when he opened the door to his apartment. "What brings you here?"

"It's not Mitchell. I'm Mitch. Mitch O'Reilly. I'm a private—"

"You're a private eye. Yeah, I know. We all knew. We figured it out Tuesday night. You did a good job hiding and all, but Austin got word his dad hired you, so we were on the lookout."

After years of tailing people, it was a blow to the ego to know they found me out. They're having been forewarned I was there gave me no sense of reprieve.

He held out his hand, and we shook. "I'm Cody Dakota." He waved me inside and shut the door.

"That has a rhythm to it. Is it a stage name?" I said. Catching myself in a sarcastic tone.

"You don't like it?"

"It's great if you star in a 1950s western."

"Good, because I think it's very masculine. I like it, and it's a hell of a lot better than my birth name." He held up his palm. "And, don't ask."

"Well, Mr. Dakota, who told Austin I was following him?"

He shrugged. "Don't know. He didn't say."

Cody was shirtless with gray sweatpants cut off at the knees. Complimenting his blond, surfer boy hair were crystal blue eyes and a golden bronze tan. He wasn't the perfectly chiseled type you see all around town. Instead, his muscular body was thick. Thick chest, stomach, arms, and thighs.

I said, "Dominique Bouchard hired me to investigate Austin's murder. She says you're packing his things. I'm hoping you can tell me, or maybe find, something that will help throw some light on what happened."

"Dominique hired you?" He placed a hand on his chin and gazed at the ceiling. "I guess that's okay."

Most of what I could see of the apartment was a long hallway with three doorways. I presumed a bathroom and two bedrooms. Next to us was an opening to a kitchenette and a series of faded yellow sheets on rods draped from the ceiling that hid a room behind it.

"Devin and I have had real mixed emotions today. We've laughed a lot about good times with Austin, but I cried more than I ever have. It's not fun around here without him, but I'm trying to act like everything is normal. This all sucks, and it's making things worse having to dig through his shit. We were best friends for years."

I asked, "Is Devin packing things now? I want to go through them first."

"Hey, Devin," Cody hollered. "Stop the packing for a few."

Cody stepped into the kitchen and pulled the sheets back to expose the living room. The three windows I watched from the outside were in the front. There was an open ratty gray sofa bed with the sheets and pillows piled in the middle, a ripped pleather recliner sat near the windows.

"This was Devin's apartment first, so he's got the large bedroom at the end of the hall. The door on the left there was Austin's where Devin and I are working now. It's only a two-bedroom place, so this is my room. I share it when we need living space, especially since Devin bought the TV last year with Christmas money." He pointed to a 52-inch screen TV attached to a blue wall. "Want something to drink?"

"Just water."

"We don't have bottled water, but there's a mango tea Snapple in the fridge. Help yourself. I want to clean this room before Austin's mom gets here."

I grabbed the drink while Cody crumpled his sheets and blankets enough to fold the bed back inside the sofa. He grabbed some envelopes and wrappers off the floor and tossed them in the garbage. Cody was charming, but not my type. However, I was disappointed when he put on a ratty blue t-shirt. It hugged his firm torso. The shirt had *Free Protein Shakes* printed on the front with an arrow pointing down to his crotch. Cody chuckled when he saw me notice.

"Austin promised we'd all get a better apartment when he started his TV gig." He lowered his head. "Looks like Devin and I will be looking for a new roommate instead."

I took a large gulp of my Snapple. "I want to meet Devin."

Cody started down the hall. "Yeah, come on." I placed the Snapple on the counter.

"Before we go. What were you doing Thursday night?"

"I guess you mean after work," he replied. "I wasn't scheduled for clean up, so I got off right at 2:00 a.m. A group of us went to IHOP on Santa Monica Boulevard. I don't know why because it's always crazy at that time, but we went and waited forever for a seat. I don't think we got out of there until just after 4:00."

"Austin's body was found before 6:00."

"Yeah, that's what the cops said." Cody wiped his eyes with his wrist. "They said I didn't have time to get Austin's body up there."

I nodded.

He said, "Come meet Devin."

There wasn't much in Austin's room except a double bed pushed against the wall next to a side window, a long oak dresser, and a closet that was nearly empty. Boxes were on the floor in the center of the room. Half of them were on their side. On the wall above the bed was a Roman Holiday movie poster.

I rarely refer to men in pretty terms, but Devin was exotic and beautiful. Being a mixed race of black and Asian, his skin was the color of honey. He had cupid's bow lips, which were wide in the center and narrow at the ends.

"I'm Devin Doss. I believe you are Mister Detective?"

We shook. "I'm Mitch O'Reilly. I'm a private investigator hired by Dominique Bouchard."

"Yes," Devin said with a long-drawn lisp. "I heard you in the hall." He twirled and put the picture frame in a box. "I heard enough to tell you I manage Fidgety and worked from 9:00 p.m. to 6:30 a.m. when Austin was killed."

"Fidgety?"

"Where have you been? Fidgety is the premier coffee house in downtown LA. You know downtown is exploding with excitement these days."

"So, I heard. The skyline sure is changing, but I never heard of your coffee house. Sorry."

Devin pointed a finger to my chest. "You'll stay sorry until you have some of my creamy mocha with extra foam."

"I'm sure I will," I replied dryly.

Cody tittered.

"Don't worry, unlike Ms. Cody, I'm just a tease," Devin said. "I got me a handsome man who treats me right."

Soft yellow highlights were applied from Devon's eyelids to his paper-thin brows which emphasized their distinctness. His cheekbones were so high, and the rest of his thin face so angular, I had a tough time deciding if it was a natural look or if he wore blush.

I said, "What can you tell me about what happened to Austin the other night. Why did he go to the club and then leave?"

"I could tell you, but everything I know is hearsay," he said. "Cody can tell you more. He was part of the whole escapade."

I turned to Cody. "Escapade?" Until that moment, no escapade or special event of any kind had been mentioned, other than Austin's disappearance.

"Come on," Cody said. "Let's go back to the living room. I'll tell you everything I told the cops forty times yesterday."

I turned to Devin. "Please don't continue packing."

"Nope. I'll keep turning these boxes on their side so you can get a good look."

When Cody and I reached the living room, we sat on his sofa bed, which was surprisingly comfortable.

Cody started the conversation.

"Here's the deal," he said. "I told you Austin knew you were following him, and he wanted to get out for the night. He asked Luna—she's the owner if he could have the night off. He went in the main employee door, talked with a couple of us and then out the side door so you wouldn't know where he'd gone."

A smart move I thought, and asked, "Where'd he go?"

"He was supposed to meet Zach and Rachel around the corner, but they say he never showed. Zach is the tall one you met at The Abbey. Beautiful hair and dreamy eyes, yet stiff as a board. You know Rachel Roundtree, don't you?"

"She doesn't sound familiar. Should I?"

"She was big once, but not so much anymore, I guess. She's a singer who started performing at Topaz last night. She and Zach dated for a short time after he graduated college, but it was never much with her being on the road and all."

"Zach is straight?"

"You don't have any gay friends?"

"I'm gay," I declared, embarrassed I was so blatant about my assumption about Zach. "I also have straight friends, so I meant no disrespect. It's just the way you all interacted at The Abbey and then went to dance at Euphoria."

"Zach is an actor. Homophobic straight actors end up lonely men. Zach and Austin were friends back in high school. That's why I think he resented our friendship because we had become close in college. In New York, Austin and I dated a few months, but it was a disaster. We stayed friends, though, which is how we wound up in Los Angeles together."

"You said you and Austin were best friends. How long did you know each other?"

"We both started school in 2012, so that's what? Six years? I guess he lost touch with Zach, and I think our friendship made Zach feel left out. Sometimes it made me wonder if he's a closet case in love."

"A minute ago, you said Zach was straight. Are you confused, or is he?"

"Hell, I don't know. Austin would get on my case because I think everyone is gay. Wishful thinking most of the time, I guess, because to me, if they're cute, they're gay."

From down the hall, Devin called, "Ain't that the truth. He's a whore for straight men."

"I beg your pardon," Cody yelled back. "I never charge."

"Yeah, yeah, girl. You're a slut then," Devin responded. "Wear the badge with honor."

Cody grinned, winked, and whispered, "I do."

"Why am I bothering to try to talk to each of you privately when you can hear everything through the thin walls in this place?"

Cody shrugged. "I've been wondering the same thing."

"Can you think of any reason Zach, or this Rachel person, would want to kill Austin?"

"I can't think of anyone who would want to kill him," Cody said. "He was so stereotypically good. I've seen him go out of his way to help old ladies cross the street. There's no one I can think of who'd be less likely to get murdered than Austin Bouchard."

"There's something puzzling. T.J. Mooney said Austin had a boyfriend. His exact words were 'he had a good-for-nothing boyfriend.' Dominique didn't say much other than his name is Hector and he was a problem. If there's a boyfriend in the picture, why haven't I seen him?"

Cody frowned. "Austin and Hector started dating about two years ago. Hector is super sweet, and oh my God, he's so fucking hot. He's a model."

Given the looks of the rest of Austin's beautiful friends, that was no surprise. "What was wrong then?"

"T.J. was right, Hector is no good—at least now. He's the kind soul when he's sober, which he was when he met Austin. They were like two scouts. Once Hector started drinking and using again, he became angry, mean, and even violent. He beat the crap out of Austin a couple of times. Almost ruined his beautiful face."

"Were they still together?"

"Kinda-sorta. Like I said, Hector is sweet when he's not using, but that's been a lot less lately. He can't hold a job, and no one is letting him stay at their place anymore, so his life is a rollercoaster. Evil one week and pure as snow the next. Every time Austin was ready to make an official end to their relationship, angel Hector would come back, and Austin wouldn't have the heart. He couldn't handle the guilt if he caused Hector to go into another tailspin, but Hector always did anyway. Someone told me he's hustling now, but I don't believe he's sunk that low—not yet. As hot as that boy is, if he was hustling, he'd be tweaking all the time from all the money he earned."

"When was the last time Austin saw him?"

"You were there," Cody said. "Hector was the guy who went nuts that night in front of Euphoria."

"He was the crazy drunk man taking swings at Austin?"

"Yes. He was bad off. Austin was in tears the rest of the night. He never stopped loving Hector."

"I wouldn't call the guy I saw hot or sexy."

"You didn't see him at his best. Get him off the junk for a few days and clean him up and he's as damned sexy as they come. If he'd keep his shit together, he'd be a world class model. Should I go help Devin now?"

"I'm sure I'll have plenty more question, but you can go back. I need to see Devin."

"Thank you, Jesus," Devin yelled from down the hall. "I need a break."

Cody went to Austin's room while Devin came up the hall and went to the fridge. He looked in, glanced at the empty bottle on the counter and slammed the door shut.

"Cody," he yelled. "Did you give this man my last Snapple?"

"He's a guest. I had to be nice."

"You thieving bitch." He slid his sock covered feet across the wood floor to the sofa, sat, and padded his hand on the cushion next to him. "Have a seat, dear. I'm not mad at you. You didn't know it was my last drink."

"I'll sit here." I plopped myself in the worn recliner.

Devin shrugged. "Suit yourself."

He crossed one knee over the other, pulling his black leggings taut against his thin calves and thighs. He adjusted his baggy mustard colored shirt to lay neatly on his torso.

"How may I assist you, sir?" He leaned forward and placed his hands on one knee.

"Call me, Mitch. Sir makes me feel old."

"Well, Detective Mitch. I heard the questions you asked Ms. Cody, and I don't think I'll help much. Austin and I were roommates. We were friendly and all, but we each had our own circle of friends before he moved in, so we never became tight. Same with Ms. Cody down there. They was friends, but I was just the roommate. Cody was right when he said Austin was as straight as they come. I didn't know any of his friends really well, but not one of them I could think would kill him. It probably was that Hector mess. He would get so crazy when he was fucked up."

"Any idea where I can find Hector?"

"Lord no. I doubt Hector himself knows where he is. Austin's been worrying himself to death over that tasty Latin man." He put a hand to his mouth. "I shouldn't say things about his death so flippantly."

"Do you have any evidence that may help implicate Hector?"

"I ain't got no evidence on nobody. Austin was a sweetie, and if I could help, I'd help. I'd like to find the bitch that killed him and snatch his head right off."

"Hey, Devin," Cody called from Austin's room. "Do you know where Audrey is?"

"Ain't she in that lunch pail."

"No, she's not here."

Devin jumped out of his seat. "Oh, good Lord. We need to find her before Dominique gets here or she'll wig out."

He scurried to Austin's room, and I followed. Cody was on the floor looking at a Wonder Woman lunch pail.

"She ain't in there?" Devin asked.

Cody opened the lid. "I told you no. See? Start digging in those boxes."

"Maybe the policemen took her." Devin said.

"Why would they?" Cody said. "Wouldn't they take the whole lunch box?"

I asked, "What is Audrey?"

"You mean who?" Devin replied.

"I didn't ask who because I don't know anyone small enough to fit in that lunch box."

"Oh dear, girl," Devin put the back of his hand to his forehead. "We're talking about Audrey Hepburn. Austin had a picture of her—a keepsake from his mom."

Cody and Devin dug through the boxes that were on their sides, spilling out the contents. They frantically sorted through each pile.

Cody said, "After the mess the police made searching yesterday, and the mess we're making now, Austin would have a fit. He was such a neat freak."

A light rapping came from the front door. "Hello? Devin? Cody? Are you home?"

Devin said. "The shits about to hit the fan now." He eyed Cody. "Hold on, Dominique."

Cody whispered, "Mitch, go distract her to give us time."

"How am I supposed to distract her? I'm not even sure what for."

"We'll be right there," Cody hollered then turned to me. "Think of anything to give us time to find the picture. There's got to be something you can think of."

"I'll try," I said, then stepped into the hall where Dominique was standing in the doorway. "Could you have a seat in the living room before going through Austin's things? I'd like to discuss this case a bit more."

When I walked into the living room, she set her purse with Rémy inside on the couch and sat next to it. I also sat on the couch on the opposite end.

"This is a tough time for you," I said. "I want you to know I understand that. We're going to—"

"Oh my God!" She stood and pointed out the window.

A shadowed face belonging to someone leaning in from the fire escape was looking in a front window. Upon hearing her scream, they ducked away.

I raced out the door and down the steps.

Nine

There was no one visible when I reached the front stoop, but a grunting sound came from above. The man who had been in the window was stepping across from the fire escape on the second floor to the top of the awning above the barbershop. The barber, seeing me staring up, came out of his store.

"That's him," the barber declared, while pointing to the man above. "I keep telling him to stop climbing above my shop."

The man flung himself from the escape, landed on top of the awning, then rolled off and hit the sidewalk inches in front of me.

"I keep telling you I will call the police," the barber yelled, standing above the man.

The guy grabbed his knee, looked at me and got up to hobble away. I grabbed the back of his t-shirt, and the force of his forward movement ripped it, causing it to dangle off his body, held only by the thicker fabric of his collar around his neck. Regaining his momentum, he attempted to flee but fell on his chest when I dove forward and grabbed him by his knees. His attempt to writhe his legs from under my body were fruitless. That didn't hold him back from attempting to kick me in the chest. The kicking stopped as a foot landed squarely on his back, knocking the wind out of him. The foot belonged to Zach, Austin's tall friend who I also met at the Abbey.

When the man lifted and turned his head to look back, Dominique's hand smacked across his cheek. "Hector Rojas, how dare you?" She exclaimed. She held Rémy in her other arm.

Devin and Cody pulled Hector off the ground. Out of fear of being hit, Devin stepped back and shielded his face with his hands while Cody held Hector by wrapping his arms around his chest.

"You're not going anywhere, sonofabitch," Cody said.

I crossed my arms and nodded. "I finally get to meet the boyfriend."

Dominique and Devin both stood aside nervously while Cody and Zach pushed Hector into the front entrance of the apartment building. I looked to the barber and shrugged.

He asked, "Should I call the police?"

Dominique slumped and shook her head. "Please don't. We'll handle it."

When Devin, Dominique and I entered the apartment, Hector was sitting on the couch leaning forward with his head between his knees. Cody stood over him holding his shoulders down with his beefy arms. Zach stood stone-faced with his arms crossed.

"What did you do with it?" Cody asked.

Hector answered, "With what?"

Cody said, "The Audrey Hepburn, *Breakfast at Tiffany's* photo. What do you think I meant?"

Hector said, "I didn't do anything with it. Austin keeps it hidden somewhere."

"And you took it, bitch." Devin waved a finger.

"Oh no." Dominique's voice trembled. "The Audrey photo is missing? Hector do you have it?"

"No, Dominique, how would I get it?"

Zach stood stoic over Hector and asked in his monotone voice, "Is that why you killed Austin, you motherfucker? For that stupid photo?"

Cody said, "That barber outside said he keeps telling you he's going to call the police. You've climbed up here before. What did you do with it?"

Hector placed his face in his hands. "I did nothing. I wouldn't know where to get it."

Dominique held Rémy against her breasts and sobbed over the dog. "I must have that photo."

I asked, "Would someone tell me about the Audrey Hepburn picture?"

"It was Austin's graduation present from me,"
Dominique said. "He had been a fan of *Breakfast at
Tiffany's* since he first saw the movie. I think he was
twelve. He fell in love with Audrey Hepburn. It's a photo
of her sitting on the sofa from the set made from half a
clawfoot bathtub. On one side behind her stood director
Blake Edwards with George Peppard on the other. George
is holding her iconic cigarette holder in his mouth, and they
are all laughing it up like the best of friends. Are you
familiar with the film?"

"One of my favorites, too. I didn't know Blake Edwards
directed it."

"He was a lovely man. I met him at my wedding when I
married T.J. It's amazing he came because they despised
each other. Then again, if everyone who disliked T.J. didn't
come, the church would have been empty."

I said, "I liked his *Pink Panther* films. Funny."

She gave me a blank stare. "If you say so." After
pausing a moment, she said, "The photo is rare. I know of
no other, and it was signed by all three of them. Do you
know what that is worth?"

"I presume a lot."

Zach had stepped back and took a rigid stance. "A whole
lot," he said dryly. "Especially to someone like Hector."

I asked, "Can you all head out while I talk to Hector?"

Hector jerked his head up. "Who are you?"

"I'm Mitch. I'm a PI Dominique hired to investigate Austin's murder."

"I'll only talk if Dominique stays," he demanded.

It took more than a little work to convince Devin, Cody, and Zach to leave the apartment building, but Dominique was able to coax them. She gave them her Starbuck's card. She sat on the couch next to Hector while I paced the floor, my adrenalin still running from our tussle.

He was one of those men who was so attractive it was hard not to stare. His smooth skin emphasized his delicate features, yet his thick, rich eyebrows, and stubble chin made him undeniably masculine. Despite the fear in his narrow eyes, their rich brown pools were hypnotic. It was hard to believe this was the disheveled, filthy drunk I had seen less than a week before. Pretty boy seemed anxious, so I chose to dive into hardcore questioning.

"Hector," I exploded. "What were you doing on that fire escape?"

His cheeks were soaked with tears. He pushed his back deeper in the couch. "Austin took my key. There's no other way for me to get in. I didn't see Cody or Devin's cars, so I thought no one was here. They must be parked around the corner."

I stomped my foot to intimidate him. "That doesn't answer my question. Why did you want to get in?"

The neighbors banging on the ceiling downstairs caused him to jump.

I pointed my finger inches from his face. "Why did you try to break in?"

"I loved Austin. I wanted to get something to remember him by."

Dominique asked, "Isn't the Audrey photo enough or do you need that for money?"

"I don't have that photo, or even know where he kept it. I just wanted something. I don't know what. Anything."

"Hold on," Dominique patted his leg and walked down the hall. Hector and I remained silent until she came back holding a maroon pullover shirt with weaves of gold vines through it. "You gave this to Austin, didn't you? Why don't you take what's left of that shirt of yours off and you can have this? Austin loved it."

Hector put the shirt on and grinned while I stood speechless. Dominique's change in attitude discounted every ounce of fear and intimidation I had worked so hard to attain. I collapsed into the recliner.

"Tell me about the other night," I grumbled. "You were taking swings at Austin and today you're telling me you loved him. What gives?"

"Do you mean Tuesday in WeHo? How do you—" he shook his head. "I was fucked up. Drinking and doing Tina all day, but I've been clean two nights and am going to an Alcoholics Anonymous meeting tomorrow."

"Tina?" Dominique inquired.

"Crystal meth," I told her.

"Why wait until tomorrow," she stood. "I'll find you an A.A. meeting right after we're done here."

Hector shook his head. "No, I'm good. Tomorrow works."

Dominique sat and sighed.

"Tell me about Thursday night," I asked. "Where were you… between 9:00 p.m. and 5:00 a.m.?"

"I don't know the exact times, but you know where Plummer Park is? It's a bad place to sleep, but I found a nearby house with hedges right up to it on Vista Street. I squeeze behind the hedge, against the house. It's next to their front window, but they're always in the back. They can't see me, and I don't snore."

I said, "Helluva weird place to sleep. Can anyone vouch you were there?"

"It's not that weird," Hector responded. "If I sleep in a park, I'll likely get run out or arrested. Even worse, people I know might see me. Maybe you think getting my throat slit in a tent city is a better option? No, no one saw me when I was sleeping. I was getting fucked up with some guys earlier, but I'm not sure who they are or what time it was."

"I'm sure your fine, respectable friends are around somewhere," I said. "Maybe you can take me to your little nest against the house too?"

"Great, you're going to get me caught. I don't want to have to find a new spot"

I ignored his protest. "Who do you think is capable of killing Austin?"

Hector shrugged. "Hell, I don't know. Maybe Zach?" He laughed. "He claims he's straight but has fawned over Austin for years. He's about as straight as a Slinky."

I looked at Dominique. "Are you aware of this?"

She huffed. "I've heard rumors. Austin and Zach had been friends for years, but I don't think it's more than that. They were almost rivals more than friends. Always competing for roles in school."

Hector stood. "Can I leave now?"

Dominique said, "Would you please bring back the Audrey picture?"

"You've been so good to me. If I had it, I would give it to you." He gritted his teeth and looked at me. "Can I go?"

Frustration and helplessness consumed me. I didn't want to let the bastard go, but there's no law that requires anyone talk to a private eye. "I can't hold you if you won't stay, but it doesn't look good for you to run off." I said. "How do I reach you when I have more questions?"

"I wish I knew that myself." He straggled out the door.

Dominique pulled tissue from her purse and wiped her eyes. She placed her white powder puff on the floor where it scurried down the hall. She walked to the kitchenette.

I said, "If you're looking for a Snapple, I drank the last one."

"No," she replied. "Austin liked herb tea. I'd like to make myself a cup." She shuffled through the cupboards. "Would you care for some?"

"Herbal teas don't have caffeine, do they?"

"Not usually."

"No thanks. I don't see the point."

She pulled down a box of chamomile tea and set it on the counter. After turning on the heat under a teapot, she sat back on the couch.

I said, "You're obviously grieving, but holding up amazingly well."

"I was a model and the wife of a Hollywood mogul. You learn to keep things together on the surface. I'll fall apart plenty back at my hotel."

"Your relationship with Hector seems...to put it nicely, weird. Dysfunctional."

She cocked her head. "How so?"

I felt the blood rush to my face. "One minute you were sweet and loving and the next you acted like you couldn't stand to be around him. I mean, things started with a slap out on the sidewalk, but a few minutes later you were gifting him Austin's shirt."

"I understand," she said. "Hector is a sweet young man, but he's very troubled. I deal with him with how he needs to be dealt with, based on the moment. I was so happy that Austin had found himself a handsome and charming young man, but that changed when Hector fell off the wagon."

"Cody said Hector started using again. So, he got clean and then relapsed. Right?"

"Oh yes. He lost his job with the fire department because of his drinking, but was sober when he met Austin, and they hit it off right away. He had no direction, and well, you saw him, he's gorgeous. I helped him get some small modeling gigs. Nothing much. A photo shoot here and there, and I think he stood looking pretty in a commercial. He got a job in some print shop over on La Cienega Boulevard to bring in spending money between gigs."

"But things went wrong," I said.

"Yes, I don't understand it. Between his jobs and his relationship with Austin, he seemed to be doing well, but less than six months ago, he started drinking and doing drugs again for no apparent reason that I can see."

"Sometimes there doesn't have to be a reason."

The pot screamed. Dominique walked to the kitchenette and poured herself a cup of tea. She didn't turn back. She leaned over the counter and sobbed instead. How she knew I was getting up, I don't know, but she politely told me to sit back down. She took one big sniff, dried her eyes with more tissue, sat on the couch with me, and put her cup down.

"Austin was heartbroken," she said without missing a beat. "Hector would be warm one minute and then have violent outbursts the next. Austin told me he was afraid of Hector sometimes. I wish Austin would have been strong enough to leave him, though I feel for Hector and what he's going through."

"It will be hard for him to come up with an alibi. Do you think he killed Austin?"

"Absolutely not. I think he has that damned Audrey photo, but I don't think he'd kill him."

"Sentimental value?"

"No," she said. "That photo is worth thousands. That's a lot of money for a homeless drug addict."

"Possibly even enough to kill."

"Where's Hector?" Cody bellowed when he Zach and Devin came back in the apartment.

Dominique said, "He left just a few minutes ago."

Devin flailed his arms and his mouth dropped. "Left? You let that bitch go? She should be locked up where someone can love that pretty little Latin ass."

"Not our call," I said. "I'm not a cop, so I can't hold him. You can call them if you want, but all you got on him is an attempted break-in. Everything else is conjecture."

Cody said, "I'll kick his ass if he comes back." He threw himself on to the couch.

"Damn, Austin," Zach said. "He kept trying to break up with Hector but was too much of a pussy. Said he didn't want to break his heart and kick a man when he's down."

"Interesting," I said. "I was going to ask why they didn't break up."

"Sorry to say, Austin never stopped loving him," Cody interjected. "I understand, I guess. I thought Hector was one of the nicest guys I ever met. Hell, I fell in lust immediately. I can't tell you how jealous I was of Austin when they first went out. But, once he started hitting my friend and breaking stuff, I was done with him. Austin was too, but couldn't say it. His plan was to get his nerve up this weekend."

"I'm going back to finish cleaning Austin's things," Devin said. "I'm sure Ms. Dominique don't want to be staying around this neck of the woods much longer."

She said, "No, I want to stay and help. Is there anything else, Mitch?"

"Not for now, but I'm staying, too. I need to search Austin's room. I don't expect much since the police have been through it all, but it'd be foolish not to look." I picked Rémy off the floor and placed him in her arms. "When I'm done here, I need to head to Topaz."

"No point in going now," Cody said. "It's closed for a private party. All you'll do is piss people off."

"Closed for a private party on a Saturday night?" I asked.

"Yeah, I guess the son of a Saudi dignitary has booked the place." Cody looked at the time on his phone. "Hell, I need to be there in an hour."

"Looks like we have plenty of time to go through Austin's things," Dominique said.

"Let's get started," I replied.

Ten

My plan to sleep in until 9:00 a.m. was ruined by an early morning banging on my sliding glass door. It was the only entrance to the A-framed guest house I rented in Silver Lake. My attempt to ignore the unwelcome guest was futile, due to their incessant pounding. I threw on some boxers and a tank top and slogged down from my lofted bedroom into the tiny living room. Harold Beavers was waiting outside.

"Have any coffee or tea made yet?" He asked.

I shielded my eyes from the sun. "It's only 7:30, I rarely make coffee while sleeping."

I was not happy to see Harold's face that morning. The last thing I was in the mood for was to be nagged into trying to go back to the support group. I was struggling with enough bullshit in my head.

"I'm surprised you're not up early working," he said. "You have that big case with T.J. Mooney."

"It's not the Mooney case any longer, but it doesn't matter because I'm still working. Hard work requires extra sleep."

"It's good you're getting good sleep. Do you know what the Dalai Lama said?"

"No, but I'm sure you'll tell me."

"He said, 'Sleep is the best meditation.'"

"For once you have a quote that makes sense. What are you here for?"

He leaned an elbow on my canary-yellow, laminate kitchen counter. "What brings me is you. You've had me worried since we talked on the phone yesterday. You seem bitter."

"Because I am fucking bitter." I dumped some water in the coffee maker and turned it on. "I thought the support group was supposed to help me. Instead, I'm thinking about shit I haven't thought about in years. I don't want to think about any of it. The group brought back the damn flashbacks, which I haven't had in three years, and even then, they were minor. A guy is dead because I'm having them."

"Wha—"

"I've told this a thousand times now, so you only hear it once—I had a flashback, I met the guy I was tracking, I had to hold back so he wouldn't see me again, I lost the guy, and he was murdered."

Harold said, "Was it possible for you to watch him every second of every day?"

"No, but—"

"Llama Surya Das says, 'Forgiveness means letting go of the hope of a better past.' Typically, the most common person to forgive is ourselves."

I rolled my eyes. "What a load of shit."

"This angry person is the man I met three months ago. You can't change overnight, but don't let go of the progress you made."

He was right; I had reverted to my bad behavior. I didn't dare tell Harold that it felt good not faking it through the day. That life was not all rainbows and unicorns. "What the hell are you doing here so early?"

"I have an appointment with a client in an hour on this side of town. Gives me the opportunity to arrange for you to go back with me to group next week."

"I was better off before the group and doing just fine. I need to deal with shit on my own. I'll work it out.

"You're not coming to group anymore?" Harold asked. "Come discuss it with us next Saturday."

"I didn't say I'm never coming back, just not right now. You and the group will survive without me."

"I hope you survive without us."

"I've been okay without you all for the last thirty years."

"I've told you before," Harold said, "You can't only go to group. You need therapy and maybe even a psychiatrist."

"I tried the psychiatry route when I was first released from the army. Digging up what was best kept buried didn't work then, and I have no desire to give it a second round. No one wants to hear my problems, and I ain't taking no goddamn pills to screw with my brain."

Harold sighed. "Maybe you're right and need a break. Three months is a long time to work on yourself in the beginning. I only ask. Actually, I'll beg. Please continue to work on being nicer to people and use the meditation tools you've learned to chase away those negative thoughts."

"I'll be fine."

I poured myself some coffee. I wanted Harold to leave, but he had been good to me since the day we met. As much as I wanted to chase him away, I couldn't do it. "Want a cup?"

"Just a half," Harold said. "I can't stay long."

I put our cups on my round, oak dining table, and we took a seat.

He said, "Wine barrel, swivel, dining chairs? These are a blast from the past."

"Don't knock it," I said. "The place is cheap and comes fully furnished."

"It wasn't a judgment. It makes me feel nostalgic." He raised his coffee then set it right down. "What happened that you lost track of this guy?"

"Technically I was off duty, but I was tired and slept in my car where he worked. Before you say that makes it not my fault, his father doesn't see it that way and neither do I."

"Sometimes shit just happens. Do you know who said, 'We never accepted that randomness is not a mistake in the equation—it is part of the equation.'? It was Jeanette Winterson who wrote *Oranges are not the Only Fruit*. I'm sure you've heard of her. It's a brilliant book, and she's a lesbian."

"For an open-minded guy, you say some of the dumbest things. I rarely read, and I don't know every member of the lesbian or gay community."

"That's not what I meant, but point taken." He stood. "I need to get going. I hope you change your mind and come back, but everyone has to work things out in their own way."

"Thanks for chilling out, because I was ready to throw you out otherwise."

"You're not done with me yet. I didn't say I wasn't coming back. Any chance you can break free to catch a Dodgers' game anytime soon?"

"Of course. With this case, I have all the time in the world."

"I'll take that as a 'no'."

Harold left without having taken a sip of his coffee.

I grabbed my fourth cup of coffee and sat with pen and paper to collect my thoughts and think through who I needed to speak with in the Bouchard case. My list was short. Cody, Devin and that other friend, Zach Pickering, could possibly help expand my search, but I had a greater concern gnawing at me. How was I going to talk to the Mooney family? Having been asked not to return to T.J.'s home made it unlikely he'd chat over a cup of tea.

I was mulling over my plans when a second visitor came to the door. It was Trent.

"Greetings," he said as he stepped in. "I come bearing gifts."

I opened the bag he dropped on the counter and took a sniff of the meaty goodness. "This is déjà vu. Wasn't that what you said the first time you ever brought me burgers?"

He laughed. "I don't know, but I'm sure I didn't bring one of these." Trent wrapped his powerful arms around me and rubbed his beard against my neck, then gave me a swift, yet tender kiss. He continued to hold me as he leaned back and surveyed my face with his glistening amber eyes.

"Wow." I stumbled back. "This is one hell of a lunch hour, though a bit early."

He flashed his mischievous grin as he ran a finger down the center of my chest. "What do you say I give you a lunch hour you'll never forget? Let's go up to the loft. We can warm the burgers when we're done."

Each time I saw Trent, it hurt more than the last. He had so much love for me that I could not return—or, refused to. I believed I loved him too, but I wasn't ready to say it. We'd only been dating three months, and I wouldn't give myself over to him the way he deserved. Yet, I played along, confused whether I was toying with him or myself.

"Going upstairs is damned tempting," I said, "but I need to head out soon. I've got a lot to do."

"You and your old-fashioned work ethics." He kissed me again. "You know, I had an uncle who worked all the

time. I think it was an uncle—maybe it was my cousin." He
stared at the wall for a moment. "We weren't close to that
side of the family because they lived somewhere in the
Midwest. I think it was Illinois. Maybe it was Iowa.
Anyway, Uncle Terrence or Cousin Terrence worked hard
every day in the coal mines."

"I don't think there are coal mines in Illinois or Iowa.
You sure it wasn't somewhere like West Virginia?"

"Don't be ridiculous," Trent howled. "West Virginia
isn't in the Midwest. Wherever he lived, Terrence worked
at least fifteen hours a day."

"And he died young and miserable, right?"

"No." He shook his head. "Terrence was one of the
happiest men you'd ever meet, and he lived to be one
hundred and one. Spry and moving about one minute and
flat dead the next. You know, the way it should be."

"What does this have to do with my working too hard?"

He placed a finger on his lower lip. "Now I'm not sure it
does." His hands began rubbing each of my shoulders.
"You seem shaky."

"Too much shit going on. I told you about getting that
kid killed. What you don't know is after the victim's dad
fired me on Friday, his mom hired me on Saturday to find
the killer. Hell, I was planning to do that on my own time

out of guilt. The money is a bonus. She's kind of funny. One of those frou-frou purse dog ladies, but down to earth and easy to talk to. So far, she's the most level-headed one in the family."

"Doesn't sound like a problem to me then. Do you have a good list of suspects?"

"Not really. I barely know the people in his life. He's got two roommates who have strong alibis. There's his dad, half-brother, half-sister, and I know nothing personally about them. He had a boyfriend who is a homeless drug addict, and that's it." It dawned on me I hadn't questioned Zach. "There is another friend I need to speak with, too, I guess."

"A drug addict boyfriend? You think he got high or something and killed him?"

"I don't know." I took a bite from my burger and washed it down with water. "The other guy I mentioned is named Zach. Other than being a friend, I know nothing about him either. That's why I've got to get out of here right away. I need to talk to more people. Whoever killed this guy knew him."

Trent asked, "Because they took him near the Hollywood Sign?"

"Of course. I mean, I guess some random sickos could take his body up there, but that's not likely."

We grabbed our food off the counter and sat next to each other at my table.

Trent nudged me with his shoulder. "How are you holding up?"

"Like I said, the case has me shook up and feeling a lot of guilt."

"That's not what I meant." He gently placed an arm across my shoulders. "I mean how are you really holding up? The longer we're together the less you open yourself to me. I'm worried about you—and us."

That was the conversation I'd been dreading, and it couldn't have come at a worse time. There was too much going on with the case. There was too much going on with me. I didn't have the time or energy to work on a relationship, but I didn't want to give it up either.

I said, "It has nothing to do with you or us. Just working through some shit with the memories is all."

"Memories of Jackson?"

"No, Jackson was killed during my second tour. He may have been my fiancé, but I wasn't there when he was shot. I think of him every day, but these memories are of my first tour three years earlier. You've seen one of my flashbacks."

Trent said, "It was scary."

"How do you think they feel from my end? I never talk about the first tour because I don't like to think about it. Every time the memories come up, I push them down again. I watched a friend of mine get shot to pieces." Tears were welling in my eyes. I faked a cough and wiped them.

"Oh, my God." Trent said, "Do you want to talk about it?"

"Hell no, I don't."

His lips quivered. "How horrible. I hate war."

"George Suzuki, who we called Suze, and I went through basic and MP training together. Other than Jackson, He was the closest friend I had in the Army. I tried to help. It was obvious the Taliban were playing with him. They were making him suffer. They fired multitudes of shots at us while they picked him off one bullet at a time. By the time backup got there, he was dead."

Trent rubbed my back. "I'm sorry. I am so sorry."

"And That! Is what my flashbacks have been. Sometimes I see something that sets me off. Sometimes I hear something. Sometimes it seems for no goddamn reason at all, but it keeps happening. I'll walk down the street, and suddenly Suze is lying in the street screaming. I can explain it over and over, but I don't think you'll get it if you haven't been there."

I wanted to tell Trent more about the locals who were gunned down, that we couldn't protect, and my other friend K.K. being shot by the fire. I wanted to explain my inability to get more than a few shots out to protect my friends and citizens, but I couldn't. I didn't say as much as I wanted. I said more than I thought I could.

"I wish I could better understand what you're going through, so I could help."

I leaned forward and put my forehead on the table while Trent continued to rub my back.

He breathed, "Don't you think that's why you should continue getting additional help?"

I jumped up and balled my fists. "No! That's exactly why I shouldn't go. I don't need to think about this shit." I stormed into the bathroom without shutting the door.

Trent knocked on the door frame and asked, "Can I have a kiss goodbye?"

I pulled my t-shirt over my head. "Of course."

Instead of a kiss, he held me tight for over a minute and stole my lips before heading out the front door. I leaned against the bathroom wall and thought through everything I had just said, plus the parts I couldn't say. My hope was it would make me feel better, but I was worse. I stared in the mirror at an unknown face with tears rolling down his cheeks. When I could no longer stand to look at myself, I took a shower.

It was time to go check out where they found Austin Bouchard's body.

Eleven

Rattler Trail ran off Tacoma Drive in the Hollywood Hills. It was the highest and closest trail to The Hollywood Sign. It was short, running to a dead end below the sign to give tourists the best photo opportunity to catch a picture of themselves with the landmark in the background. The length of the trail from where Tacoma Drive ends, to the bench where Austin Bouchard's body was found, was slightly over a quarter mile.

Matias Castro, the police detective overseeing the Bouchard case, refused to give me any information, so I put in a call to my old friend Detective Dirk Turner, who worked with me before. He said there was little information to give. The body had been dragged most of the way, covering all traces of the culprit's footprints to the bench. Because of the popularity of the trail, attempts to distinguish the killer's prints when leaving the area, from the hundreds of tourists who hike the trail, had proven fruitless.

In 1923, Real estate developers built the massive sign, which originally said HOLLYWOODLAND. At the time, Los Angeles was as bigoted as the rest of the country, so it promoted an exclusive white only housing development on the slope below. Despite standing for the glitz and glitter of Tinseltown, there wasn't much glamor to the sign's history. Since it was nothing more than a cheesy billboard, its expected lifespan was only eighteen months, and it deteriorated fast. Over the years it had been saved numerous times from being torn down. The condition of the sign fluctuated until the 1970s when much of the first O crumbled away, making it look like a U, and the D tipped over. Structural engineers reported the sign was un-repairable and needed to come down. Celebrities, studios, and business leaders united and raised the money to replace the old monstrosity with a bright, beautiful, and far sturdier sign. In 1978, HOLLYWOOD vanished from the hillside for three months before it was born again.

Sitting on the bench where Bouchard's body had been found was a familiar face – Hector Rojas. He bolted upright when he saw me and held his hands out. "Don't touch me. I'm not doing anything."

"Chill out," I said. "I'm not looking for you, or to hurt you. I didn't expect to see you here."

His body shook and the veins in his eyes were thick and red. His pupils were as large as a cat's at night. The guy was strung out on meth.

Hector's voice faltered. "I heard they took the police tape down last night. I wanted to see where Austin was. I hear he was on this bench."

"The police say he was set on this bench, probably looking down the hill toward Hollywood, but he had fallen over. His body was found on the ground there next to it."

It was a clear day, and rain the night before drizzled enough to clear some of the smog. The view was outstanding. Down the slope of the hill were multi-million-dollar homes, most of which were simple ranch houses. Just beyond that was the Hollywood Reservoir, also known as Lake Hollywood. The city beneath the reservoir looked beautiful, and peaceful, from the distance, and I believed the shimmering at the horizon was coming off of the Pacific. Behind us, the Hollywood Sign stood grand.

Hector sat back on the bench and lowered his head. He muttered, "I didn't kill him, you know. Everyone thinks I did, but I loved him. He was my soulmate."

"You didn't act like you loved him the night I saw you in WeHo. You looked like you were out to hurt him."

"I was fucked up. Really drunk. I've hurt him a couple of times and will never forgive myself for it. That doesn't make me a killer."

"When was the last time you saw him?"

"That night you saw me."

"Before then?"

"We sat and talked in West Hollywood Park. He never said it, but I could tell he wanted to break up with me. I almost said it, but I couldn't. It was a strained conversation. I could feel his distance. I had lost him."

"Did you fight?"

"No, it was polite. That's the problem. It was too polite. Rigid."

"Do you have the Audrey photo?"

"How many times do I have to say no?"

"General consensus is you're lying. Even Dominique isn't sure you're telling the truth."

"She has every reason to believe that. She helped me a lot, and I let her down. Doesn't matter, though. I didn't kill Austin, and I don't have the photo. I wish I did."

"You need the money?"

"I could use the money, but I wouldn't be able to sell it. It meant too much to him. He was obsessed over Audrey Hepburn. She's the only thing I got tired of hearing him talk about."

"I hear she ate tulip bulbs during World War II."

"Yeah, yeah. She and her mom made flour from them. Her dad was a Nazi sympathizer, so he dumped them for the cause. Trust me, there's nothing I don't know about her."

At Austin's apartment, my attempt to strike fear in him didn't work, so I was trying to earn his trust. It was easy since I'm a sucker for hard luck cases, but also difficult. He reminded me too much of a time in my life that was best forgotten. I broke free from meth before it was too late, but I had almost crossed the line of no return.

"What are you doing?" He asked.

I was on my hands and a knee snooping around the bench.

"A likely fruitless attempt to see if I can find some evidence. It doesn't sound like the cops found much, but I have to look anyway."

"Why are you being so nice to me? You were an asshole at Austin's place."

"I wasn't an asshole. I was trying to get information out of you, and you weren't cooperating."

"Resistance is normal when you're under attack. Everyone was at me. I thought Cody was going to go for my jugular."

"Fair enough." I stood and paced around the bench. "How badly do you want that photo, Hector?"

"So badly I'd do almost anything, except kill someone. I didn't want to steal it from Austin. I want it now, so I can remember him." He hesitated. "Are you finding anything?"

"Nothing. As expected."

"Isn't it real hard to get a body from the road to here? Austin would have been heavy."

"It looks like the body was dumped in the bushes at the end of the road. At the beginning of the trail. It was probably left there while the killer parked somewhere and walked back to drag the body here."

"Why wouldn't they have just left it there?"

"That's the big question. Likely, they were making a statement by putting him here below the sign. Especially since they put a tourist shirt on him with the Hollywood Sign printed on it."

"I didn't hear that part."

"I'm guessing you don't read or watch the news."

"The only news I get is what I overhear."

"Based on all that, my theory is the killer was trying to make a statement. I can't for the life of me come up with a reason for you to make that kind of statement. What was it?"

"You're a sonofabitch. I had no statement to make. I didn't kill him."

"I'm heading back down the hill. Why don't you let me drop you off at an AA meeting somewhere?"

"I want to stay here longer. The bus stop is only two miles away. I'm going to go to a meeting tomorrow."

"I hope tomorrow comes for you someday."

"What does that mean?"

"It means I don't want to see you die."

Twelve

Though considered the spot for Hollywood's rich and famous to party and play, The Sunset Strip was an eclectic mix of clubs. The well-known music establishments, such as The Viper Room, The Roxy, and the Rainbow Bar & Grill were housed in buildings from the 1960s and 70s and looked it. Though known for these monuments to rock-and-roll, most of the strip had become upscale looking chic bars and restaurants mixed between expensive boutique shops, like Armani and Fred Segal.

Topaz was a blend of the two worlds, combining an upscale bar and restaurant downstairs with a music theater upstairs. The club was housed in a contemporary cube building. A wall of glass on the lower level gave diners a full view of the happenings on the famous boulevard. The second floor was windowless sheet metal with Topaz emblazoned across the front in the style of handwriting embedded with yellow-gold inlays. Through the large glass doors facing Sunset, I entered the lobby which had stark white walls and yellow-gold floor tiles that matched the signage out front.

I had called to meet with the club owner, Luna Salcedo, and scheduled an appointment at noon. Being forty-five minutes late, I hoped she would still be available. The slim and perky young woman with golden brown hair had me wait at the host stand for her boss. She was singing and swaying to "Single Ladies" by Beyonce, which was playing in the lobby.

Within a few minutes the owner greeted me. "Mitch O'Reilly, you have perfect timing." She took my hand and gently patted it. "Had you arrived at noon you would have waited for some time while I handled a minor crisis in the kitchen. I don't know why on earth I scheduled us to meet during our lunch rush. Please follow me."

Luna escorted me into the dining room, the entrance of which was flanked on each side by opaque yellow-gold glass sheets with streams of water flowing down each. The color matched the sconces which sat at each of the many tables lined formally from the enormous front window to the back of the room.

"I'm surprised by your color scheme, Luna."

She turned, placed a hand on my chest and chuckled. "Don't tell me you were expecting a blue themed club."

"Yes, actually I was."

"Oh Mitch, you have been taken in by modern retailers. Sadly, blue topaz has become one of the most popular stones, but most are not natural. They use radiation to get them that color. If you knew anything about birthstones, you would know the light golden color is most common in nature. I'm a November baby, which makes it my birthstone. Come back to my office, and we can talk."

Luna glided across the restaurant greeting customers at nearly every table as she sped along. She took long, methodical strides and kept her chin held high.

A hallway that led to the kitchen had a door on each side facing each other. One marked Accounting and the other had a sign that simply said Luna. In the immaculate accounting room, a man was half hidden behind a computer monitor set upon a large oak desk.

"Mitch O'Reilly, this is my accountant, Wesley Stumpf." Luna placed a hand on my shoulder and gestured to the man. "He's been with me for years since before I had my old club in Hollywood. I stole him from my former employer."

"It's a pleasure to meet you Mitch." He stood to shake my hand and knocked a pen holder on the floor, scattering the pens under the desk. "How embarrassing."

His oval face turned as bright red as his thinning hair as he eyed the mess on the floor. His toothy smile never left his pockmarked face.

He turned his head back to me and gazed with his lime colored eyes. "I can be such a klutz sometimes."

I chuckled. "I understand. I knock a massive pile of papers off my desk at least once a day."

"Oh, that won't happen here," he guffawed. "Luna would never allow a mess to collect on my desktop." He grabbed a manila folder and placed it in a side drawer. "I hear you're investigating Austin Bouchard's death."

"Yes, I'm going to talk to Luna for a while, but I'd like to meet you when we're done."

"I've eaten lunch, so I should be available all afternoon."

Luna brushed the front of Wesley's white, buttoned up shirt. "That's right. Don't you go anywhere," Luna teased. "You're glued to that desk until you spend time with Mitch."

Luna's office was slightly larger than Wesley's with more upscale furniture. I knew little about materials, but I could tell high end fabric, and had once had sex on top of a rosewood desk almost identical to hers.

"Have a seat, please," she said.

I eased myself into a square shaped brown leather chair with silver studs. It was an old style with a modern update. Rather than sitting behind her desk, she sat in the matching chair next to me, placed an elbow on the side, and rested her chin on her hand. "It gives me chills sitting next to you."

"Excuse me?" I thought she was making a pass.

"You understand. Knowing you're here to gather information about Austin's death is beyond belief. Who would kill such an amazing young man?"

A strand from her short, curly, brunette hair hung down her forehead. She gracefully pushed it back up where it belonged.

"From everything I hear, he was a boy scout. I'm sorry for your loss."

"I was so angry when he told me he would be leaving to be on a TV show. Not angry at him, of course. I was delighted because he deserved it. I saw him perform at a small theater in North Hollywood. He wasn't the lead, but he stole the show—and I don't mean he was the type to ham it up. That wasn't like him. He had a look and charisma that was hard not to be drawn to." She gave a nervous titter. "I guess I'm saying it wasn't his fault he was so striking. I knew I'd lose him, eventually."

I'd heard plenty about Austin being handsome and charming. Handsome like all of his friends, and there I sat next to his strikingly beautiful boss. Her wide, brown eyes were hard to look away from. It was obvious she noticed me staring, yet she didn't flinch. Clearly, she was used to it.

I asked, "How long had Austin worked for you?"

She placed her hand on top of mine. Her light bronze skin almost glowed. "Two years right out of college. It was his first job, so he applied as a busser. I'm selective in whom I hire, but I knew right away he should be a waiter despite his lack of experience. I haven't hired anyone off the cuff like that before or since. It was an incredibly good decision. We're still new around here. Topaz may be the hottest spot on The Strip, and has been since we opened two years ago, but some are still saying we're a flash in the pan. The Whiskey A Go Go opened in 1964, and I plan to hold firm for just as long. I hope to be running this place from my bed in the nursing home in fifty years." She put a hand to her mouth and laughed.

It was hard to picture her ever being old enough to be in a nursing home.

I said, "You're not like the other rock-and-roll joints around here."

"That's because we're not a rock-and-roll joint," she replied. "Whiskey A Go Go and The Viper Room have had the corner on that market for years and serve their clientele well. I knew if I was going to make it, I must be different.

Since House of Blues closed, I knew a different style of venue was a risk, but I took it. I decided the one thing missing in this town is what people turn their noses up to, and that's pop music. Everyone says they hate it, but it's the pop songs you sing in the shower. We bring in pop stars from the 80s until today, and the people eat it up. They practically ripped the doors off the hinges when we had Tiffany."

"Tiffany?"

"Don't you like the oldies, Mitch?"

"Absolutely, I'm a Nirvana fanatic, plus Alice in Chains, and Soundgarden, and—Well, they're not really oldies to me"

"You can't be so young that you don't know Tiffany."

"I'm thirty."

She laughed. "Thirty years ago was the time she was a hit, but I would have thought you would have heard of her. We'll do the grunge bands from time to time, but they're not really our style. There were lots of other hit stars from the 90s. Hold on."

She walked behind her desk and turned up a knob on a speaker on the wall.

"That's 'What is Love,' isn't it?" I asked.

"Yes, by Haddaway. It was a hit here in the U.S. but reached number one in many places throughout the world. It will be in your head the rest of the afternoon, won't it?"

"I'll thank you later for that."

She turned the volume off. "That's the music we play here."

"Getting back to Austin," I said.

"Of course." She sat.

"You were here on Thursday, the night he disappeared, right?"

"I'm told he was here. He requested the night off, and I told him that was fine. The staff says he came in at his usual time anyway but visited with friends for a few minutes. Then he walked out the back door in Wesley's office, which is strange. I have no idea why he didn't go out the employee entrance. They're not supposed to use any other door. I didn't see him, though. I was upstairs with Vanessa Carlton. She performed that night, and we hit it off and talked until long after Austin had gone."

"Do you know why he came here?"

"I have no idea. That's what I told the police detective too. Perhaps he forgot something in his locker, but that's just a guess. Have you talked with Cody Dakota? They were the best of friends. He should know."

Cody had already explained it was Austin's way of ditching me for the night, but I had hoped Luna could shed some more light on the story.

"When does Cody come in again?"

"He's scheduled to work this afternoon. I offered to let him off for a week, but he insisted he'd rather things get as back to normal as possible. He's one of the friendliest men you'd ever meet, and one hell of a flirt, so both the ladies and the men adore him. I'm thrilled he's coming back so soon, but realistically, I think he'd be better if he stayed off."

"Could you hum something for me?" I grumbled.

"Excuse me?"

"That God-awful song is still killing me."

She howled. "I'm so very sorry, but I was trying to give you a taste of what Topaz is all about."

"Please, don't give me another bite." I closed my eyes and took a big sigh. "When does Cody come in?"

"I don't know, but it should be soon. He usually bar tends upstairs in the club, but he's early today because he traded shifts with someone here in the downstairs bar. Wesley can give you his schedule."

"What I haven't asked you is an important direct question. Who do you think would kill Austin?"

"Oh, I don't know. Like you said earlier, Austin was a boy scout. No, more like Captain America. Honest, caring. Do you think he could have been a victim of gay bashing?"

"That's very unlikely. Bashers do their job and run. They don't drag their victims to the base of world-famous landmarks."

"I guess that's true."

"Unless you have something else to add, I want to talk to Wesley."

"That's fine. Let me get out of your way so you have some privacy here. His office can be Grand Central Station during shift changes."

I sat patiently while listening to Luna and Wesley discussing schedules, accounts payable and ticket prices in the outer office. Nearly ten minutes later, Wesley strolled in, sat at Luna's desk, clasped his hands, wiped his nose with a tissue, then clasped his hands again.

"I hope there's something I can say that will help you," he said. "I can't imagine how, but I'll do whatever I can."

I said, "I appreciate your cooperation. I'll start by asking who would kill Austin Bouchard?"

He blew his nose. "Good Lord, how would I know? I do the accounting and hand out paychecks, but that's as far as I get to know these people. He was always a polite young man. One week his check was wrong. Significantly so. Yet, he didn't get upset when I told him it'd be a day before I could get around to printing him a new check. My printer was broken. He took it in stride and thanked me. Beyond that he was another employee to me, but I don't mean to sound callous."

"I understand he was a nice guy, but it's not a big deal for a waiter to disregard a paycheck. They live off tips. Their hourly rate is a pittance."

"I was trying to point out how nice he was. I didn't think I'd offend you."

"Not your fault. I just think the below minimum wage pay for tip earners is bullshit." I took a deep breath and shook my shoulders. "Though you didn't know him, did you see or hear anything that would make you feel suspicious? Perhaps it didn't sound like anything, but looking back you can see how it could be a threat."

Wesley shook his head. "No, nothing at all. I don't recall anything like that."

He raised a tissue. "I apologize. I have these terrible allergies." He blew his nose, but when placing his hands down he spilled a water glass over on to the top of Luna's desk.

"Oh dear," he said as he mopped the desk off with his sleeve.

I grabbed a towel sitting on an extra chair by a window and tossed it to him.

"I can't use that. It's Luna's workout towel." He jumped up, ripped some papers out of her printer, rather than from the stack sitting next to it, and used them to mop up as much water as he could.

Once finished with his poor job of drying the desk, Wesley blew his nose again and sat back down. "You were saying?"

"We were done with the last question. I need to know about Austin coming in your office and going out the back door."

"That was odd. Our associates know they're only allowed to go in and out of their entrance, so I was surprised that he, of all people, would come in to break the rules like that. What little I know; it was unlike him. Unfortunately, I told him it was fine, which got me a chewing out by Luna."

"What's outside that door?"

"There's a small alleyway with a little space where Luna and I park. That's why it's so odd for him to go out there."

"You don't seem like a rule breaker, Wesley."

"It was an unusual circumstance and lack of good judgment."

He looked down and noticed his sleeve was sitting in a small puddle of water still on the desk. He used his shirt to mop it again and then shook his arm vigorously to his side.

"What time was it that Austin came through here?"

"I was extremely busy, but I believe it was around 8:00 p.m."

"Aren't you second in command here?"

"The managers run the operation. I only take care of the office."

"Allowing an employee to go out a wrong exit seems like quite the blunder."

"I already said it was a bad decision. I took heat from Luna over it. There's no reason to belabor the point. Austin said it was important that he use that door because someone was waiting for him at the employee entrance that he had to avoid. I didn't think it was anyone out to hurt him. I assumed he just didn't want to talk to someone, so I was surprised because it seemed immature for someone his age. He was laughing like it was all a game to him."

It was a game for Austin, and the name was "Get Away from The Private Eye." It hit me in the pit of my stomach and did not feel like a game to me.

"But, you didn't stop him from going?" I asked

"I didn't think it was that big of a deal. It was a onetime only thing. I guess I'm more trusting than I should be, especially given my job." He blew his nose again.

"What were you doing that night after Austin left?"

"I stayed here in the office late to catch up on some things. My wife took the kids to Disneyland, and I had them stay at the Best Western Inn to avoid the long drive after the park closed."

"Who saw you here after Austin?"

"No one. I locked the office door to avoid further interruptions and left a little after 10:00 p.m."

"And you went home to an empty house. That seems convenient."

"I see where you are going with this, and I can assure you—"

"I can't think of any further questions for now. If more comes to mind, I'd like you to give me a call." I reached out my business card.

Wesley stood quickly, which caused the rolling chair to fly back and smack the wall, causing a frame to hit the floor.

"Thank goodness," he said. "It's her business license and not something personal."

He placed the broken item on the desk and took my card.

"Did you ever dream of dancing ballet, Wesley?"

"No. Why do you ask?"

"No reason. Thank you for your time."

Wesley blew his nose again.

When I reached the front lobby, I realized I forgot to ask when Cody Dakota was coming to work. I figured I'd wait at the bar until he showed up.

Thirteen

The Topaz downstairs contemporary bar area was long and narrow and smaller than I expected. It appeared to be a necessary evil. The larger focus was on the dining room and the club upstairs. Cody looked sharp behind the long, light bamboo bar, wearing his red paisley vest. His hair still had that look as if he were standing along the surf. Kelly Clarkson's "Since U Been Gone" was playing throughout the lounge.

There were three people sitting at the end of the bar. Along the wall were six four-seater tables. Only two were being used. One had three women and a man all dressed in business attire. The other table had a man and a woman dressed in casual jeans. The way they beamed at each other and laughed, I guessed it was a first or second date.

Cody's eyes widened, and his smile stretched across his face when he saw me. "Mr. Mitch O'Reilly, I didn't expect to see you here. Take a stool, and tell me what's your pleasure."

"I'm going to pass on a drink, but thanks."

"You're assuming when I asked for your pleasure that I was talking about drinks." He winked.

"Are you ever not horny, Cody?"

"What a terrible thought." He snickered. "Seriously, the drink is on me."

"In that case I'll have a Rolling Rock."

"Just a beer? You're going cheap." He popped a top and placed the bottle on the bar. I refused a mug. He said, "I'm guessing you're here for a reason."

"I met with some people and want to talk to you a little, too."

"Or, you could just sit there and look pretty—uh, I mean strikingly handsome."

"I need to talk about Austin leaving again."

The smile erased from his face. "Before you do, I have something for you. Hold on."

He walked to the other end of the bar and filled drinks for the three that were there, checked on the ones at the tables and held up his index finger before walking out of the bar. "Wannabe" by the Spice Girls came on the speaker, and the young couple at the table swayed and mouthed the song to each other. One woman at the end of the bar began dancing while her cohorts continued a conversation and ignored her.

When Cody returned, he was holding some sheets of paper.

"I've been hanging on to these for you in my duffel bag," he said. "Devin and I found these stuffed in a book after you and Dominique left our apartment."

I shuffled through them.

He said, "Hold those down. Don't let anyone see you."

"What are they?"

"They're reports from here: finance reports, or something like that. Austin must have gotten it from Wesley's office."

"Why would he have these?"

"I don't know for sure, but he did tell me he thought Wesley was screwing us over. He said he'd been tracking his hours and the money has been a lot lower on his paycheck. He had me start tracking mine, too, but I haven't been paid yet, so I don't know if there's a discrepancy or not."

"How serious do you think this is?"

"I don't know. If it's off as much as Austin said it was then I guess it'd be serious big time if he's scamming off everyone."

I said, "I can't see how he could make enough money off skimming your wages to make it worth the risk. It wouldn't be much, but I'll look into it anyway. Have you talked to anyone else about this?"

"No."

"Don't. Continue keeping track of what you should be earning, but keep it between the two of us. When is your next payday?"

"Friday of next week."

"When you get the check, I want you to bring it to me with what you wrote and we'll go over it."

"You think Wesley had something to do with Austin? I mean, come on, that guy is a big doofus."

"I didn't say that." I didn't say it, but I had to take it into account. "Things like this are important to check out as a normal part of my job. You know, I'm required to investigate anything I think may be illegal." That's actually the police's job, not mine, but I banked on Cody not questioning my statement.

The four people at the table along the wall stood to leave. Cody ran around the bar to thank them for being there. When he approached, one of the women, a tall brunette in a silver dress, lost her footing when her heels came into contact with a napkin on the floor. She fell with a look of terror on her face.

I was in Afghanistan. Outside Kabul to be exact. I was back with K.K., Suze, and the rest of our unit when it was besieged by an ambush. For a flash, the brunette was getting on her knees to raise off the floor, and then, she turned back into Suze being picked away by bullets.

I shut my eyes and repeated to myself over and over that I was at a bar in WeHo. The scene was still before me, yet I kept my hands firmly on the bar top to remind myself of my true surroundings. My entire body quaked, and tears rolled down my cheeks.

"Mitch? Hey, Mitch, are you okay?" It was Cody shaking my arm which I quickly pulled away.

"Are you sick? Do you need a doctor?"

I held up a palm and shook my head. "Leave me alone for a minute."

The flashbacks went away, but I continued to tremble as the panic attack remained. I have no idea how long. I don't know whether it was five minutes or thirty, but I was finally able to grab the edge of the bar with each hand and take several gulps of air. My cheeks were still wet, but the tears had stopped flowing.

Cody was a dozen feet away, regularly turning his head to watch me. Noticing I was regaining my composure, he ran up from behind the bar.

"Anything I can get for you?" He asked. "Some water?"

I held still while he slowly backed away. Finally, able to speak, I said, "Water would be good. I'm okay."

He set a tall glass in front of me. "What was that? Some kind of seizure or something?"

Not wanting to reveal I was struggling mentally, I played along with his assumption. "That's it. I had a seizure. I have epilepsy, but rarely get them anymore with my medication. Guess it's just an unlucky day." Cody continued to stare. "Would you mind stepping away, so I can get my head together and rest?"

After giving myself another twenty minutes, I called Cody back.

"There's someone else I need to ask you about. The other friend who was with you at The Abbey. His name was Zach."

Cody chuckled. "Zach and I aren't exactly friends. We were both friends of Austin, and that was it. I wouldn't be surprised if we never see each other at this point. There's nothing wrong with the guy, but he's damned stiff. Besides, he still doesn't seem over Austin and me being so close."

"You weren't joking when you said you think he's gay?"

"You know what they say. The only thing straight about him is straight to bed."

"How close were he and Austin? Any reason he would hold a grudge? Angry?"

"Oh, hell yeah. That role Austin just got in that sitcom—it was Zach's first. They both tried out for it, as usual. They were competitive, but Zach got the role and was parading around acting like Joe Hollywood. He rubbed all our noses in it but was especially mean to Austin."

"What happened?"

"I don't know. Two weeks ago, they called him and said he was out, and within minutes Austin got the call he was in. We were all together when it happened, but Austin was cool not to say anything. He walked away when the call came in. He talked to Zach privately, and he said Zach tried to act cool about it, but he could tell he was going to blow."

"Do you know why the switch?"

"Not specifically. Zach hasn't said anything, and I'll be damned if I'm going to ask. They only told Austin they thought he was a good fit for the role."

"Back to your belief that Zach was in love with Austin. Did he ever say anything to you?"

"No. Never. But, you could tell." A couple was seated at a table and were waving at Cody. "Hold on, I'll be right back."

"Not necessary. I'll be back in touch, but I've got everything I need for now."

"You're sure you're feeling okay?"

I patted my hand on the bar top. "Everything is cool. You've given me a lot to go on."

"Mmmbop" by Hanson started playing. I couldn't have picked a better time to leave.

When I got in my car, I called Harold at home. "Any chance you're going to be on this side of the hill in the next couple of days?" I asked.

"Not planning on it," he replied. "All my appointments this week are here in the valley. What's up?"

"I've got some financial paperwork I need you to look over for me," I said. "I need to know if there's some discrepancies or funny accounting going on."

"What is this for?"

"I'll send it to you express in the morning. I'll explain it then."

Fourteen

In the rolling hills above Bel Air, where Stone Canyon Reservoir meets scenic Mulholland Drive, sits The Stone Canyon Tennis Club. Jared Mooney and I scheduled time for a meeting there. He arranged for the clubhouse to allow me in.

Having labeled itself specifically as a tennis club, I expected a tennis version of a no-nonsense free weight gym. I imagined rows of courts as far as the eye can see, an equipment facility and probably a small snack bar. Given the area where it's located, I should have known better. It looked more like tennis was an afterthought. The stone, three-story, Victorian style clubhouse was built soon after World War II, a few years before the reservoir was established. Reaching Jared entailed walking through the circular entryway, past the extravagant, four-star restaurant and bar with green chairs and mahogany walls, and down the stairs adjacent to the Olympic size pool. At the far end of the property, bordering the reservoir grounds were the club's ten tennis courts. Next to the courts was an outdoor dining pavilion with a small hut surrounded by white tables with white umbrellas above each.

Jared was in a singles match with another man. While I know little about the sport, I know skilled players when I see them. After being acknowledged by Jared with a wave, I ordered a six-dollar bottle of water and grabbed a seat in the pavilion. They don't take cash at the club, so I had it billed to Jared's account. At the opposite end of the patio were a man and a woman wearing gray business suits who were discussing too loudly the restructuring of their corporation. At the table next to mine was a slim, blond woman wearing a tennis outfit with a pink top and white skirt. She was on her phone switching from texting to talking every few minutes. Rarely did she stop giggling.

After a thirty-minute wait, Jared raised his racket and swung his hips in an obvious sign of triumph. Unsportsmanlike in such a facility, I believed. Before approaching me, he stopped at the giggling woman's table and kissed her on the cheek. She placed a hand where his lips touched her and smiled.

"Hey, babe," Jared said. "I've got a little meeting here. Why don't you go inside and have a salad on me?"

"Oh, pooh," she replied in an exaggerated tone of disgust before sulking away.

He pointed at my water and waved to the attendant before sitting down. "I'll have what he's having."

"Thanks for taking the time to see me," I said. "I know you're busy."

"That was my trainer. I have a tournament in Beijing coming up, but I must spare some moments for the man looking for the person who killed my brother. I'll have to get back to it after lunch, though. I've got to keep Father proud."

"I've never been to China. The places I've been outside the U.S. are not popular vacation spots."

"Work has taken me all over the world, but it sounds more glamorous than it is. Most of that time is spent on one court after another, and most look the same. I do enjoy pleasure traveling as much as I can. It feels like I've been most everywhere, but then I look at a map and say to myself, 'Well, there's that place.'"

"I'm fortunate if I make it down to San Diego once a year."

"That's not fortunate at all."

"We can't all be world class tennis champions."

He laughed. "I guess not. We Mooney's can't help ourselves. My father is who he is, I'm a tennis champion, and you know, Austin finally landed a big role."

The server brought over Jared's water and asked if we'd like menus. "We have a special today on salmon or our delicious chicken and kale salad. May I get either for you gentlemen, or would you like a menu?"

"I loathe kale and am allergic to seafood, Lawrence." Jared said to the server. "How about herbed chicken." Jared smiled and looked to me. "What about you, Mitch? Did you want one of the specials or a menu?"

"Do you have just a burger?"

"We have our incredible steakhouse burger with brie and caramelized onions. You won't regret it, sir."

"That sounds delicious," I replied. "I'll take that but how about cheddar and hold the caramelized onions."

"Of course," the server sniffed. "Would either of you care for anything other than water?"

We both told him we were fine with water, and he scurried off to the pavilion.

"I don't eat burgers often," Jared said. "But you should have got it with all the works. As Lawrence said, it's incredible."

I said, "I think I'll survive with it the way God intended a burger to be." I scooted upright in my chair. "I'm going to ask some questions. Keep in mind it's all part of my investigation."

"That sounds like a dour warning disguised as reassurance."

"That's up to you, Jared. When was the last time you saw Austin?"

"That time you saw us together just days before the murder. When we had dinner at Providence on Melrose. It was his favorite place but became out of reach when he chose his life as a pauper. It'd been awhile before that, and we had a good time catching up."

"Had you talked to him after that?"

"We hadn't talked, but we texted. He thanked me for dinner."

"Are you willing to show me the text?"

"A friendly man who's now getting down to business, I see."

Jared thumbed through his phone and handed it to me. I looked at their text exchange. They did chat about dinner, as he said. I nodded, and he put the phone down on the table.

"About the night he was killed—"

Jared rubbed his palms together and laughed. "I've been waiting for this."

"You seem happy to want to talk about your brother's murder."

"I didn't mean to sound flip because that's not what I meant. I thought it was funny because I was anticipating the moment you asked me that question to see if I killed him. I take no pleasure in that."

"Some of us take joy in the strangest of things. So, where were you?"

"I was with Gretchen that night at the Beverly Place Hotel. I rented a bungalow for the two of us."

"The woman who was sitting there." I nodded at the empty table next to us.

"No, that's Brittany. I think."

"Where do you live?"

"I'm living with my father. I moved out of my old place last year after some severe storm damage. The homeowner's association was taking their sweet time getting bids for repairs, so I got fed up and moved out. Since I've been on tour so much, I haven't gotten around to getting a new place. My father likes having me around, but he doesn't like me bringing girls home, so I rent rooms frequently."

"And the woman, Gretchen, can verify this?"

"Of course. I gave her a night she'll never forget."

"I'm happy for you both. Have you given more thought to who may have killed Austin since we talked last?"

"Not much, to be honest, but that's because I don't know anyone in his life except for Hector. Austin grew up

in Palm Springs, and I grew up here. I went away to
college, and then he went to college. I go on tours; he went
on auditions. As for Hector, I only met him once, and he
was a nice and polite guy. I only know about the drinking,
drugs, and violence from Austin. Like I said, we had love
and respect for each other and wanted to be closer, but
circumstances never allowed it." He lowered his head.
"Now it's too late."

Jared continued to lament his regrets over not having a
better relationship with Austin. He bragged about what a
good man Austin was and what a waste that his life ended
so early. Once he was done talking about his dead half-
brother, he continued to brag but about his tennis career. He
rambled quickly, not allowing a moment of silence between
us. I was relieved he quieted down when our food was
brought out.

"I think that's enough questions," I said after a bite of
my burger tasting of sawdust. "I'm sure I'll have more
later. I'll let you get back to having fun with Brittany after
lunch."

"Brittany? I don't think so. I'm taking her home right
after this. Tonight, it's dinner with Chelsea."

Having had more than my share of one-night stands, I
wondered if I was as cold and callous about men as Jared

was about women. The men I hooked up with over the years never were given the pretense it was for anything more than sex. I doubted that was true for Gretchen, Brittany, or Chelsea.

After finishing our lunch, I asked, "Do you have the number for the woman you were with at the hotel?"

"May I text it to you later? Brittany's probably sulking over her salad."

"You're not giving me a vibe of any sense of urgency regarding solving this case."

"The text is not going to lead you to a result any quicker. I suggest you worry about other things. Is there an alternate reason you want her number so badly?"

"If you're implying what I think you are, that's not an issue. I'm gay."

"Here I was going to ask if you'd like Brittany's number, too."

"You're a gallant man, Jared."

Fifteen

Zach Pickering's Silver Lake apartment was less than three blocks from my place. The home he lived in was an odd mix of Victorian and adobe style, with the wood painted blue and the stucco a natural putty color. As he directed me over the phone, I walked around to the side of the house where the door to his apartment was built into a small alcove.

He said, "You're early." He was wearing blue jeans and a ratty button down with smears of paint on them.

"Something people rarely ever say about me."

"Sit down. There's some juice in the fridge if you want. I need to get changed."

Zach stepped into the other room, and I took advantage of his offer for juice. It was orange and tasted freshly squeezed. His place appeared to be one of the many illegal apartments that was built in the area over the past fifty years. At one time a family sectioned off a couple of bedrooms for tax free income as the neighborhood value increased. The stove and refrigerator didn't meet the standards that I would call a kitchenette. They were lined against one wall, jutting into the room by a couple of feet. The living space itself had that put-it-together yourself fiberboard furniture that had gotten so popular. It didn't last long, but at their low prices many considered them disposable. Once an old table became wobbly, just toss it out and buy a new one for only thirty bucks. The apartment was humble but immaculate.

For twenty minutes I shuffled on Zach's futon before he came out from the other room wearing gray slacks and a stiff powder-blue shirt.

"Sorry for the time," he said. "I had a phone call."

"It was a shock not seeing you so polished. I heard you're a painter."

"No, I'm an actor. Keep that in perspective. What I do to make money is paint. It pays the bills, and that's it."

"I own a store in addition to being a private investigator. It could use a new paint job. Can you paint over old wood paneling?"

"It's done. Some people like the look, I guess. I think it's better to rip it down and redo the walls."

"Maybe we can work out a deal. Right now, we need to talk about Austin."

He leaned against the bedroom door frame. "Hit me."

"Did you kill him?"

"Fuck no." Despite his obvious anger, he remained stiff and spoke in his typical muted tone. "Don't play games with me. You'll lose."

"Not trying to pull anything. Trying to get the direct questions out of the way. Do you know who might have wanted to kill him?"

Zach reared his head back against the frame. "I've been trying to wrap my head around all this since I got the news. He was goody two-shoes. Even back in high school he never got into trouble or partied with the rest of us. He'd come along but was always the designated driver."

"You were close in school?"

"We met while we were sophomores. We took theater together at Palm Springs High School and became best friends. We both loved acting and would practice together and do scenes. Overall, we were pretty normal, but I guess we had our geeky side." He gave a hint of a smile. The first I had seen from him. "Looking back now, we were real geeks – theater geeks."

"Where were you the night of his murder?"

"That's what's weird. We were waiting for him near Topaz. He snuck out to ditch you, so we could all go bar hopping."

"All? Who's all?"

"Me, Austin and Rachel Roundtree."

"Who's Rachel Roundtree?" Cody had already told me who she was, but I wanted to hear about her from Zach's lips.

"She's a friend of ours. You know her. She was the lead for The Titmice before they broke up."

"The Titmice?"

"Don't be surprised if you never heard of them. They were a one hit wonder, but you'd know the song if you heard it. It was 'I Want a Man Who.'"

I asked, "A man who what?"

"All kinds of things. The song was full of innuendo, which made it so popular.

> I want a man who's a master debater,
>
> I want a man who's got good diction,
>
> I want a man who's a cunning linguist,
>
> I want a man who talks cockamamie."

"I remember it," I said. "The video had sexy shirtless men attending a spelling bee."

"Yeah, that's it. I think it reached number three sometime in 2015."

"None of it rhymes."

"That's why some people thought the song was funny. It was the irony. It's about linguistics, it sounds dirty, and none of it rhymes."

'Yeah, it was a real laugh riot."

He said, "It was lame."

"So, tell me more about the three of you."

"What do you want to know? We were all friends. Rachel and I date sometimes, but nothing serious. Friends with benefits mostly. We couldn't be more if we wanted to. She's always on the road. She starts a gig at Topaz on Thursday night."

"What was she doing in town when Austin was murdered?"

"She was playing at a club in San Diego and would drive up on her nights off."

"Tell me more about your relationship with her. Doesn't sound like your type."

Zach shook his head. "You've been talking to Cody and some others about my deep abiding love for Austin."

"Something like that. It's not true?"

"I'm an actor, and that means I'm around gay men and women all the time, but don't make me guilty by association. I loved Austin like a brother, but it was nothing more than that."

"Bisexual?"

"Straight as an arrow," he replied.

"Where were you and Rachel when you waited for Austin?"

"We parked on Cory Avenue, right around behind the Jaguar dealership."

"When were you there?"

"We got there right at 8:00 when Austin said he'd park at the Topaz. Rachel called him at 8:15 and he told her he would be right out. At 8:30 she called him, and he said he was still tied up. We waited a little longer. She tried some more. He wouldn't answer, so we got pissed and took off."

"She called on her cell phone?"

"What else? A phone booth?"

"That seems out of character from everything I've heard of Austin. Surprising that you drove off like that."

"He was the good boy but could flake out like anyone else. We were glad, actually. She and I bought some wine and came here."

"What time?"

"Hell, I don't know. Nine-ish. Probably a little later."

"Can anyone vouch you were home?"

"You mean other than Rachel? I don't know. Maybe my landlords. The walls are thick here, so we don't hear each other much. I haven't got a clue if any neighbors saw us. She left at 10:00 the next morning, just before I got the call about Austin."

"Let's get back to Austin," I said. "I hear he stole a role from you."

"Stole? He stole nothing from me," he protested. "That's the way Hollywood works. I did the pilot, and it sells. Then, somebody doesn't like me—I'm out and Austin's in."

"You seem laid back by it all."

"No, I'm pissed. I had my big break in a sitcom, and then, some asshole didn't think I fit the role. It sucks, but it's not Austin's fault. He didn't sneak in and steal it. He wasn't nearly as talented as me, but he had a look they were going for, I guess."

"Your humility is refreshing."

He waved a dismissive hand. "Whatever. Is there more?"

"I'm having a hard time believing there was no conflict between the two of you."

"Hell, I am human. It hurts, and yes, I'm resentful, but logically, I know he had nothing to do with it."

"And the singer's name. What was it again? Rachel something? How do I reach her?"

"Roundtree. She's staying at The Primrose Inn on La Brea, or you can catch her at Topaz."

"Is there anything else you missed telling me, Zach? Something that might help."

"I'll call if I think of anything. Right now, I need to get to a job."

"At night? What's the job?"

"Don't see how it matters, but I'm giving a quote on some old lady's kitchen in Los Feliz."

I gave him my card before walking home, passing his business pickup truck in the process.

Sixteen

When Jared's alibi for the night of the murder, Gretchen Overton, gave me her address over the phone, I knew exactly where she lived. Her place was one building over from my sister Josie's place in the same condominium complex. I was surprised Jared gladly handed me her number and was equally surprised she was open to see me.

The condo was near the intersection of Third and Fairfax. An intersection well known due to the Farmer's Market that had been sitting there for over eighty years. There wasn't much left of the original huge complex, but it remained with shops selling candies, peanuts, old fashioned sodas and even a few vegetable stands. It stood humbly next to the newer outdoor shopping plaza, The Grove, with its Pottery Barn, Banana Republic, Cheesecake Factory, and other more expensive shops. The Grove is where Josie goes to spend money she doesn't have.

I rapped on Gretchen's door several times before she answered. At that point I was no longer surprised to see another stunningly beautiful person. With a name like Gretchen, I expected a platinum blond, but she had deep dark brunette hair that was nearly waist length. It swooped across her back and hung to one side. Her fresh face glowed and was enhanced by her engaging smile and honey-colored eyes.

She held out her hand. "You must be Mitch." Her smile broadened. "I'm Gretchen."

I took her hand and gave it a gentle shake. She then gracefully pulled it away and sashayed to the living room. "Please, come with me and have a seat." She leaned over a red chair, padded the seat cushion, and brushed off its low back. Her impressive breasts nearly fell out of her low-cut top. You know, you may not be into tall buildings, but the One World Trade Center is still impressive.

It was not my norm to feel insecure, but there was an air about her that was stately. As if she were royalty. I strutted to the chair and sat.

"Would you like a drink? Water, juice, or something stronger?"

"I'm fine."

"Then I'm fine, too." She settled on the couch and crossed her feet at her ankles, revealing the long slit that rose up her flowing white dress. "You said on the phone you wanted to talk about Jared. How may I help you?"

"This is going to seem personal, but I need to ask about the night you spent with Jared in the bungalow at the Beverly Place Hotel."

She giggled. "There's nothing personal about that. At our age we're expected to have a sex life, aren't we?"

"Of course."

"My question is which time at the hotel are you referring to? We've been there more than once."

"I'm referring to the night his brother, Austin, was murdered."

Gretchen's eyes widened, and she placed a hand to her mouth. "Oh, that was so horrible. When Jared told me about it, I couldn't believe anyone could be so awful. I'd never met his brother, but I was in tears."

"I'd like to know when you and Jared arrived at the hotel."

"It was early. I think around 5:00 p.m. We planned to order room service and stay in that evening. He picked me up at 4:45."

"When did you check out?"

"I have no idea. It was immediately after Jared got the call about Austin. Things were so chaotic with us both rushing out of there that I didn't notice."

"What was Jared's reaction when he got the call?"

"He clutched his phone so hard I was afraid it would shatter. He threw it into a chair and then sat at the end of the bed and cried. I wanted to help him but had no idea what to do. We see each other, but I can't say we're really close."

"Did he take you home?"

"He offered, but he was upset, and the hotel isn't far from his home. I took a Lyft, so he could get to his family."

"Where do you work, Gretchen?"

"I'm a business consultant. Why do you ask?"

"No reason. What type of consulting do you do?"

"Oh, you know. Consultation on business. Retail mostly."

"I'm curious because I own a business, and I'm struggling. It's a small shop called Eye Spy Supplies. Think you can coach me?"

Gretchen stalled. "You couldn't afford me, I'm afraid. I am a consultant for major corporations like Banana Republic, Macy's, and Nordstrom. That sort of thing."

"That must be interesting. I own a little stock in Toys "R" Us. Do you work with them?"

"Yes, I do. It's so fun consulting with a toy store. I have an appointment with them next week, as a matter of fact."

"It's going to be a lonely meeting. Toys "R" Us closed all its store less than six months ago."

"Really? No wonder they're not answering my calls." She cackled. "I wondered if you were going to fall for that because I knew you couldn't own stock in a company that doesn't exist."

"Cut the bullshit, Gretchen."

"Bullshit? That's extremely rude. I think you should leave."

"I'm sure you do consultations, and my guess is you charge by the hour."

"What on earth are you implying."

"Sit down and relax. What do you make for consulting? One thousand? Fifteen hundred an hour?"

She collapsed back on the couch. "Okay, we'll cut the bullshit. What do you want to know?"

"Were you truthful about the times you were with Jared."

"One-hundred percent truthful."

"A man like Jared Mooney, who has all the money and women he wants, hires an escort? What gives?"

"You do realize the number of celebrities who hire and have been caught with ladies in my business. Powerful men like to enjoy the company of a woman who doesn't want anything from them. Jared is a playboy going from one girl to the next, but when he wants to relax, enjoy an evening of fine dining, maybe some television, and yes, likely some sex, he calls me. He knows I'm not after fame or fortune. I love what I do, and I do it damned well."

"My sister lives right around the corner here. This is a pretty cheap place for a woman like you."

She laughed. "You don't think this is where I live, do you? Dear God. Other women work from home, but not me. I need somewhere away on those rare moments I can relax and enjoy my personal space. I bought this condo for business only. With the rise in the housing market, it's turned into a good investment as well."

"It's true you arrived at the hotel at 5:00 p.m. and neither of you left until morning?"

"Scouts honor."

"What about dinner?"

"I told you. We ordered room service. And before you ask, it was probably around 7:30. After that we watched that terrible remake of *Murder on the Orient Express.* Snooze."

"I don't suppose you have any receipts, do you?"

She laughed. "Honey, you don't think I pay for anything, do you? You'll need to speak with Jared about that."

"I guess I will."

I stood to leave.

"You know I can hook you up with a sexy and charming young gentleman who I think would be just your type. He owes me a favor, so it would be free of charge."

"Excuse me?"

"He's a bisexual former gymnast named Dick, and you can only imagine the things he can do."

"A hustler named Dick? That's fitting. What makes you think I'm gay?"

"Don't sweat it, baby doll. I knew you were gay within two minutes after you got here. When I opened the door, your eyes bugged out when you saw my tits. I'm used to that."

"You're right, but how does that make me gay?"

"You never even glanced at them afterward."

I said, "You're observant. You should be a PI."

"You have to be observant in my job. You sure don't want me to give him a call? You'll like Dick."

"I do like dick, but I do fine on my own. I don't need your Dick."

She was still laughing when I shut her front door.

Seventeen

At Topaz that night, Rachel Roundtree's set was scheduled for 9:30 p.m. with the doors opening two hours earlier. I left the store immediately after closing, so I could get a second chance to talk with the accountant, Wesley Stumpf. I didn't know what kind of information I could get out of him. I didn't expect him to come out and say he'd been skimming payroll, but I hoped to get something. The littlest things can help. That day I had a long chat with Harold. He said the paperwork I gave him from Cody didn't have enough information to tell him if something funny was going on with the books.

I got to Topaz shortly before Wesley's normal quitting time. I rapped on the frame of his open door. "Hello, Wesley."

Catching him off guard, he jumped and knocked his mouse to the floor. He banged his head on his desk when he retrieved it. At least he was consistent.

"Hi, Mitch. I'm sorry, but Luna has left for a while. She'll be back around 9:00 p.m."

"That's okay, I'm not here for Luna. I came to see you."

Wesley tapped a stack of papers on his desk to organize them and slid them in his out box. "I don't have long. I have to pick up my daughter from gymnastics within the hour."

"It won't take much time. I have more questions to ask about Austin Bouchard."

"I believe I told you all I know, but go ahead."

"I don't know if you're aware, but you seem to be the last person to have seen Austin alive."

"Yes, the police mentioned that. There's not much to tell. He was very much alive when he walked through my office and out the exit door. I can't tell you more beyond that."

He was searching around his desk, on the file cabinet and a side bureau.

I asked, "What are you looking for?"

"I can't seem to find my glasses."

"That's because you're looking in all the wrong places. They're on your nose."

He raised his hand to his face, felt his glasses and laughed. "I feel foolish. That happens more than I care to admit."

"I'm sure it does."

I sat on the metal framed chair in front of his desk. "Wesley, do you do all the accounting here?"

"Almost. Luna gets her hands in some, too, of course. Why?"

I decided to shake things up. If he was messing with accounts and thought someone knew it, it could impact his behavior. Harold said it could also cause him to stop whatever he is doing which can expose his earlier actions.

"I found a note in Austin's bedroom with scratchings about your accounting."

"What type of scratchings?"

"I wish I could tell you. I forgot to hold on to it, and it was thrown out with a lot of his things. I don't know much about numbers."

"I don't understand why you would even mention it then."

"It seems important that he had some kind of concerns, and then, you're the last one to see him alive."

"Are you implying I'm a suspect to murdering a man I didn't even know for some kind of ridiculous scratchings I don't know about? That's ludicrous."

"I'm only implying you're a suspect in the sense that everyone is a suspect, Wesley. Digging, no matter how ridiculous it may seem, is my job. I'm sure you've had numbers that don't match and have to search every possible reason, no matter how silly. It's the same thing."

Wesley stood and tugged at a jacket hung on a wall hook. He yanked several times before inspecting it to see that a tag was caught.

"I guess you're right," he said. "It is similar. We both work with puzzles, don't we?"

"That's a good way to put it."

"And, I'm off to see my beautiful daughter. You have a good evening."

"One favor before you go. I texted Luna, but I don't know that she got it. Could you ensure I have access to the club upstairs? I have questions I need to ask some people up there."

With reluctance Wesley made the calls and found that Luna told her staff I had full access to the entire establishment.

Wanting to fit in, I had chosen my most party-like clothes in the morning, which happened to be an outfit Josie bought for me. It had been awhile since I hit the party scene, and I felt good in my olive chino pants and black button up shirt with tiny flecks of green, yellow, red, and blue.

Rachel Roundtree was nowhere to be found in the small backstage, I was told she could be there any minute, which was a polite way of saying there's no telling when she'd show. Cody wasn't at the club bar, and Luna was still away. Hungry from having left my store quickly to get to Topaz, I headed to the quieter downstairs bar for a bite and a drink. My chicken fingers appetizer and greyhound were eighteen bucks. Good thing I was charging Dominique for expenses. I had hoped Luna would show up and take care of my tab, but I wasn't so lucky. As I popped the last piece of chicken in my mouth, I got a call from the assistant stage manager that Rachel Roundtree had arrived.

I found her sitting on a stool behind the curtains, drinking a margarita and humming to herself. She was further proof of my deduction that Austin attracted beautiful people. Her rectangular shaped face was light skinned, similar to mine. That was no surprise. With her golden copper hair and last name Roundtree, it seemed likely she also was of Irish descent.

She wore a plum colored long-sleeved t-shirt that hung to her knees. High heeled dark teal boots were zipped up to the bottom of the shirt. Her rocker look was enhanced by the way she slung forward with her legs spread open.

"Ms. Roundtree, I'd like to talk to you for a moment."

"Who are you and what about?" She replied in a throaty voice.

"I'm Mitch O'Reilly. I'm investigating the circumstances of your friend, Austin Bouchard's death."

"Oh shit." She stood and shook my hand. "I'm not a fan of cops, but if you can catch the bastard, you're my dearest friend."

"I'm not a police detective. I'm a private investigator hired by Austin's mom."

"You not being a cop makes it better. I hope that means you don't suck. I hate sucky people."

"Should we talk somewhere private?"

"They've got a closet over there that they say is my dressing room. I think there's a couple of folding chairs."

We walked into the room and sat. Between the cheap folding chairs, tiny dressing table and mirror, it was surprisingly basic compared to the club and restaurant.

"Do you want a drink?"

"No thanks. I had one downstairs, and I'm limiting myself these days."

"Whatever," she snorted.

She yelled to an older man working on some cabling to get her another margarita. He grumbled, shook his head, and continued what he was doing.

"I think that was one of the stagehands," I said. "I wouldn't hold my breath for that drink."

She picked up a house phone and demanded one from the bar. After hanging up she said, "You got things to ask me?"

"Yes. When was the last time you saw Austin?"

"Hell, the last time I played here. Over a year ago. We're more about hanging out than friends."

"You're friends through Zach Pickering then?"

"Zach and I are sort of friends, but a little more. He's a good lay."

"I'm happy for you."

"You can say that again."

There was a knock at the door, and a young waitress stepped in before Rachel could respond. She handed Rachel the requested margarita.

"These are good," Rachel said. "You want a sip?"

"I'm good, thanks. Back to Austin. Tell me what went on the night he was murdered."

"Not much to tell. Zach made plans for us to pick him up near here. He didn't show up. We left."

"You weren't concerned?"

"I've got feelings, mister, but there was nothing I could do. I called him to find out where he was, and he didn't answer. I figured he'd been picked up by some hot boy for playtime."

"What times did you call him?"

"I don't know the times. You need to know?"

"It would help."

"What the hell." She pulled out her phone and checked her history. "8:14 and 8:30. I talked with him both of those times, but when I called later, he never answered."

"What times were those."

"Damn, you're annoying. I don't see that it matters, but it was 8:42, 8:55 and 9:03. After that, Zach and I went to his place. He got some wine and made snacks and stuff. I called Austin in the morning too, but I guess he was dead then."

"Do you have those times?"

"Hold on." She looked through her history again. "9:40 a.m. and 9:50. I split after that, and Zach called me thirty minutes later and told me what happened."

"Can I look at your phone?"

"You calling me a liar?"

"It's part of my job. You don't have to tell me, but I can call the police and tell them they should check your records."

"Damn, you were nice before. Now you're being sucky." She held out her phone. "Here."

I swiped through her phone history. The times she gave me were accurate.

"It doesn't seem you made calls or got calls between 9:30 p.m. to 9:40 a.m."

"I turned it off when I got to Zach's. Didn't want any interruptions if you know what I mean."

"I'm smart enough to figure it out. Can you think of anything else that might help me?"

"I liked Austin. He didn't suck." She paused. "Well, he was gay, so I guess he did, but you know what I mean." She cackled then suddenly stopped herself. "If I knew anything else, I'd say it."

I gave her my business card and searched for Luna Salcedo. I found her busy helping out in the kitchen, so I only had time to tell her hello and thank her for giving me full access to the club. On the way home I called Dominique and scheduled time to meet her the next day.

Eighteen

It's rare I enjoy a slow day at work. The break was nice, and it allowed me some time to research Jared Mooney's professional background. My biggest accomplishment was sending a bill for an advance from Dominique. I hoped she wouldn't delay her response.

There was a slight drizzle of rain, and typical for Los Angeles, people drove as if it was a blizzard. I was a few miles away from Dominique's hotel when my phone rang. It was Devin Doss.

"Oh, Mitch," Devin exclaimed. "Thank the Lord I reached you. Someone has been in our apartment and ravaged it."

"What happened, Devin? Did you call the police?"

"No, I wanted to talk with you first. Especially, since I ain't talked with Cody. I can't find her."

"Is she…uh, he at work?"

"She's supposed to be, but she ain't there. Won't answer her phone or texts either."

"I'll see if I can get ahold of him and head your way."

"Thank you, Mr. Detective. I'm scared being here all by myself."

I sent a text to Cody to see if he was working but got no response. It was likely he didn't hear his phone buzzing in the crowded club. I tried calling several times, but he didn't answer.

I was able to reach his boss, Luna Salcedo.

"I have no idea where he is," she said. "I've called and have had no answer. It's not like him to be irresponsible. I hope he didn't have an accident or..."

"What time was he scheduled to work?"

"6:00 p.m., and he's usually here ten minutes early."

"Over an hour late for his shift is a pretty good sign that he doesn't plan to come in."

"I would agree," Luna said.

"I'll swing by his place and let you know if I find him."

"Please do. I'm worried."

Because of the rain, the neighborhood in Koreatown was dark and empty. I was surprised and excited when I found a parking space in front of Devin and Cody's apartment building. It's those little things that made us Angelenos happy.

The light on the second landing of the stairwell was out. That with the tapping of the sprinkles on the window gave me chills I hadn't felt when I had been there during the day. My steps quickened up to Devin's door at apartment 302.

I asked, "Any word from Cody?"

"Not a thing," Devin huffed. "Come on, I'll show you the damage."

"I talked to Cody's boss. She hasn't heard from him."

"Oh Lord! I hope nothing happened to her. She best not lose his job whoring around. I can't afford this place on my own, and Cody's already late with rent. She better hope she's in trouble." Devin put his hand to his lips. "There goes my mouth again. What a terrible thing for me to say."

"Do you want to show me the damage? Everything out here looks okay."

"Come with me."

I followed Devin as he sashayed to Austin's room. It was empty except for four open boxes sitting on the floor.

I said, "How can this room be ravaged?"

"Hold on."

Devin opened the closet door. Two more boxes sat with their flaps open, and the rack was full of hanging clothes.

"All the things in these boxes were neatly stacked and flaps were closed. Look at them now?"

"Hardly looks like they were ravaged."

"Ms. Cody hasn't been in this room since the last day you were here. It upsets her too much. Austin's death finally sunk in. Everything here Dominique left for us to take to Goodwill, but I ain't done it by myself. I came in to grab Austin's old rain jacket, and this is how I found the place. Boxes open and clothes moved around."

"It's probably a good thing you didn't call the police over a messy closet."

"I don't leave things messy, Mr. Detective," he hissed.

I asked, "Do you know where Cody parked his car?"

"In this neighborhood there ain't no telling. If you don't have a driveway, which we don't, you park in the first place you can find. Sometimes that means a block or two away. Sometimes more."

I went out the building and walked two blocks down the street in each direction. Cody's car was nowhere to be seen. I stepped back inside to see Devin.

I said, "Cody's car isn't out front. Where else would he park?"

"Sometimes she goes and parks on James Wood Drive. I keep telling her she's crazy to do that. Cody goes out the back to get there. Totally cray cray."

"Show me where."

I followed Devin down the hall on the first floor. In the rear of the building was a door that opened into a courtyard between the buildings.

"Where does he go?" I asked.

"Straight down that alley, but you're on your own. It's getting dark, and I won't go out that way."

The courtyard was barely visible from a small yellow light hung on the side of the building next door. There was a basketball hoop, but judging by the board hanging sideways it looked like it hadn't been used in a long time. In one corner was a homeless camp with blankets rolled out and several piles of garbage bags. No one was there to stake their claim. From the courtyard, I took a slow walk up the alley leading to where Cody's car was parked. The entire alley was free and clear except for a pile of debris midway to the street. There were several garbage bags opened and with trash spewing out. Some broken furniture and an old box spring on its side leaning against a gray stucco building.

Finding bodies is not a habit I enjoy, and I was worried I'd find Cody's body there. Could also be rats, or some crazy man with a knife or a broken bottle. When I got close my heart sank. Sticking out from behind the box spring was a pair of bare feet. As I got closer there was heavy breathing and grunting sounds. Goddamn in hell, they were still alive.

When I tilted the box spring forward, I found a haggard, grungy woman lying silently while holding a shopping bag from Target. I carefully let go of the box spring and backed away so as not to wake her.

I cased James Wood Drive for five minutes before I spotted Cody's dark green 2012 Ford Focus parked in front of Ultra-Fast Check Cashing. *Cash in Minutes with Low Fees* the sign promised.

A car is just a car, and I should have had no qualms approaching it, but experience had taught me that sometimes there are dead bodies inside. It was a day I wasn't feeling up to reliving.

Like a cat creeping toward its prey, I inched my way quietly toward the vehicle. I gave a long exhale with each step. I closed my eyes when I approached and stood next to the passenger window. Nervously I looked to each side and behind me before I could look in. Four puzzled looking customers in the check cashing store were eyeing my every move. When I felt as ready as I could get, I braced myself and glanced down in the car. Cody, wearing his Topaz uniform, was sitting in the driver's seat with his head slumped over into the passenger side.

A bottle of whiskey was tucked between his thighs.

"Ms. Cody, you smell like shit!" Devin wailed while waving his finger at the man's puke covered shirt and tie.

"I ish got to get to work," Cody slurred.

I said, "I don't think Luna wants you in stinking like that."

Cody dribbled. "Sheesh depends on me."

Each time Cody would start to slump sideways, Devin would punch his shoulder. "Don't you be getting' no puke on my couch."

"Devin, do you want to take his shirt off?" I asked.

"No sir, she ain't my type."

"I mean to keep you from fretting about your furniture."

Devin backed away with his arms up. "You touch that mess. Not me."

I stepped to the kitchenette and grabbed a hand towel.

"Oh, no you don't," Devin protested. "I don't want that touching her."

"Do you want your rag ruined or your couch? You tell me."

Devin crossed his arms and muttered, "Go ahead.'

With the towel in hand I undid Cody's tie and tossed it in the sink. I then undid each button and pulled off his shirt. The white tank underneath was damp, but not as extreme as his uniform."

Devin said, "I've seen her tipsy, but never this drunk before."

I put a hand on each side of Cody's face to hold his head up. "What's going on? Are you okay?"

Cody wailed, "My best friend ish dead. I mish him."

"Oh Lord," Devin howled. "I told you she was all shook up about Austin."

I asked Devin, "Could you go in the other room and call Luna Salcedo. Explain what happened to Cody, so she won't worry."

"Oh no. Ms. Cody will lose her job."

"No," I replied, "I know Luna well enough to know she'll understand. One thing she does is care for her employees."

Once Devin was out of my way, I continued to question Cody.

"Do you know anything about the closet?" I asked.

"What closet? I been out of the closet a long time," Cody mumbled.

"No, I mean Austin's closet."

He opened his eyes wide for the first time since I found him. "What about Austin's closet? I don't go in there."

"When was the last time you were?"

Cody blew out a long stream of air. "Haven't been since you were here thish last week-weekend."

"You didn't go in there and open the boxes?"

Cody scoured and growled, "I haven't been in any goddamn boxes. What are you talking about?"

"Woo," Devin said as he entered back in the room. "I never knew Ms. Cody was an angry drunk. Then again, I ain't ever seen her drunk."

"Assuming he's sober enough to understand me, it looks like someone did get in that closet."

Devin put a hand on each hip. "You know who it was."

"Hector?" I asked.

"Of course, it was. Who else would it be?"

Cody slurred, "What boxes did Hector get in?"

I lowered Cody gently on his side on the couch. "Don't worry about it. Get some rest. Devin, you don't know that it was Hector. He seems likely, but I make no assumptions."

Devin asked, "Are you going to run him in?"

"I'm not a cop, so I can't *run him in*. As soon as I can find him, though, I'll ask him."

"When will that be?"

"Not tonight. I'll be with Dominique, and I'm already late."

Devin swished down the hall with his arms crossed, calling as he went, "Forget you. You gonna let that pretty Latin mess come and go here as he pleases."

Nineteen

Built in 2004, the Hotel Willoughby was a half block from the Hollywood & Highland Center shopping and entertainment facility. It was constructed as part of the mildly successful plan to redevelop Hollywood Boulevard and revitalize the strip along the Hollywood Walk of Fame. While tourists were shocked to see closed, metal storefront security gates strewn with graffiti, cheap souvenir shops, and open air drug deals along the boulevard, the grounds above the subways stations at Hollywood and Highland, and Hollywood and Vine, had been successfully revitalized.

The Willoughby, an all-suite hotel where rooms start at five hundred dollars a night, is where Dominique had been staying since the death of her son.

When I entered her suite, she looked at me and cocked her head. "You look puzzled," she said.

"I'm surprised is all," I responded. "I've only been to this hotel once, and it happened to be this exact same room."

"That's quite a coincidence."

I didn't add that I had been there for one hell of a hot hookup. It was with a guy from Frankfurt. He didn't speak

a lick of English, but verbal communication was
unnecessary.

"Also, a little surprising is finding you in here," I added.
"This is a beautiful suite, but it's like all the others. I would
have expected you to get something larger."

"Why? So I can have a bunch of extra rooms that I don't
use? I'm only staying a short time. I'm not moving in. I
appreciate being wealthy. I know I'm blessed, but I don't
see the need to show it off merely for the sake of doing so.
This lovely room is all I need for me to sleep and Rémy to
stretch his little legs."

The living room was decorated in the overly used retro
midcentury modern style. A bright yellow couch with no
arms faced two lime green chairs. A coffee table sat in the
middle. Dominique and I each took a chair.

"Not knowing what you like, I ordered a mixed
appetizer plate from room service." Her little dog Rémy
jumped on the couch and squeezed between her and the
chair's arm. "It should be here anytime now."

"Mind getting started while we wait? I have a lot of
questions."

"Okay, no small talk." She lifted Rémy and placed him
on her lap. "Let's get to it."

"Tell me about Zach Pickering."

She laughed. "Oh, you would start with him. What a mess he's always been. He's been envious and competitive with Austin since the day they met."

"Perhaps in love as well?"

"In love?" She chuckled. "Oh, you're bringing up that rumor again. Many think that skirt chaser is overcompensating, but had he been secretly in love with Austin, it would have explained many things over the years. Our first year in Palm Springs, which is right after I divorced T.J., Austin attended private school, but he begged me to let him go to the public school in the next school year. He always knew he wanted to be an actor and Palm Spring High has an amazing theater production company. It was there that he met Zach, during Austin's sophomore year."

"It was better than the private school?"

"We are talking Palm Springs. A lot of wealthy donors helped get that program started years ago. Knowing how much he loved acting, it was impossible to say no. T.J. had a fit, of course. Austin immediately enrolled in theater production, and that's where he met Zach. They became instant friends and instant enemies at the same time. They competed against each other over everything, but you can imagine that was especially true of the theater. If you saw them, most of the time you'd think they hated each other, but the next thing you know they're hanging out and laughing and joking. Despite that, Zach was a great influence on Austin and helped him transition into the new school. It was early that year that Austin came out, and I was scared he'd lose Zach as a friend, but I don't think he batted an eye." She leaned forward and whispered, "Everyone knew anyway," and laughed.

"Do you know anything about this big television role that Zach had taken from him that was given to Austin."

"Nothing was given to Austin. He was an amazing actor. He became whatever part he played. I don't know the details about the switch. I only know that Austin was disappointed when he lost that role on the TV pilot and Zach got it. He was devastated, actually. He spent a weekend with me. Then one day he called and said the role was his. I have no idea what happened with Zach; other, than turnabout is fair play."

"What do you mean?"

"In their junior year, Austin earned the lead role as Joe Hardy in the school production of *Damn Yankees!* He was extremely excited, but during rehearsals he came down with the flu. It upset him, but he kept studying his lines and rehearsing with me. Zach convinced the director that they couldn't take a chance that Austin would be ready. Next thing you know, Zach was Joe Hardy, and Austin was cast in a small role. I don't think he ever forgave Zach for that, but they remained friends. I was relieved when they went to separate colleges and lost touch, but they both wound up in Los Angeles and were friends again."

"How do they both know Rachel?"

"Rachel who?"

"Rachel Roundtree? She's a singer. She and Zach said they're all friends."

"I don't know who she is. She doesn't ring a bell."

Room service arrived and brought in a mixed platter of fried green beans, chicken wings, cheesy potato skins and mozzarella sticks: all for only forty-three dollars.

I said, "Uh, I'm—"

"You don't have to say it. I have an amazing metabolism and was one of the luckiest models in the world. There was no starvation when I was on the runways. Now that I've hit fifty, I have to watch what I eat a little, but still nothing like most people." She pulled her hair back away from her mouth and bit into a chicken wing. "Help yourself to anything."

"I don't keep up with the Hollywood gossip, but you were modeling when you married T.J., weren't you?"

"Yes, we met in 1993 at the premier of *Sleepless in Seattle*. Sally Field was there and introduced us. I was twenty-four, and he was forty-eight, but I didn't care. I was so star-struck and in love, but nothing happened, of course. He was still married to his second wife, Lucille. That was a year before she drowned in their pool, and I was too captivated to find it odd we married six months after her death."

"Are you suggesting T.J.—"

She laughed. "Oh, despite the rumors the tabloids spread, I don't think T.J. has it in him to murder somebody. I meant it was odd that he was able to cast her aside so quickly, and we began dating almost immediately after her death. That's probably why you knew about us even though you don't follow entertainment news. It was such a scandal that year. I was modeling and worked long thankless hours to get to the top. I was no Cindy Crawford or Kendall Jenner, but I was on my way. Then, I gave it all up for T.J"

"You gave it up for him?"

She cackled. "Yes, for T.J. I was in love and starstruck, but I only thought it was him. It wasn't for him, or his money like everyone thinks—it was tinsel town. The power and the fame. I felt fulfilled; being Mrs. Hollywood was exciting. But Mrs. Hollywood didn't last long. I quickly learned I was just Mrs. T.J. Mooney, and the only thing that got me glory was being his lap dog. I was ready to divorce him but became pregnant with Austin. After that we went through the motions in a loveless, lifeless marriage." She turned her face and gazed out the window. I believed it was an attempt to hide her tears. The room was silent for a moment until she belted, "Have you seen *Gold Teeth and Silver Spurs?*"

"No. I don't think so."

"That's no surprise. No one has. It was T.J.'s first and only attempt at a comedy. A musical western comedy to be exact. It starred Dom DeLuise in drag as a saloon keeper, which was the film's only redeeming quality. It was beautiful to watch him, but an actor can only work with what they're given, and even Dom's brilliance wasn't able to save that horrible film. The film released the year before our divorce and was the last straw. T.J. became more insufferable than ever. Mean and cruel."

"Abusive?"

"To me, in a sense. Never physical, but I spent days in my bedroom in tears. He wasn't so awful to the children. He was a strict disciplinarian but would never do anything to harm them. Have you met them yet?"

"Yes, the morning I met you in the front yard of the mansion."

"Oh yes." Dominique rubbed her temples. "I'm sorry, that entire day is a fog. I want it to stay that way."

"I got to know Jared more than Erin."

"No, you didn't," she snapped.

"I stood right in the driveway and talked to him."

"I imagine Erin acted just like her dad. That's who she is. I'm guessing Jared was your best friend."

"Not inside with T.J., but he came out to the yard right after you went in and was chummy."

"Don't buy into it. I married T.J. twenty-four years ago, and I still don't know Jared. I don't think anyone does. The boy...man, is self-serving. He lives to be everyone's best friend, but if it suits his needs, he'll put a knife in your back in a heartbeat."

"Are you saying he might be Austin's killer."

"Don't take me literally. I only mean that Jared lives for Jared. He loves wealth and women and all the attention he can get."

"I'm perceptive. I got that feeling."

"Stick with your gut."

"We haven't talked about Hector Rojas."

"I noticed that and was hoping I'd get through this without talking about him." She grabbed a tissue from the box on the coffee table. "He was clean and sober when he met Austin and so proud of himself. He had problems getting back on his feet, so I helped him. You saw how beautiful he is. I've known many actors and models, and he could be the most handsome man I've ever seen, so I made some calls and got him some modeling gigs. He was becoming a hot item in a short time, and he and Austin were happy together."

"What happened?"

"You know what happened: he fell off the wagon. Hector had worked as a fireman in the valley for two years, but then drugs and alcohol got the best of him. It's tragic really. Crystal meth is ripping the gay community apart. I don't know what he did for the year after that, but he survived somehow. He ended up hitting his bottom, I guess, because he started going to A.A. He met Austin at a coffee house and was trying to turn his life around but couldn't find a job. He was so charming I had to help him out."

"He didn't seem very charming out on that sidewalk the night I saw him trying to kick Austin's ass."

"When he wasn't drinking or using, he was a loving and caring boyfriend. It's the only reason Austin stayed with him so long. They were twenty-three, and even though they'd only been together two years, I secretly hoped they'd get married. Once he started using again, I knew there was no reason to continue to hope. Austin tried awfully hard to help, but it was over. He was going to tell Hector."

"Do you think it's possible he did?"

"I don't know." She paused and looked out the window. "Do you think Hector killed Austin? No matter how bad things have gotten for Hector, I can't imagine him killing anyone, especially Austin."

"It's possible Hector killed Austin, especially if he has that expensive autographed photo, but it could have been a lot of people."

"You have a lot of suspects?"

"I was speaking in general terms: it's a big city with a lot of crazy people. I have a few who stand out, but it's early in the game, and everything is conjecture on my part."

She grabbed a handful of fried green beans.

I said, "I googled and found articles about Austin and a friend of his. A boyfriend? It was a scandal involving a congressman's son?"

"Oh, I haven't mentioned Grant Ridgeway at all, have I?" She dropped the beans she hadn't eaten. "Oh, dear God!

I think of the rocky road between Hector and Austin then thinking of Grant is nearly unbearable." She pulled her pup tighter against her with one hand while wiping huge tears from her eyes with her tissue. "He never got over what happened. You are familiar with Congressman Galvin Ridgeway from Texas?"

"Only what I read in the papers. He's still in office, I believe."

"Ridgeway is a man you should know everything about. One of the fiercest anti-gay men on the hill. He fought tooth and nail against marriage equality, fully supports keeping transgender individuals from serving in the military and wants to see gays out of there, too—not that there haven't always been gays in the military. I thought for sure Ridgeway would change his tone after what happened to Grant, but he became worse than ever. His wife Mary is one of the founders of the Mothers for Morality. Whew, what a load of tight-ass bitches those women are." She put her hand to her mouth. "Excuse my language."

I chuckled. "I believe I can excuse it."

"Grant Ridgeway, Galvin and Mary's son, was Austin's first true love."

"I bet the shit hit the fan at the Ridgeway home when his parents found out Grant is gay."

"He *was* gay," she corrected me. "Grant's grandparents
lived in Bel Air, not far from T.J. He used to visit them
every summer and met Austin when they were sixteen. I'm
not sure where they met, but I believe it was some event at
the country club. Austin fell for the boy, and they spent
nearly every minute together while Grant was out here."
She giggled. "When Austin was in college, he admitted to
me that was the year he lost his virginity. I wasn't
surprised, but acted like I was because I could tell he was
trying to shock me. You know how kids are." She hesitated
and wiped her tears. "The following summer…let me think.
It was probably 2012. That summer Grant came to stay
with his grandparents again, and the two boys acted as if
they hadn't been away from each other for more than a
minute. The truth is they barely had talked to each other
over the school year. Grant couldn't risk getting caught by
his parents. Austin was always an outstanding student, but
his grades did go down that year, and I believe it was from
his pining and moping over being away from his boyfriend.
That seems odd. I've never said that before or heard Austin
say it, but they most certainly were boyfriends. Like the
year before, they were inseparable until they hit the papers.
Under most circumstances, it wouldn't have been big news.
Likely something that would have been in the celebrity rags

is all, but because Grant was the son of two famous radical evangelicals, it was out everywhere. They had gotten caught."

"The pictures were taken at the Hollywood sign."

"Exactly, they were photographed kissing while sitting on a ridge, which is why I'm shocked it escaped me. I guess because I would never think of Galvin or Mary as potential killers. I mean it was six-years ago, and it's not like it was Austin's fault their son was gay. I should rephrase that. You and I know that Austin wasn't what made Grant gay, but his parents did. You see, the person who took the picture of the boys kissing was a staunch anti-Ridgeway man who rushed that photo to all the papers in Texas. The next day it was national news. I blame that man. I know he thought he was doing good by sticking it to Galvin, but he's the one to blame for Grant's death. Not Austin."

"Grant's death? What happened? I didn't see that."

"Rather than retreat from the public eye, the Ridgeway's decided to battle the situation head on. They didn't have Grant mention Austin by name, but he was on TV with some televangelist saying he'd been seduced by the devil. Galvin became even more anti LGBT than ever. Mary stepped down as the head of Mother's for Morality, but she remained in a leadership role. They turned up the volume on their anti-gay rhetoric, too."

Dominique paused thoughtfully then continued. "That family was too much. Sadly, as I understand it, Grant was caught by his parents with another boy, so they shipped him off to camp. They rarely saw him and never let their daughter see him. They called it a camp, but it was one of those damned conversion therapy places where he was expected to 'pray the gay away.' Instead of turning their son straight, the Ridgeway's boy hung himself a week after being sent off. He was found hanging from a pipe in a restroom with an extension cord around his neck." Dominique sobbed into her hands. She walked to the fireplace, put her arm on the mantel and stared out the window for at least three minutes before sitting back down. Seeming uncomfortable with the whole scene, Rémy scurried into the bedroom. "Austin was devastated," she continued. "It was hard on him being referred to as the devil, but he understood Grant had been forced to say that. Grant's death, though, was something he never got over." She gave me a stern look. "Did you not know any of this?"

"Only from my investigation. I missed it in the news. I was in the military at the time. There's also a guy Austin worked with."

She laughed. "You're not talking about Cody?"

"No, Cody is off the hook. His alibi is solid."

"Are you certain it was one of them?"

"Not at all. There's more I need to talk to, especially the family. They may know more than they think, but I need to get to know them better. Erin will be tough, but I don't know how I'll get to T.J. I'd fear for my life stepping up to him."

"I'll handle T.J. Don't you worry about him. I still have enough pull that I'll get him to talk to you."

"I need to get going now."

"Oh no you don't," she said sternly. "Not until you help me finish off more of this food."

Twenty

Blake Quarles was one of the best casting directors in the business and a busy man, but he cleared his calendar to get me in as soon as possible because it was about Austin.

His assistant Felicia took me to a large open room where auditions were being held for what seemed like the ninety-eighth rendition of *Annie*. There wasn't much to the space. A screen against one wall with a single raised platform in front and a spotlight shining down. At the other end of the room, four padded chairs faced the screen. A piano with a pianist sat in the front corner. A line of girls were wedged in a hallway off to one side.

They were casting some of the orphan children. A young girl, under the light, was asked to sing. She sounded like a ball of cats shoved in a bagpipe.

"Cut!" Blake yelled. "Thank you, young lady. We'll give you a call."

The girl ran out the door in tears as the next girl walked forward. She had an incredible voice, like that of an opera star. I thought she was a shoo-in, but she got the same response.

"Cut! Thank you, young lady. We'll give you a call."

Unlike the first girl, this one puffed her cheeks, crossed her arms, and stomped out of the room with her mom following close behind.

As the next girl came forward, Blake was interrupted by his assistant, who pointed me out. He nodded his head.

"Thirty-minute break, everyone," Felicia announced.

Blake mopped a handkerchief across his dark brown-skinned forehead and rushed to me so fast that I thought he was going to whiz right by.

"You're the detective? O'Reilly?"

"Yes, I'm the private investigator. Thanks for giving me the time. I hear Austin's loss is a big blow to the show."

"You're not kidding. This show is going to be big, but it hasn't been easy to sell to the networks. I'm lucky the producer kept me on with the hiring screw up. I'm respected in this town, but one mistake and that's all they remember. Follow me, I've got a lot to do, and my stupid assistant just gave me only thirty minutes."

"What screw up are you referring to?"

I jogged behind Blake to his computer where he started checking his emails. His office was worse than mine, piled high with papers on his desk and in white shelving on his wall.

"Austin Bouchard was on our short list, but I chose another guy for the role. He's a good actor and all but wasn't right for it." He paused to finish what he was typing then hit send. "When the network bought the pilot, it was on the basis we toss the guy. I brought in Austin, the execs loved him, and I saved my ass." He picked up the phone and nodded to me. "Just a minute."

His phone conversation went on for several minutes. He was sweating profusely and kept wiping his face.

"The guy you let go was Zach Pickering?"

"That's him. I think he has an okay career ahead of him. He's a handsome fella and a good actor, but not much range. I should've seen that."

"I read in the trades that the show is *Stock-car Kid*. There's a lot of skepticism about it."

"I wouldn't be involved in a show if I didn't believe in it. I would have never dreamed up a show about a twelve-year-old race car driver, but my kids have read the books and loved them. There was no hesitation on my part to accept when they asked me to be casting director."

"What role were Zach and then Austin going to star in?"

Without acknowledging my question, Blake picked up the phone and made another call. After hanging up, I repeated myself.

"The stock-car kids' older brother Willy Trimble. Willy is the head of the kid's pit crew. It was a small part in the books, but we made his character equal to the kid himself for the series. We need someone handsome and charming to bring in females and those thirteen to twenty-four. That Pickering guy is handsome enough but doesn't have the charm."

"How did Zach handle it when you told him he was off the show?"

"I don't know how he acted when he was told. That isn't my job. But I felt the heat of his resentment when he barged in here the next day. I don't even know how he passed security, but he got right here, in my office, and attempted to rip me a new one. I wouldn't play his game, but I mean, come on, it was his big break, so I understand. Unlike many in this town, I don't have a heart made of coal, but sorry, it is a business."

"What did you do?"

Blake ignored my question and sorted through his emails.

"Mr. Quarles," I implored. "I know you're busy, but I need your time."

"You have all the time you need. You've got my full attention." He hit speed dial on his phone and yelled at someone regarding being behind on casting another show. The conversation went on for five minutes. He placed his hand over the phone and looked to me. "You were saying?"

"I really need your time."

"Of course, of course. You've got it." He returned to his phone call. After another couple of minutes, he disconnected and said, "What were you asking?"

"What did you do when Zach barged in on you?" I replied.

"I sat quietly and let him have his say while I dialed security. I don't know who he thought I was dialing, and he didn't seem to care. He kept yelling."

"Was anyone else here?"

"I was," a stern looking woman with long gray hair spoke up as she walked in Blake's office. "He was out of control and made all kinds of threats."

I asked, "Threats? What kind of threats?"

"This is news to me," Blake said. "What threats, Caroline?" He stood and rushed to the next room with Caroline and me jogging behind. He stopped to leaf through some hanging clipboards.

She said, "As he was being dragged out by security, he was screaming Blake was a dead man. He said we all were going to regret it."

I said, "I'm sorry. Who are you, ma'am?"

"I'm Caroline Yonkers. I also work casting and made the same mistake as Blake. We all initially agreed Zach was our man."

"You all act like it was an obvious mistake now," I said. "Why didn't it seem obvious before?"

"We got caught up in the physical," Blake blurted. "Do you know Oakley Cashman?"

"No."

"One of the best child actors out there, but he's not so little anymore. He's sixteen playing a twelve-year-old. He's still got the boyish face, but he's gotten tall for the role."

"How's Zach fit into this?"

Blake's phone rang, and he answered it.

Caroline said, "Zach is six and a half. We were taken in by his handsome face and that he would make the shorter Oakley look smaller, younger."

"And you knew nothing about the threats?" I asked Blake.

He held up a finger. "Yes, sir," he politely said into the phone. "No, I assure you it will be taken care of. I'll have them all in place next week."

He disconnected the phone, threw it in his pocket and gave a huge sigh. "I don't have much time. What did you ask?"

"I asked if you knew anything about Zach's threats," I said through gritted teeth.

"He kept screaming it was his role and he was getting it back, but he never made an actual threat. He only said I'd be sorry."

"I take it he's not getting the role back."

Blake and Caroline both burst out laughing.

Blake said, "He wouldn't have gotten it even if he didn't throw a fit. The network execs couldn't stand him."

I said, "Caroline, Zach threatened Blake and the rest of you, which is not his usual demeanor. Did he say anything about Austin?"

Blake ran back to his office with Caroline and me close behind. He pulled something up on his computer and started screaming into his phone again.

"Nothing threatening," she replied. "He said we were fools for taking a hack over him. It seems to be his impression that he's God's gift to the arts."

"This is all surprising," I said. "I met Zach twice, and he seemed cold, but composed. He doesn't sound like the guy you two are describing."

Blake covered the phone with his hand again. "That surprised us, too. He was cool and steady through the whole casting process. Like he knew it was his. His self-confidence is another thing that drew us to him. I don't think any of the staff would have thought he'd do a one-eighty like that."

"Probably wouldn't have happened if the role went to someone other than Austin Bouchard."

"Excuse me?" Caroline asked.

"Oh, it's nothing," I said. "I was thinking out loud. Too loud, I guess."

"Do you have anything else?" Blake Quarles asked. "We're busy around here."

"I thought you said you'd give me your time."

"I'll give you all the time in the world, but you need to hurry."

"You've given me all the time I need."

Twenty-One

It had been an unusually busy day at Eye Spy Supplies, and I was looking forward to a chilled evening at home. My landlord's driveway wasn't wide enough to accommodate my car as well as his, so I had to park about a block away from the house. For my weary feet it may as well have been a mile. There was nothing in my mailbox except for some sales fliers and an overdue electric notice. It was going to have to take priority over other bills.

My landlord Wilkins, a gaunt, seventy-eight-year-old former college professor, was cleaning the pool late that night, which was not unusual for him. He tended to do things whenever the urge hit. My experience has been most retired people have a regular routine. Sometimes more regular than when they worked, but not Wilkins. I gave him a wave and walked back to the guest house I rented.

The lights didn't come on when I flicked the switch at the entrance. Neither did the overhead dining nook light. The clock on the microwave was blank. I was surprised the electric company didn't give me much more of a notice.

I stepped back outside and yelled to Wilkins, "Are you having any problem with your lights?"

He took a puff from his joint, pointed to the glowing light coming from his kitchen window, and the bright spotlight shining across the pool deck. "Everything looks good to me."

"No problem at all today? No flickering or anything?"

"Not a thing. Check the circuit breakers on the right wall."

"Hopefully, that's the problem. Otherwise, I'll need you to take a look at it."

"Nah. It's just the circuits." He took another hit off his joint.

I turned the cell phone's flashlight on and went back in the house. Despite the small light, I stumbled into a chair, before making it to the circuit breaker. I discovered that was the problem, and after flipping the switches back on, I also discovered my house was a wreck. All the pillows were thrown off my couch. Some of the cushions had been unzipped and lay exposed on the floor. The few books I had that sat on the shelf in my side table were ripped and strewn across my dinette table. All the cabinets were open in the kitchen, but there I was lucky. The intruder had carefully placed each dish on the countertop.

Typically, I don't like involving the police in my matters, but this was a situation that called for it. I held my gun to my side while I dialed 9-1-1 and told them what happened. I was advised to step outside and wait for an officer to arrive. I didn't listen.

With the kitchen pantry wide open and disheveled, the only place to hide downstairs was behind the couch. I hit the floor and as quietly as possible crawled across the front of it, gritting my teeth when I clipped my metal floor lamp as I turned the corner. I pointed my gun behind the couch and rolled forward prepared to pull the trigger.

No one was there.

Despite the old brown shag carpet on them, the stairs leading to my lofted bedroom creaked with each step. No sound came from above. I turned quickly when I reached the top of the landing where the stairs turn up to the loft. With gun drawn, I believed I was fully prepared for anyone that might jump out. I should have been prepared for anything instead.

When I reached the top step there was a flash of something that hit me square in the face. It was only a few seconds of falling backwards and down the stairs before I blacked out.

◆ ◆ ◆

Officer Darleen McGee sat with me on the rickety, chipped wooden bench outside the sliding glass door to my house. Wilkins had been in a tailspin over the incident and was asked to leave to calm things down. I could see him in his house peeking through the kitchen curtains every few seconds. He had finished with the pool and gone into his home soon after I entered my place.

"We've been unable to reach Detective Castro, Mr. O'Reilly," Officer McGee said. "With him being in homicide, I don't see how he can help you in this matter."

I pulled the blood-soaked toilet paper out of my nose and put another bundle in each nostril. "He understands a murder case I'm working on is all. This looks like a plain old robbery, so I doubt there's much more than that."

My head was thumping like my brain was going to explode, and the sting in my face wouldn't subside. Every muscle in my body screamed with each movement. What pained me most was my pride. Having been a military police officer for three years, I had no excuse for being taken by surprise like that. I had become sloppy.

She said, "It looks like a robbery to me, but if you think there's more to it, you should tell me now."

"I've got nothing to tell."

"You can go back in now," a male officer said as he came out the door.

Officer McGee stayed in the living room while I scoured the apartment. Somebody seemed to think I had something worth stealing because nothing was untouched. My fry pans were out of their cupboard and laying on the floor, all the food in my fridge and freezer had been rearranged, everything from my medicine cabinet was sitting on the toilet lid, and all my bedding was sitting on the floor beside my dresser which had every drawer open. I went back to the living room.

"Anything missing?" Officer McGee asked.

"Nothing, off the top of my head, but it's hard to tell when everything is dumped like this. Does it look like I'd know something is missing?"

"I'll get forensics here tomorrow to dust for fingerprints, though don't expect much to come from it. Are you going to hang around here tonight? You need to be careful and not touch much."

"No, I'm not in the mood to clean up. I have somewhere to go."

I called Trent to tell him I was going to stay the night.

♦ ♦ ♦

"Oh, my god, honey," Trent said. "You look worse than you said on the phone. "That lamp across your face has it bruised and swollen."

"Thanks. It's good to know I'm still sexy."

"If there's one thing I'm sure of is that you'll always stay sexy. Are you hungry?"

"Not much. Do you have any Honey Nut Cheerios?"

"I've still got the box you bought a few weeks ago. Should still be good."

"I'll take a bowl." I put my elbows on the table and leaned my forehead into my palms. "You wouldn't have real milk, would you?"

"Just the usual—unsweetened almond milk."

"If that's the best you can do."

He put the bowl in front of me and sat across the table.

Trent said, "We've got to get your store business up, so we can get you out of this detective business."

"The way it looks now, I'll be a PI long after I'm forced to close that store. Besides, this looks like it could have been a simple burglary. I don't know that it had anything to do with the Mooney-Bouchard case."

I didn't really believe that. A burglar wouldn't have been so tidy. In and out would have been their M.O.

Someone was looking for something specific. If it was related to the Mooney-Bouchard case, then it had to be the Audrey Hepburn picture. Hector was my first suspicion, but it could have been anyone who thought I may have had the valuable photo.

Trent said, "Well, if it's not that case, it seems awfully coincidental."

"Life is full of coincidences."

I ate my cereal, each bite sending shockwaves down my neck. Any movement of my face or head was overwhelming. Trent sat at the table leaning on one hand smiling as he watched me eat.

He broke the silence. "I wish you'd let me take you to the hospital."

"I'm banged up is all. I'll be fine. Besides, hospitals don't take kindly when you can't pay. I just need to lay down."

"Follow me." He took my hand and gently led me into the bedroom.

Trent pulled down the sheets and blankets and eased me down to the edge of the bed. He kissed me. He then slowly undid each button on my shirt. Each time I tried to speak, he'd put a finger to my lips and would say, "Shhhhh."

My shoulders ached, and it was hard to move them to allow him to get my shirt off. Once he succeeded, he laid me on my back with my feet still dangling off the bed. He kissed me again on the lips, then on my neck and then nuzzled in the hair in the center of my chest.

I tried to speak, but again he placed a finger over my mouth.

My neck muscles screamed as I leaned my head back, but the pleasure had overtaken the pain as he slowly moved down my body and carefully released all my tension.

Neither of us said a word when he raised my legs and turned me fully on the bed.

While I slid over from the edge, he pulled the sheets and blanket on me, leaned over, and gave me the final kiss of the night.

I was asleep within minutes.

Twenty-Two

Eye Spy Supplies opens at 10:00 a.m. Tuesday through Saturday. My sister Josie works for me on Saturdays, which gives me three full days to devote to investigating each week. Though Josie is typically at least a half hour late to work her shift, I was surprised to see her Volkswagen Beetle in the plaza's parking lot only five minutes after the hour. Instead of the store being open, she was leaning over Frank, sleeping in my vestibule, as always. I pulled up to the curb in front and got out of the car.

"What's going on between you and Frank?" I joked.

Frank was not in his usual fetal position. He was on his back with all his limbs sprawled out. Josie poked him in the shoulder every few seconds and spoke his name.

Josie said, "I'm pretty sure he's dead. I keep shaking him, and he won't budge. I've been trying for minutes."

"I've been through this before. He's fine."

"I don't think so." She wrapped her arms around herself and shuddered. "This is so gross!"

"There's nothing gross about a man sleeping," I said as I grabbed the front of his jacket and shook him.

"See, I told you he was dead."

"What have I told you to do when this happens?"

"I don't remember." She was hyperventilating.

"Watch this."

I put my hands on Frank's rusty shopping cart full of treasures and rolled it's creaky wheels back and forth."

"Huh?" Frank sat up. "What the hell is going on?"

I said, "You told me you weren't going to drink late. It looks like you got pretty sloshed last night. Josie thought you had gone to the great beyond."

"I just had a few drinks with some friends," Frank said as he pulled himself up with the cart. "Sorry, Josie."

"Just glad you're okay," Josie said.

As soon as Frank moved away from the door, Josie and I rushed around the store to set things up. Within ten minutes she was unlocking the door while I rolled up the security gates.

"Now we're open," Josie said. "And I get to stand here for eight hours with nothing to do."

"Business hasn't been bad lately. You might have to get off your ass for a change."

"I'll make sure I read only the shorter articles. I hate being interrupted in the middle of the longer ones." She set a pile of magazines on the counter next to the register. "How's the Mooney-Bouchard case going?"

"As always, slower than I want."

"You and I haven't talked much since our discussion about Trent and how you're going to fuck things up. Things any better?"

"I don't think I'm fucking things up. He came by my place not long after our talk, and I shared with him what I've been going through regarding the military and PTSD."

She put a hand to each cheek in an exaggerated manner. "Oh, my God! Are you saying you actually…dare I say it? Did you share your feelings?"

"Cut the dramatics. Yes, I shared my damned feelings. Plus, I stayed at his house the night my place got trashed and my face was bashed in."

"Great, I hope you two got to screw for a change."

"I was in too much pain to screw, but he showed me a good time. Since then we've been busy and haven't seen each other much, but he's coming with me to Topaz tonight."

"Topaz?" Josie clapped her hands and jumped up and down. "Can I go? Please? Let me go with you."

"Sorry, I'm doing a little investigating and spending some time with my man. There's no room for you."

"You suck."

"And Trent hasn't complained once."

Josie threw a magazine that hit me in the chest and collapsed on the floor. She whooped.

I chuckled at her reddening face as she gasped to breathe from laughing. "What's the deal? It wasn't that funny."

"I'm in a giddy mood is all. I was going to wait and surprise you, but Stu and I are moving in together."

"Move in together? That's fast."

"It's not that fast. We've been dating for months. I've really fallen for him. Besides, we're not getting married, but even if we were, he's much sweeter than Cal or Bob ever were. I don't know why I married either of them."

"You're that in love with this guy?"

"I don't know about love, but he's more fun than you think he is. He may be a complete geek, but he's so good to me. Plus, you wouldn't believe the things he's able to do in the bedroom…or the kitchen…or the bathroom…"

"That's enough. No more details."

Josie laughed. "I thought that'd shut you up, but it's true."

"Who's moving in with who?"

"I told him there is no way in hell I'm driving down to Torrance every day, so he's moving into my condo—and he's bringing his stuff. I'll have furniture in my place for the first time since I divorced Cal."

"Wow, you'll get your mattress off the floor and everything. I hope I don't get a wedding invitation next week."

"Speaking of wedding invitations. Look who's in the parking lot."

Trent pulled his jeep up next to my car. He shook the store door several times to tease us with the twinkling bells on the knob. He was successfully annoying.

"Hello, you two crazy kids," he said. "I hope you're getting along for a change."

"I get along fine with Mitch," Josie said. "How about you?"

"We get along just great." He wrapped me in his arms and gave me a deep kiss that felt like it went on for minutes. I opened my eyes long enough to catch Josie smiling.

"That's sweet and all," she said. "but if it starts to get more than that you two will have to go to the backroom."

I said, "We can hold off since we're going out tonight. Even if it is partially for work."

Trent frowned. "Uh, about tonight…"

Josie instincts went into gear, and she jumped off the stool. "I'll go into Mitch's office and play on the computer. You two have your talk."

She walked into the backroom and closed the door. I held a finger up to Trent and whispered for him to keep quiet. After a thirty second wait, I tiptoed to the door and smacked it as hard as I could with the palm of my hand.

"Ouch!" Josie screamed from the other side. "That hurt."

I yelled, "Back at least three feet from the door and mind your damn business."

Trent bent over laughing.

I gave him a minute. "Now that you've regained your composure. You started to say something that sounded like you were bailing on me tonight."

"It's Saturday night. It's our busiest night of the week," he said.

"Yeah?"

"Sorry, Mitch. Three servers called out sick, and there's no one else who can fill in?"

"There's no other supervisors working? Inga works with you on Saturdays."

"Inga will be there but being short three people is more than one supervisor can handle. We'll probably switch off waiting tables."

"That sucks. I wanted to be with you tonight."

"It breaks my heart to hear you say that. You're usually not so sweet."

"Harold and Josie are working at getting me to speak how I feel these days, but it is weird as hell."

"You said you were going to be working part of the time while at the club anyway. What's up there?"

"Some employees think the accountant there is being fishy, and I was able to get some bookkeeping information. I sent it to Harold."

"And?"

"He said there wasn't enough for him to tell if something was going on. He wants me to get more paperwork. Somehow I have to do that during Rachel Roundtree's concert."

"I really like her. I hate I'm going to miss it."

"Why am I the only one who doesn't remember her?"

"You don't know who Rachel Rountree is?"

"I do now, since I've been told."

"She was the lead for Titmice before they broke up."

"Yes, I know."

"So, you know their song, 'I Want a Man Who?'"

"I remember it. It sucked big time."

"You can say so, but it was huge when it came out. Personally, I like their other version of the song. It's 'I Want a Man Who Can't.'"

"Please, don't start singing it."

"I'll spare you." He snapped his fingers. "You'll be in my neighborhood. Why don't you stay at my place tonight? I'll probably be off work before you're done. If you stay for the whole show."

"I don't know how long I'll stay."

Trent raised a finger and told me to shoosh. He tiptoed to the door to my office and whispered, "What do you think? Are you two going to stay for Rachel Roundtree's entire show?"

The door swung open.

"You bet your sweet ass we're staying," Josie gushed.

While Trent laughed hysterically, she and I argued over her listening to our conversation. By the time he sobered up, Josie and I weren't speaking.

"I've got to go now. I'm sorry, baby." Trent hugged me and gave a quick kiss. "I'll see you tonight though." He winked.

"Josie, you have a good night, too."

"Whatever."

He stood in the doorway looking at the two of us standing silently. After many seconds he said, "Mitch, what time are you meeting Josie at the club?"

I sighed, looked at her and said, "Does 8:00 p.m. work?"

"I'll be there at 7:59," she replied.

Twenty-Three

It was 8:15 p.m. when I pulled into one of West Hollywood's new parking garages built along the strip. With garages' low flat fares every night, the days of forced valet parking were numbered. Though, there will always be lazy ass rich folk who think it's worth paying over twenty bucks rather than walking a block.

Josie said she'd be there just before 8:00, so I didn't expect to see her until half past at the earliest. She surprised me when she arrived only a minute after me.

"I've got two things to do," I said as we walked. "One, is to try to talk to Rachel Roundtree somehow. I guess during one of her breaks. Two, and most important, is to get into Wesley Stumpf's office, so I can grab some paperwork."

"Stumpf is the accountant?"

"Yes."

"No one has paperwork anymore. He's going to have spreadsheets on his computer."

"That's why I brought this thumb drive." I tossed it up and caught it behind my back.

Josie said, "Good catch. You think he'll be nice enough to leave his password laying on the desk for you?"

"I haven't figured out how to get around that one yet.
I'm hoping the owner, Luna, is here and will have the
office open and possibly the computer on."

"That's a lot of hoping, Lil' Bro."

"It may be unlikely, but it's a first step. If it doesn't
work, then I'll move on to the backup plan."

Josie stopped and put her hands on her hips. "You have
no backup plan, right?"

"Let's hope I can come up with one if we need it."

Wesley was not in his office, so I told Josie we'd go up
for the show and look for him later. I showed the guard the
passes Luna Salcedo gave us and had to run up the stairs to
reach Josie. As was typical, she was able to walk past a
guard at an event without being questioned. It was her
super-power. The thick crowd in the club had a significant
larger number of women than men. Clothing and hairstyles
ranged from Melrose Avenue chic, to Target shirts and
jeans. Carley Rae Jepson's "Call me Maybe" blared
throughout the hall.

"I'll buy the first round," Josie said. "Do you want a
greyhound?"

I nodded rather than attempt to be heard over the music
and the crowd. During my fifteen-minute wait, I stood
looking foolish, but occasionally would move my arms and

feet, which was equally embarrassing. After fifteen minutes, Josie returned with our drinks.

"Sonofabitch," she grumbled. "The bartender said Rachel probably won't start her show until 10:00 or 10:30. Why'd you get us here so early?"

"I know bands start long after the doors open. You're the one who clubs all the time."

"Coming here had me too excited to think about it."

'N Sync's "Bye Bye Bye" came on, and Josie danced with a thin woman in her fifties wearing a sparkling, golden, short dress. The song made me want to go bye bye, but I had work to do.

"You wait here," I said. "I'm going to see if Rachel is backstage."

"Can I come?"

"No, this is business. I can't have some fan slobbering all over her. Go find yourself a nice man."

"I already have a nice man," she yelled as I squeezed through the crowd.

"Whatever," I mumbled.

The guard at the stage door said there was no reason to go in. Rachel was nowhere to be found, and added, we'd be lucky if she showed by 11:00. Josie took the news surprisingly well.

"That's cool. This is a fun crowd. Go get me another sea breeze."

"We should go downstairs and see what I can get from accounting."

"That doesn't sound like much fun." She twirled, spilling the last of her drink. "Get me another one, and go yourself."

"If Luna is here, I might need to distract her by introducing her to my lovely sister."

"Fine. It's a deal. Get me that drink, and we'll head back downstairs."

"Walking on Sunshine" by Katrina and the Waves came on as we were leaving.

Rather than fight the crowd coming in, we took the elevator to the lower level. There were at least twenty people waiting to be seated at the restaurant. We walked around them and through to the end of the main dining room and found the office doors locked. I grabbed a nearby table."

Immediately, the attendant marched over and huffed. "Excuse me, but we have a list of people waiting. This isn't a seat yourself diner."

I stood and reached out my hand. "I'm sorry. I should have introduced myself. I'm with the Sunset Strip Community District Subsidization Program."

Josie choked on her drink.

"The what?" The attendant asked.

"The Community Subsidization Program. Let me find my card." I started digging in my pockets. "We're the division of the city of West Hollywood that oversees the enforcement of the consortium standards and operations of this sector. I'm here to meet Ms. Salcedo, so I can audit your establishment."

The woman put a hand to her mouth. "My apologies, sir. Luna said she'd be gone for a bit. I don't know when she'll be back."

"This is a surprise visit. It's not her fault. We will patiently wait here for her return."

"Whatever, it's still not cool that you took over a table like this."

"You can have Ms. Salcedo file a complaint with the city if you'd like. While we wait would you please have someone come over. My cohort and I are famished."

Within minutes a server rushed to our table to take our order. Josie was nursing her sea breeze. I ordered a water for myself and a plate of hummus and pita bread.

"You're supposed to be detecting, not making a spectacle of yourself," Josie said. "Why'd we come barging in here like that?"

I pointed to the nearby hallway. "That's where the offices are. This is the closest table, and when I saw it was available, I had to jump at the opportunity to get it. If we waited in the lobby too long, the attendant would have been suspicious."

"That District Subsidized whatever you thought of was brilliant. It's like I thought of it myself. But it put us in the spotlight didn't it?"

"Sometimes in the spotlight is the best place to hide."

"What does that mean?"

"I don't know, but it sounds like something Harold Beaver's would say."

As our server brought a third plate of pita bread, Wesley came in from the front lobby toward his office. I jumped out of my chair and met him at the door.

"Mitch, what brings you in?"

"I'm here to commune with Luna, but given that she's not available at the moment, I wonder if you and I may have a tête-à-tête.

He chuckled. "How many drinks have you had?"

It was at that moment I realized I had not changed my inflection or manner of speech since toying with the seating attendant. Josie and I continued speaking that way out of fun. I grabbed my stomach and belted out the best fake laugh I could. "I'm so sorry. I must sound ridiculous."

"You think so, too?"

"I don't know if I told you before that I participate in community theater. The company I'm with is doing a Victorian play titled, uh, *On the Hill*. I guess I got a little carried away. Funny isn't it?"

Wesley chuckled. "I took some drama classes in high school. It's easy to get caught up. I spent weeks talking like a Scotsman."

He unlocked the door and stepped in.

"May I wait with you inside?"

"Uh, sure. Have a seat?"

"I'd rather stand if it's okay. I've been sitting all day."

"You said you were at a community theater rehearsal."

"Yes, but my character sits through the entire production. I was on my butt for hours today."

"That must get tiresome."

I paced from the entrance to the office to the side of his desk. He kept looking over like he was distracted, but never said anything. Each time I walked, I'd go a little farther past his desk and a little closer to the exit door, so I could unlock it.

I broke the silence. "Do you mind if we talk while you work?"

"As long as it's not too distracting. It's not more about your investigation, is it? I don't know how much more I can tell."

"This is about Rachel Roundtree."

He swiveled his chair toward me and crossed his arms. "I know Rachel very well."

"You do?"

"Yes, every six months to a year she performs here. I make out her checks and hand them to Luna to give to her. In other words, I know how to spell her name and that's it."

"You've never met her at all?"

"No."

"How about Zach Pickering? What do you know about him?"

He dropped the pen in his hand on to the desk. "The answer to that is even more of a nothing. I don't know anyone with the name Zach, or with the last name Pickering. I don't think I can help you further, do you?"

It was at that moment my opportunity arose. Wesley stretched out his arms to crack his knuckles, knocking his inbox to the floor in front of his desk.

I asked, "Do you need a little help?"

"No, thanks. Everything goes in a specific order."

While Wesley fumbled with his paperwork on one side of his desk, I cautiously backed up on the other side until I reached the exit door. I stepped forward when he was half standing, but papers slipped out of his hands and back to the floor.

This time I wasn't so hesitant. I looked around and turned the tiny lock on the doorknob. A glance over my shoulder showed me he was still scrambling on the floor, giving me enough time to unlock the deadbolt. I slid back beside his desk just as he stood again.

"What a day this has been," he said.

"Maybe it'd be good for you to relax at home."

"You know what?" He smiled and smacked his hand on the desk. "I think you're right. It is time for me to go." His cell phone rang.

"Hello? Yes, it's Wesley...I don't need to come up there. It's not my responsibility... ...No, Luna is not here...No...No, I will not come up there...No...No, I will not...I'll be right there."

"Trouble?" I asked.

"It sounds like an employee, or likely a guest, got their hands into one of our tills upstairs and the supervisor is out of his mind. Says he doesn't want to go to jail for the missing money."

"Happen often?"

"It's rare, but no time to talk. I need to get up there." He grabbed my elbow. "Why don't I notify the bartender that you're waiting for Luna, and you can have a couple of drinks on the house. How about we leave a voicemail for her to find you there?"

Wesley left Luna the message and escorted me through the restaurant to the front lobby. Josie jumped from her seat and followed several paces behind. When we reached the seating station, the young woman who chastised me earlier spoke up."

"Wesley, this man—"

"I'm in a rush, Anna, would you please escort Mr. O'Reilly to the lounge and set him up with some drinks."

"You know who he is?"

"Of course, I do. Please tell the bartender the drinks are on Luna." He trotted up the stairs to the club.

"Goodnight, Wesley," I said.

"Follow me, sir," the attendant said. "I'll talk with the bartender."

"One moment, please, miss. I need to have a discussion with my cohort."

She backed away, grabbed some menus, and escorted a family of five to a table near the front window.

"I'm going outside, Josie. I need you to stay back and ensure Wesley does not get into his office before I get out."

"How are you getting in there. He locked it."

"No worries, I can get in from outside."

"How do you expect me to stop him if he comes back?"

"Trip him."

"What?"

"I don't know. Anything. Tell him you want to apply for a job. He'll tell you he's too busy, and you'll need to demand the right. Be crazy. You know, act normal."

"Not funny, Lil' Bro."

I told the woman at the front desk that I was leaving for a while, but Josie was staying behind to wait for Luna. I exited the building and strolled around to the small alley between the club and the bank building next door. As expected, the door opened with no hesitation when I turned the knob.

Wesley's mad rush out of the office left a nice unprotected computer for me to get my hands on. My biggest concern was that a lock screen would have been timed to close before I got there, but apparently, he didn't have one on. I threw my finger down on the space bar the instant I hit the room just to be on the safe side.

Having no idea what I was looking for, I put in my thumb drive and dragged every spreadsheet I saw into it. Wages, invoices, profits and losses, tips, and more.

As I waited for a file called Inventory 2, Wesley started clamoring in the hall outside the office.

"Young lady, I told you, I do not take applications. The people at the front counter will be happy to help you. Now let go of my arm."

I dove behind a file cabinet when I heard a key going into the lock.

"Oh, Wesley, please don't be so mean to me," Josie cooed.

"Excuse me? Who are you?"

The file completed downloading, so I dragged the next one into the thumb drive.

"You don't recognize me, Wesley? I'm so hurt."

"I've never seen you before."

"I sure have seen you. I see you a lot."

"What on earth do you mean?" Wesley was flustered.

"I sit right over there, at that dining table several times a week, so I can watch you come and go."

"Are you a mad woman?"

"I don't know about mad, but I'm crazy. Crazy for you."

There was a loud thud against the door. I believe it was Wesley's back being pushed against it.

"Dear God. Is this your insane way of finding a job?"

"It's you that I want to give a job, but not the kind that has you waiting tables."

I clenched a hand across my mouth to keep from laughing out loud. Fear and hysteria were battling inside my head. Josie was doing a great job of stalling the man, but she was going to get me caught if I couldn't hold back from cracking up. There was another bang against the door. It was softer this time.

Wesley said, "Move away from that door before I call security. I'm giving you ten seconds."

"Don't you find me attractive?" Josie wept.

"Oh, for the love of God! I think you're a lovely young woman, but I'm a married man."

"Happily?"

"Yes, very happy." His voice had gotten more tense and stern.

"I'm happy that you're happy, but I have no doubt I can make you happier."

"I've had enough of you. I'm calling security. You need to be in an institution."

There was a smack followed by a crack.

"Look what you did to my cell phone?"

"I didn't mean for you to drop it."

"What on earth do you mean? You slapped it right out of my hand."

"Janet," Wesley called out. "Would you call security immediately." His voice quivered with a mix of fear and anger. "Now you've done it. Security will be here any second."

"I'm giving up, Wesley! It's obvious you're unable to love me the way I love you."

The sound of Wesley hitting the door happened again. "Let go of my shirt. What are you doing?"

"I want a kiss goodbye, but I know you won't give it to me," Josie sobbed. "I guess I should go."

"That would be a good idea. Let me escort you out."

"You're going with me?"

"Right out the front door."

While they walked away, I took the chance to download at least one more file. I wanted to ensure I got as many as I could to Harold. Once it completed downloading, I locked the deadbolt and doorknob, and cautiously stepped into the hall. I locked the office door behind me as Wesley came around the corner.

"What are you doing here? You were going to wait in the bar for Luna to get back."

"I was, but I need to get going. I was just going to leave her a note."

"I need to get out of here. Call and leave her a voicemail or send her a text."

"Good idea. I'll try that."

Wesley unlocked his door and stomped into his office.

"Good night, Mitch." He slammed the door.

"Good night, Wesley," I said under my breath as I walked to the lobby.

I forwarded the files to Harold that night.

Twenty-Four

I was locking the door to Eye Spy Supplies when Frank pulled up with his shopping cart. He was unusually cheerful and was singing "I Believe I Can Fly" by R. Kelly. Though he had to hum through half the song.

"Frank, my friend," I said. "I've never seen you here so early. I'm usually long gone before you show up."

"I told you I was turning over a new leaf. I ain't staying out late getting drunk anymore. Now I get drunk early, so I can get up fresh in the morning. A better way to start the day."

I chuckled. "Any requests for breakfast in the morning?"

"No, just something good and hot."

"You got it," I said as I was walking to my car.

"Hey, O'Reilly," Frank called. I turned to see what he wanted. "Thank you."

Just as I was pulling up close to home, I got a call from Zach Pickering.

"Mitch, can you come over? I've been robbed."

"What'd they take?"

"I don't know, but the place is trashed, and the police are here now."

When I reached Zach's place, Officer Darleen McGee was there. She was the same officer who went to my place when it was broken into.

"I forget your name, what was it?" she said to me.

"It was Mitch O'Reilly, and still is. You were at my place a week ago. It's three blocks from here."

"Yes, I remember. Looks like we have some local burglars in this area."

"How many robberies like this?"

"Just you and this place."

"And I know Zach."

"Who's Zach?"

"Zach Pickering. The guy who lives here who I presume you've talked to."

"I deal with a lot of names. It's hard to keep them straight. Are you friends?"

"Acquaintances mostly," I said. "But what a coincidence we're the only places hit, huh?"

"Could be a coincidence. Could be someone doesn't like the two of you."

"If you knew me, you'd know that's likely."

Zach came out of the front door. Officer McGee went in.

"Thanks for coming, Mitch," Zach muttered. "I know who did this. It was Hector."

"Was he here. Did you see him?"

"I saw him walking down this street the other day."

"That's no proof at all. Did your landlords see anything?"

"No such luck. They're out of town for the week."

"I guess you would expect Hector to know this?"

"I have proof enough. You know him. He hangs out in West Hollywood most of the time. I heard he goes to MacArthur park sometimes, too, for drugs, but what would bring him to Silver Lake?"

"A trick, some drugs, there's some AA meetings here. It could be a thousand reasons."

"Why my street?"

"Why not your street?"

"Thanks for nothing. You're no fucking help at all."

Zach walked back in his living room. I followed.

Whoever ransacked his apartment was more thorough and desperate than mine. The cushions on the couch weren't neatly unzipped, they were cut to shreds. Dishes had been broken, bedsheets were on the floor and there were cut marks in the mattress. Everything in his linen closet was scattered on the floor. Leaving an ocean of towels.

Zach was shaken but was fighting to maintain his cool composure. He stood in his painters' outfit. "I don't have renter's insurance. I have no money to refurnish this place."

He picked two of the few plates that weren't broken off the floor.

"You may be able to be roommates with Cody and Devin."

He smashed a plate on the counter. "Are you trying to be funny?"

"Sometimes I find myself hilarious. But, maybe I'm wrong. Anything stolen?"

"Not that I can see so far. The only thing I have worth stealing is my laptop, and it was with me. Even my TV is a piece of shit."

"Were they looking for the Audrey photo?"

"Who is they?"

"I'm leaving that open to whoever. You've been a friend of Austin's for years. Did you have custody of the photo?"

"Look, I have had custody of it before. A couple of times. Austin needed some loans and insisted I keep the photo as collateral."

"That's shocking when you think how much he loved it."

"Not really. You know by now he never wanted to go to his parents for money. He was humble, but that's one thing his pride wouldn't let him do. Not even from his mom. The last time I had the photo here was about five or six months ago."

"You loaned him some money?"

"Yes. Five hundred bucks. He gave me the picture to hold. He paid me off in three months, and I gave it back. I haven't seen the damn thing since."

"You think Hector thinks you have it? Is that why you're blaming him?"

"It's the best guess I can come up with and the only one. When I see him, I plan to kick his ass. I'd sue, but the only thing he can afford to give me is a bag of meth, and he sure won't give one of those up."

"Do me a favor."

"What's that?"

"If you see him, leave him alone. I want to talk to him, and it won't be easy if you beat the shit out of him. He's running scared already."

Zach did several deep breaths and reclaimed his usual stoic composure. "It won't be easy."

"You're a big boy. You can do it. I'll find him."

The question was why someone would tear apart both my apartment and Zach's. What were they hoping to find? It seemed likely they were searching for the missing photo, but why assume either of us had it?

Twenty-Five

I was on time for a meeting, for a change. I waited in the reception area outside Erin Mooney's office for forty minutes. Her assistant, a thin man with blond hair and glasses, wearing a powder blue sweater vest, offered me herbal tea twice. I asked for coffee, but I was told they don't serve caffeine drinks in their office. I never understood the concept of tea, especially herb. If I want tasteless hot water, then I will drink hot water. No need to pay for an overpriced bag of twigs.

Erin's company Vankka Foods' main office was on the eighteenth floor of a high-rise on Wilshire Boulevard in the expensive Westwood district of Los Angeles. The office was furnished with teakwood furniture. The salmon carpeting, light teal walls and wooden flute music was too New-age, and maddening for my tastes. I was relieved when Erin brought me into her office to get away from it. It was the same style, but without the sickening sounds.

Like her staff, Erin was dressed business casual. She wore her plum jacket open and was accented with a white blouse that had blue stripes matching her blue slacks. She asked me to sit with her on a denim couch in front of her desk.

"How may I help you, Mitch? I presume you're here to discuss Austin's death."

"You presume correctly. Dominique hired me to investigate his murder."

"I'm well aware she did, or I wouldn't have seen you otherwise. An unfortunate choice on her part, but as long as you're here..."

"Yes, as long as I'm here. First, thank you for the payment for my services to your dad. Regarding Austin, what was your relationship like?"

"There's nothing I can tell you. I hardly knew him. Austin was only ten when I went away to college. By the time I graduated, my father and Dominique were divorced. Beyond that, I only saw him on the holidays. There really was no relationship between us at all."

"What was your relationship before you went to college?"

"Not much different. My father married Dominique less than a year after my mother died. Austin came a year after that. As a seven-year-old girl, do you believe I'd want anything to do with them?"

"So, bitter."

"It's not bitterness. It's the sad truth for a little girl growing up in the Mooney household. Thank God, our home was big enough that I was able to avoid them as much as I could for ten years. As an adult, I see things more clearly, but I shouldn't be questioned about my feelings at that age."

"When was the last time you talked to Austin?"

"We saw each other for all of thirty minutes at my father's on Christmas."

"No communication with him for eight months?"

"None. You must understand, at this point in my life it wasn't a dislike for Austin, it was indifference. I'm certain he felt the same."

"I'm not questioning your relationship with Austin, but it's starkly different compared to Jared."

"Yes, Jared." She chuckled. "I've told him many times to get over his contempt for Austin."

"Contempt?"

"After the divorce, Jared and Austin would be at my father's during the summer. I understand at one point Austin convinced Jared to give him some tennis lessons, but that's the only time I recall they tolerated each other. While I had, as I said, indifference, towards Austin, Jared abhorred him. I told him repeatedly to move on, but he refused."

"But my understanding is—"

I was interrupted by a knock on the door. It was Erin's assistant, bringing her a pastrami sandwich and fries for lunch which he put on her end table.

"I'm sorry, Mitch. The sandwich will wait, but I hate cold fries, don't you? I hope you don't mind that I'll enjoy them while their hot."

"That's quite the meal for a woman who owns one of the largest organic and health foods companies in the U.S."

"What do you know about my business?"

"Enough to know that your sales from your Heaven Sent Snack Bar's alone is greater than the GNP of many countries."

Erin put her fries down and walked to a cabinet behind us. She came back with a box of Heaven Sent bars in mixed flavors.

"This is for you and some of your friends. I created this one myself. It's delicious and one of the few products we make that I'll eat. I do not concern myself with gluten free, organic, or other health foods, but I do know an opportunity when I see it. I'm sure you see it as hypocritical, but I think my success as a business leader speaks for itself. I take pride that I can be an inspiration to girls and young women around the world."

"You are your father's daughter."

"You don't mean that as a compliment. Are you intimidated by strong, independent and successful women?"

"No, quite the opposite. I respect women. I have respect for anyone who's strong, independent and successful, but not as much for those who are lucky enough to have a daddy who provided millions in seed money to get started."

"That's a smart mouth for a man asking questions. I may not have known Austin, but I do care that he was murdered. If I didn't, I'd have you leave."

"Then let's get back to questioning, so you can get to your sandwich. Jared and Austin had dinner together not long ago, despite how Jared felt about him."

"I don't know what that was about. Jared said he didn't either, other than an attempt of Austin's to have a closer relationship. Jared said he went through the motions, but he was done."

"Do you know where Jared was the night Austin was murdered?"

"It's impossible to keep up with Jared, but I assume he was with a woman."

"Your brother is quite the ladies' man."

"My brother is charming, but he's also stinking rich. The few of the ladies I've met didn't seem to have more interest than that."

"You are incredibly straightforward."

"You said I'm my father's daughter. I keep everything above board."

"And it is appreciated. I thank you."

"Is that all?"

"One more question. Where were you the night of Austin's murder?"

"We had a reception for major retailers at the Doubletree. I was there until around midnight, and a group of us went for drinks at The Wellesbourne and closed it."

"I'm guessing that's a bar, and you mean at 2:00 a.m.?"

"You guessed correctly. You said that's your final question, and my sandwich is getting cold."

"I thank you for your time."

"Tell my father 'hello' for me."

"He told you we were meeting today?"

"He and I share everything."

Twenty-Six

"It's good to see you again, Mr. O'Reilly," Paul, the butler, said when he opened the door. "I was heartbroken when we all thought you'd never be back."

"Do they teach you to be this cocky at butler school?"

"No, I watch a lot of TV sitcoms."

"You're a funny man."

"Mr. Mooney is waiting for you in the north lawn."

"How come everyone calls him T.J., but you?"

"T.J. is his brand. It's how he's known by his fans and throughout the industry, which is why he insists on it. However, when I was brought on, we agreed to the same, but changed it quickly. It felt forced. Odd for a butler to sound familiar with his employer in that manner. I insisted on switching back, and he agreed."

"The reality is not that it sounded familiar, but you didn't want to be that familiar."

"Again, your investigative skills are astounding."

"Don't sweat it. I know what an ass the man is," I said. "While I have your attention, do you mind if I ask you a question or two?"

"I may not answer, but ask away."

We started down the hallway.

"How well did you know Austin?"

"Not at all. I rarely saw him."

"I'm hearing that a lot from this household."

"It's not my place to share the family's business. I will only say that it was a rare event that Austin was here, and that broke his father's heart."

"Broke his heart?"

"I wasn't employed here when Austin lived at home. However, Mr. Mooney spoke highly of him."

"Thanks."

"Follow me. I'm sure you'd like to get this over as soon as possible."

"You're damned perceptive yourself."

We walked to the end of the grand hallway where extra wide double glass doors were open, allowing the breezes in.

"Mr. O'Reilly to see you, sir,"

"Paul, could you have someone bring me a drink? What about you, O'Reilly? What's your drink of choice?"

"Water or juice is fine with me."

"That's right, you're an alcoholic."

"I told you before I'm not an alcoholic. I've cut back is all."

"You're not cutting back today. I need a drink for this meeting, and I'm sure you could use one as well."

I looked to Paul. "Give me a greyhound."

"Your drinks will be right out, gentlemen."

Much of what Paul called the north lawn was a putting green. Other than the front yard, it appeared to be the smallest yard space around the mansion. A staircase wound around the corner of the home to a slightly lower level backyard which could be seen from where I stood. It had an enormous square pool with a large deck, and extensive gardens. T.J. leaned to pull a golf ball from one of the holes and stood with his putter in hand.

"You're lucky I'm a weak man when it comes to Dominique. She's a master at persuasion, and you can thank her for being allowed back in my home."

I didn't want to press my luck, so I bit my tongue and was cordial. "I appreciate you taking the time to see me, T.J. I didn't know you were a golfer."

"I'm no golfer. It's a boring game, and who has the time? I'm a putter. It's an underrated form of meditation. I can put all my thought and concentration on the ball." He sighed. "I've been spending a lot of time here since Austin died."

T.J. walked to a gazebo that stood next to the outdoor stairway. It sat above the backyard and gave a full view. The gardens past the pool were larger than they initially appeared. They seemed to go on forever with a mix of red and purple flowers that I didn't know the names of. We each took a seat at the cast iron Victorian style dining table.

"It didn't take you long to get here from Erin's office. Traffic must be light today."

"I drive fast."

A young woman, no more than twenty, her brown hair pulled into the tightest bun I'd ever seen, brought our drinks to the table. She didn't speak and neither did T.J. She did get a nod from him, which seemed the best he would offer.

I began, "I'm not one for chit chat, so let's get to it Why did you hire me to follow Austin?"

"What?"

"Why did you hire me. You said it was to make sure Austin didn't get into trouble. What kind of trouble?"

"I was concerned. He changed his last name from mine to his mother's. He wouldn't allow me to help him financially, which means he made a personal choice to live as a poor man. I didn't understand that. His choice to live the life he did made me concerned about the type of people he hung out with. I assumed he must be involved in something that would make him choose to live that way: Drugs or something. I wasn't sure."

"Bullshit."

"Concern for my son's safety is bullshit?"

"I say it's bullshit because Austin was gentler than Clark Kent. No one has a bad thing to say about him. Other than your other children, I can't find anyone who disliked him. You may not have known him well, but you knew him well enough to know that."

"He chose to live in a slum rather than comfortably here. That makes no sense."

"He didn't live in a slum. He lived like three guys right out of college. They're all trying to make their way. That's the biggest reason I know there's more behind you hiring me. You grew up in a small Iowa town. You busted your ass to get to college. You worked ridiculously long hours on film studies projects—"

"What does that have to do with anything?"

"You, of all people, know what it's like to pull yourself up from the bottom and the thrill of succeeding by your own merits. Austin's not the only celebrity child who changed their name, so they don't ride their parent's coattails. Austin Mooney, son of the famous director T.J.

Mooney, wouldn't have guaranteed him jobs, but it sure as hell would have gotten his foot in the door. Dominique, who is a B-List celebrity, not even close to your fame isn't even known by her last name. Few people know what it is. I know you're smart enough to understand this."

"Not only did I understand, it made me proud and increased my already tremendous respect for him. You're right. It's not a matter of him having chosen to live as a poor man. He chose to strive for success on his own. It was frustrating only because I know how talented he was, and I wanted the world to know that he was my son."

"So, then I'll ask again. Why did you hire me?"

"Do you think it's easy for a man to admit his son rejects him?"

"What?"

"Austin never let me down. I let him down. His mother is the best thing that ever happened to me. He grew up to be an incredible young man despite my being absent in his life. I rarely saw him when he was in Palm Springs or in the summer when I had custody. I was often on location somewhere, usually overseas. I'd fly him out from time to time, but even then, I never had the time to spend with him that he deserved. Despite my absence, Dominique raised an incredible man for whom I had the utmost respect. His denying my assistance and demanding he was going to make it in the crazy town on his own filled me with enormous pride. The part that pains me is to know he wasn't rejecting only my fame and wealth. He was rejecting me as his father."

"It would have made things a lot easier if you told me that from the beginning."

"I asked you to track him. I didn't see the why as important."

"How did Jared and Erin get along with Austin?"

"Erin never paid him any mind. When Lucille drowned, Erin blamed me for her mothers' death. I loved Lucille, but I couldn't control her drinking. Our marriage was no marriage at all, so I started dating Dominique. Because Dominique and I married so soon after Lucille died, Erin held it against Austin. She was never mean, never kind, just cold. Jared was a different matter altogether; he wasn't indifferent to Austin. He couldn't stand him. Because he was the older brother, I thought it was normal, but it wasn't normal at all. The hate he felt for Austin was deep. I don't know where it came from, but Jared was always a disappointment."

"How so?"

"He had no desire to do anything but have booze and babes. It was my fault for letting it happen. It was my money, after all, but I don't know how to be close to children. I don't know how to be close to any of mine. I mean, look where Jared has wound up."

"He's a well-respected professional tennis player."

"He's well respected if your expectations are low. Right now, he ranks only at number fifty-six. You know what ranking at fifty-six got him last year? Less than six hundred thousand. Ridiculous."

"To a guy like me that's a lot of money. Many parents would be proud."

"I would be proud. I'd be proud as hell if he worked his ass off the best he could to get where he is, but Jared is a magnificent player. He should be in the top of the ranks and a household name, but he doesn't take life serious enough and never has, no matter how hard I pushed him. Do you know where he was two weeks before the Washington Open? Having himself a good time in Ibiza. That's where he was. Before the Geneva Open, he was in Rio. I could go on, but you get the point."

"If it's your money, why do you continue to allow it?"

"I don't know. I guess because I blame myself for him being such a mess. My God, he's as loved and charismatic as Austin was. If he were at the top of his game, his charm would have him overwhelmed with endorsements. I did tell him it's time he pulled his life together. After living here a year, I insisted it was time for him to get his own place and move out. I've been pushing him for months, but he hasn't budged yet."

"But you wanted Austin to move in."

T.J. huffed, "Austin was more of a man than Jared will ever be, and I told Jared that myself. I was trying to help Austin while he busted his ass to make something of himself."

"Did you know any of Austin's friends?"

"Not a one. That's what I hired you for." He finished the last of his drinks and pushed an intercom button on the gazebo rail next to him. The lady with the cockney accent responded. T.J. ordered her to have another set of drinks brought out for each of us. He refused my protest that I was fine. I was about to speak when the sounds of a tennis match could be heard in the distance. Jared was on the court teaching a young blond woman how to serve.

"See what I mean?" T.J. growled. "He's got a tournament coming up in some Oriental country somewhere. He's trying to impress me like I believe he's practicing. I'm smart enough to know he's merely ogling that girl. Where's his manager while he's down there messing around?"

"Maybe you need to get him a new one?"

"I don't pay a manager's salary. I make him do that from his own earnings."

"Kind of doesn't matter much when you let him live here in your palace free of charge."

"I'd bust your ass for saying that if it wasn't true."

I stood as the same woman from earlier brought out our second round of drinks.

"Don't leave before you have your other drink." T.J. pointed at my seat.

"Why T.J., if I didn't know better, I'd think you want my company."

"Don't be ridiculous. Now sit back down."

For the next forty-five minutes, I sipped my greyhound while T.J. shared his pride and remorse over Austin.

Twenty-Seven

I was lying across my couch with a Rolling Rock in hand. I gave room service at the Beverly Place Hotel a call. A gruff voice answered that sounded familiar. "Room service, this is Vincent, how may I be of service?"

"Hey, Vincent, this is Mitch O'Reilly."

"How may I help you, Mr. O'Reilly?"

"Vincent, it's Mitch O'Reilly. Remember me?"

There was hesitation. "About six feet tall? Scruffy face and dreamy, rich brown eyes? That Mitch O'Reilly?"

"Some would say that describes me. How have you been?"

"I've been great except you broke my heart. I thought I was going to be more than a one-night stand, you naughty bastard."

"Hey, I hear that a lot. You know studs4studs.com isn't the place to go to find true love. It's not my fault that I aim to please."

"And you succeeded. I wasn't looking for love. I only wanted more fun. Anyway, I'm surprised you even remembered me. It's been what? Almost two years? I haven't seen you on studs4studs.com in a long time. You looking to hook up?"

"Not right now, Vincent. Relationship wise I'm in a state of flux."

"Hmmm. That doesn't sound good. Boyfriend troubles, or are you married?"

"Neither at the moment."

"Then what kind of flux do you mean?"

"It's complicated."

"It's always complicated. Do you need someone willing to just listen?"

"I didn't call for therapy."

"Well, whatever then. What can I do for you?"

"Do you remember I'm a private investigator?"

"I don't think you ever told me your occupation. I'm amazed you remember mine."

"I remember because you promised me a deal on a room anytime I wanted one."

"I was hoping you'd take me up on the deal, and a certain someone would be your guest."

"At your hotel, even your employee discount is out of my range."

"Humph. Mine and the rest of the staff, too. I don't know why they even bother to give us the discount when they know that none of us will ever take advantage of it. I guess that's their expectation. The sneaky bastards."

"Yeah, that sucks. Look I—"

"You still haven't said what you want."

"That's what I was getting to. I need you to look up an order for me." I gave him the date Jared and Gretchen stayed and their bungalow number.

"That's confidential information. I'm not supposed to give that out."

"I just need to know who signed for it."

"Sounds fishy to me. I hate this place. I hate it with a passion, but the money is damned good."

"Sorry you hate it."

"I'm not going to tell you what I make a night in tips. You wouldn't believe it. You really wouldn't believe it."

"I'm sure I wouldn't, but I was calling for that favor."

"That's what I was getting at. If I give out personal information, I could lose my job."

"Is it easy for someone to find out what you did?"

"Not tonight. It's my turn to take the orders. The other servers are out delivering most of the time."

"So, you have the time."

"I guess so. We're busy. They just grab their food and go. A lot of people eat in here. Unbelievable at our prices."

"I'm sure, but—"

"Do you know how much a sandwich costs?"

"No idea."

"A burger is twenty-nine dollars. Just a burger. Can you believe it?"

"That's a lot of money. You're right. If no one is usually around, do you think you can find out what I'm looking for."

"We'll see. Hold on."

I was on hold for fifteen minutes and grabbed myself a second beer in the process.

"Sorry about that. An influx of orders came in. Damn, I wish I were the one making tips tonight."

"Were you able to get the info I need?"

"I have an order for champagne, two lobster tails, one side salad and cheesecake."

"Tell me about the signature."

"Before I say anything, who was in the room?"

"Jared Mooney."

"You're right, but if you know who was in the room, what do you need from me."

"I want to know exactly who signed for the check."

"This must be a big case for a PI if a Mooney is involved. Does this have to do with that other Mooney kid being murdered?"

"No, nothing that serious," I lied. "That's way too big time for me."

"If you want to know who signed for it, you're going to make me look through all the signed checks and some servers let Mooney get by without signing."

"Could you at least check?"

"For you, I will, but you're going to have to take me on another date…or, at least a good hard fuck."

"Vincent, I told you I'm in a situation. If I wasn't, you'd be the first one I'd call."

"Okay, I'll search for it, but you're going to have to give me some time. We got some orders to run, and I'll have to get in the file to find that receipt."

"Time as in hours? Days?"

"Before I leave work. That will be around 11:00 p.m. Hopefully, sooner than that."

I gave Vincent my phone number and went about making some car rental calls to pass the time. I was trying to see if there was an agency that rented a car to Jared Mooney the night of the murder. I had Josie doing the same under Gretchen's name. There were only a couple of small-time rental offices open that late, so it didn't take long. I turned on the tube and watched an infomercial for a men's body razor. I was repulsed and intrigued at the same time. An hour later I got a call from the hotel.

"Mitch, it's Vincent. I found what you're looking for."

"Great. Who signed it?"

"It's signed in his name, but I know it wasn't him. I remember this delivery now."

"How do you know?"

"Because I did the delivery. Jared Mooney usually answers the door and signs for it, but not that night."

"How would you remember that?"

"Because he always gives a minimum of a twenty-five percent tip. I remember the bimbo who signed for it only gave me five dollars. Can you believe that shit? Five dollars for a hundred and fifty dollar bill. How the fuck can I forget her. I thought she was joking at first, but that was it. I almost called her the 'C' word, but I need to keep this job."

"Vincent, I can't tell you how much I appreciate your help."

"Maybe someday you can show me how much."

"Maybe, Vincent, maybe."

Twenty-Eight

It had been a busy morning at Eye Spy Supplies. I'd been open for three hours, had three customers, and made three sales. I sold a hidden camera in a picture frame, a hidden camera in a smoke detector and a Goodbye Eavesdropper bug detector.

As soon as I got a lull, I called Josie to ask her to continue to call car rental companies to see if any were under Gretchen Overton's name. I knew calling the big names like Avis, or Hertz would be a waste of time. They would have policies in place where they'd require proof of your rental before releasing any information. It was unlikely Jared would use a major one anyway. The fly-by-night operations were a different story though. I believed they wouldn't be so thorough in ensuring someone's privacy.

Josie protested, but as always, I persuaded my sister to continue to help me out.

My fourth customer of the day was a hunched over old woman who looked to be in her mid-eighties. She had stringy gray hair that hung to her shoulders and a face that looked like a map of Manhattan. I asked her twice if she needed assistance. Both times she waved her cane and told

me no. I took to dusting the shelves behind the cash
register, periodically looking back to see if she was ready
for help.

After twenty minutes she tapped a ring she was wearing
on the glass countertop to get my attention.

I said, "What can I help you with, ma'am?"

She mumbled something so low that I couldn't
understand her. I asked her to speak up.

She spoke too low again, and I had to ask her to talk
louder.

She waved me closer, so I leaned down near her face.

"You have a large selection of handcuffs," she
whispered. "Do you have any that are fur lined?"

"It's okay. There's no one else here. You don't need to
speak so low."

She tapped her ring on the glass again. "Just answer the
question."

"No, ma'am," I said. "I don't sell those types of cuffs,
but I can tell you who does."

"Go to hell," she growled as she hobbled to the door.
Trent was coming in and held it open for her as she left,
without thanking him.

"She looked bitchy," Trent said. He placed a bag on the
counter.

"In the wrong store and a little embarrassed, I think, is all."

"Huh?"

"Don't worry about her," I said. "You didn't bring me more burgers, did you?"

He leaned across the counter and gave me a kiss on the cheek. "No, not this time. You've hardly been to the gym since you started the Austin Bouchard case. I figure you need something healthier. It's turkey with curried yogurt in pita bread."

I rolled my eyes. "Wow, that sounds mouthwatering."

"Eat it and like it. You're the one who's been complaining that you're getting pudgy."

"You don't think so?"

"Not enough to complain about. I think it looks good on you."

"Thanks, but I feel fat. Any chance you can get off work this weekend?"

"It's the weekend so it's hard to say. There's a couple of supervisors who owe me favors. I can see if they can take my shifts if Aunt Ada will allow it. What's up?"

"I'm going to Topaz Saturday night and then driving to Palm Springs to meet Dominique Bouchard on Sunday. With all that's going on, I could use a weekend getaway. I wouldn't feel I have the time otherwise. Plus, I should take advantage of the time away from LA."

"Clothing optional hotel?" he begged.

"What the hell. If you can get us a room then go ahead."

"Hot damn. I'd be proud to strut around the place showing off my handsome boyfriend."

"You mean showing off your body and dragging me along."

"That's not true," he scoffed. "You look fantastic, and you know it."

"Do you really think it's necessary to spend extra on a nude hotel?"

"Why not?"

"Because I do plan on us being naked, but don't anticipate leaving the room much."

He put his brawny arms around my waist and nibbled my neck. "Music to my ears."

"Say My Name" by Destiny's Child was playing when Trent and I entered Topaz. Without hesitation he started swaying his hips, snapping his fingers, and singing the song out loud—badly. It was miraculous he could move his hips at all. Being a Saturday night, the place was busier than the last time I was there. Certainly, fire codes were being ignored.

I said, "Get us some drinks while I see if I can find Rachel backstage."

"Sure," Trent replied. "Do you think I'll get a chance to meet her?"

"I'll see what I can do."

It felt like it took hours to snake through the crowd to the stage door. Luna Salcedo was coming out as I was going in.

"Mitch," she shouted above the noise. "Come inside so we can talk." She took my hand and led me up the two steps and through the door to backstage. She smiled and straightened out the collar on my shirt. "I'm sorry I keep missing you when you stop in. What has you continuing to investigate here at the club?"

"I'd be negligent not to. A lot of people were here, and it's the last place he was seen alive."

Luna placed a hand against her cheek. "I keep forgetting that. It makes me depressed thinking about it. You continue to have full access here. I wouldn't consider holding you back in any manner. What brings you backstage, though?"

"Rachel Roundtree and Austin were friends."

"I didn't know that. Do you think she was involved?"

"Friends never know that they may have information that can help. They may have seen or heard something that seemed innocent at the time."

"I see. That makes sense." She faced me, took my hands, and raised them. "I do hope you catch the person soon. Austin had so much life ahead of him."

Luna and the stagehands all told me that Rachel Roundtree was in her dressing room. I rapped on the door three times, the last one for an extended period. There was no answer. I assumed she was drunk or passed out, so I turned the knob and opened the door. I didn't expect to find her on a blanket on the floor with her legs in the air. From the looks on their faces, it appeared Zach Pickering and Rachel weren't expecting me either. With no sense of urgency, Zach stood, tucked his cock inside his pants and pulled up his zipper. Rachel was not so calm. She grabbed her drink off the floor as she got up and waved her finger at me.

She growled, "Who the fuck do you think you are busting in like that? Are you some freak who likes to watch?"

I played with the lock on the door handle. "I never trust these cheap things. Looks like it didn't latch."

Zack was silent with his hands clasped behind his back while Rachel screamed. "This is my private room. You have no business walking in, whether it's locked or not."

"I'll remember that rule of etiquette next time," I replied. "If you're done with your little fit, how about answering some questions."

Zach stepped forward. "You're not a cop, so we really don't have to answer your questions, do we?"

"Answering my questions is up to you, but I'd be happy to turn everything I have over to the police and let them question you."

"You're full of shit," Rachel belted. "You got nothing, and you don't scare me."

"Zach, you seem like a reasonable man, and you've said you hope I catch Austin's killer. Certainly, you want to cooperate."

He relaxed his arms and sighed. "Tell the man anything he wants to know, Rachel. There's no harm."

"What do you want to know, Mr. I Thought You Were a Nice Guy?"

"I've been thinking about the phone calls you made to Austin. We've established your last call the night he was murdered was at 9:30. You didn't call him again until 9:40 the next morning. Weren't you the least bit concerned where he was during that time? He seemed like a man responsible enough to let you know when he couldn't show up as planned."

Zach said, "I told you Rachel and I went back to my place and spent the evening together."

"I told you that, too," Rachel screeched. Plus, Austin was popular. He probably found some other friends or some cute guy."

"You mentioned that before," I said. "It doesn't seem to fit everything I've heard about Austin. I hear he was a responsible fellow."

"So what, that we didn't call. Why does it matter?"

"It matters because if Rachel had made those calls while in the hills, the cell towers would trace that's where she was. It wouldn't have been a smart move to call if she was up there."

Rachel sucked down the last of her drink and called the bar to deliver another one.

"Are you saying you think Rachel carried Austin all the way up to the Hollywood sign? You're crazy."

"It's not so crazy if she had help."

"I've been cooperative with you, Mitch. Now you're getting way out of line."

"Just a theory. I can't leave any stone unturned, you know."

After I was thrown out of Rachel's dressing room, I found Trent dancing to "U Can't Touch This" by MC Hammer. I let him have his fun until the song was done, and then off we went to Palm Springs.

Twenty-Nine

Traffic was heavy along the 10 freeway to Palm Springs.
Trent asked about my case, and I told him about the cold
reception from Erin and T.J. Mooney, compared to the
openness of Jared. I wanted to relax for the evening, so I
did leave off that Jared was nothing but a rich playboy
phony. I also didn't think it was my place to tell him about
Gretchen, the hooker Jared hired from time to time. Trent
had no need to know the guy's personal business.

Trent gave me a detailed description of when he was ten
at his Uncle Kostas' fiftieth birthday party. It was a thirty-
minute story, involving him getting in trouble for hiding the
birthday cake in the linen closet. Typically, the elaborately
detailed story went nowhere, but there were enough funny
parts that he had me laughing most of the time. Despite my
inability to say I loved him; I was concluding I did. It was
his playfulness, ability to make me laugh and his positive
attitude that endeared him to me. Three things that didn't
come naturally at that time of my life. It'd been far too long
since I allowed myself to loosen up and focus on the good
things. It wasn't for lack of trying. I tried hard to be the
person Josie, Trent, and even his aunt Ada said I was. I was
exhausted from morphing from joy to bitterness in a matter

of minutes. It hadn't been until Josie explained to me that Trent was a *fixer* that I understood why Trent stayed with me. It made me wonder what would happen if I was fixed. What the hell would that look like? What if he succeeded in making me embrace the good things in life? I considered the possibility that he'd move on to the next guy to fix. I didn't believe it'd be a conscious thing for him, but he'd get a feeling one day that it was time to move on. Just as things would get better, I would lose him.

It wasn't until we hit the windmill farms about twenty minutes outside of Palm Springs before more serious discussion began. We were in Trent's Jeep, and he let go of holding my hand and put his on my thigh.

He said, "There's no way to express how much I'm enjoying this trip. We've both been so busy that it's been awhile since we've got to talk and joke, and you putting up with my silliness. Holding your hand for over an hour felt good. It felt like the way things should be. We both need to try harder to ensure we get together more often. We've been so distant physically that it's made me feel you've been distant mentally, but I know you still care."

He was right, I did care, but he was right that I had been distant. I couldn't decide if it was on purpose or because of everything that was going on. My nightmares, the flashbacks, the store, and my PI business. But it was more than that. No matter how much I liked being around him, it scared the shit out of me. No, it wasn't fear, it was a general discomfort that was difficult to pinpoint. I was starting to consider it was because I didn't have time for him.

I said, "You don't need to worry, babe. I do care."

"Babe? This is a red-letter day. You have never called me babe before. This is a side of you that you rarely let me see."

I said, "You know me well enough to know not to make a big deal of it, kiddo."

"That I do."

It was near midnight when we reached the Palm Breeze Inn. Although we would be there for only a few hours to sleep, Trent insisted we stay at an upscale clothing optional gay hotel that was more than either of us could afford. He put it on his credit card.

"Is the pool still open?" Trent asked the blond, tall twink behind the front desk.

"It closed a couple of hours ago, but if you promise to be quiet, I can let you slide."

"Deal!" Trent exclaimed with a broad grin on his face. He looked at me and winked.

I'm not a fan of clothing-optional hotels. Not that I dislike them, but walking around naked, even when I was at my fittest, was never that big of a deal. Technically, that's untrue when I considered how much time I had spent in the bathhouses five years before, but nude beaches, resorts and such were not my style. That night was different because I got to see my man, Trent Nakos, parade from our room, across the patio and ease himself down into the pool. Not that I hadn't seen his beautiful muscled body a thousand times before, but I wanted others to see that delicious looking, olive skinned, strapping man was with me. I was embarrassed by the thought. It was childish. Even worse, it was insecure. But it made me grin.

I lowered myself into the pool beside him, and we wrapped our arms around each other and kissed. We embraced for over half an hour whispering stories to each other and trying not to laugh out loud. With time, we grabbed each other's dicks and gently stroked them. We'd laughed a bit and kissed a bit for about an hour. A few times he ducked under the water to suck on me until he had to come up for air. He wrapped his arms around me and gave me the most passionate kiss I ever had. It was a weak moment for me, and I almost said the words he wanted to hear.

Instead, I whispered, "I love…this."

Trent's eyes saddened and I gave him a kiss.

When we climbed out of the pool, he held my hand and led me back to our room. I gave myself completely over to him, and he took full advantage.

By 2:00 a.m. our sheets were soaked from water, sweat, and a multitude of ejaculations. Trent put his head on my chest, and we both drifted off.

At 3:30 I woke up screaming. The night terrors had hit.

My appointment with Dominique was at 9:00 a.m. Trent talked to the front desk to request a late check out until 1:00 p.m. That gave me plenty of time to spend with her. I felt welcomed the minute I stepped into Dominique's Palm Springs home. Despite its ultra-contemporary furnishings and straight lines, the natural wood flooring and ceiling, large stone fireplace, and warm yet vibrant purple and yellow furniture gave me an "at home" feeling. Seeing that was her style, I could imagine how the cold Mooney Mansion, which looked and felt like a museum, must have been miserable for her. The stone fireplace at the end of the room broke up the complete walls of glass that lined each side of her long living room. The windows looked out to desert grounds with succulents placed to give a natural feel. She had non vocal, acoustical guitar music playing softly throughout the home.

She graciously met me at the door and motioned from the intimate foyer to a seat on the armless purple couch. She asked if I'd like a drink and brought out my glass of water. She had a cup of coffee herself, which I regretted not asking if she had, but I didn't want her to go to the trouble of making any if she had not.

I said, "Thank you for taking the time to meet with me, Dominique."

She smiled whimsically. "Don't speak so formally with me. We've chatted enough that you know I'm a laid-back person. Besides, why wouldn't I give you the time? You're working for me, aren't you?"

"Good point."

"How is the investigation coming along?"

This was a question I dreaded a client to ask. No matter what the answer, they were sure to be disappointed. The only time they were happy was if and when I was able to solve a case. I had the suspects, but nothing conclusive to draw me to suspect any one over another. My goal that day was to shed some light on some of the individuals involved.

How much to reveal to a client to gather information without them knowing you don't have a clue was a delicate balance.

"The investigation is coming along great. I'm focusing on a few suspects."

"When do you think you'll be done."

"That's a tough one to answer because I can't know what I don't know. Although I have a list, it could take some time to narrow it down."

"Who are the suspects?"

I couldn't tell her the suspects. It was a bad, yet frustrating, way to operate. To tell her my list included her former stepson Jared, Austin's close friend Zach, and Zach's crazy kinda girlfriend Rachel, was more information than she should know at this point. There was also Hector and the accountant at Topaz, who she'd never heard of.

"I prefer not to say, if you don't mind. I don't like to rouse your suspicions over an individual which could make you be subconsciously biased when I ask you questions. That can hurt my investigation. Though, it's likely you'll be able to have an idea about some from our conversation today."

"It's confusing that you won't give me more details about the investigation that I hired you to conduct."

"Trust me, okay?"

As she nodded her head, her fluffy, white pooch Rémy trotted up the hallways behind me, into the living room and threw himself on to the couch next to her. She stroked his fur while he laid down and nuzzled against her.

"Who do you want to ask me about?"

"I don't want to ask specifically about an individual. Rather, I'd prefer you tell me more of Austin's story. Primarily his teen years through and after high school."

She walked to table against a glass wall and grabbed a box of tissues. Rémy stayed on her heels and got back into his cuddled position when she sat back on the couch. "I'll probably end up needing these," she said. "Let me think. We talked about his relationship with Jared and Erin, and the odd, loving feud with Zach. I don't think I left anything out about Hector. Plus, I told you about Grant's suicide."

"Tell me more about Grant."

"Grant and Austin were here in LA while I was in Palm Springs, so I never met the boy. I knew little of him until the photograph was taken and they wound up on the news."

"Is there anything you left out about Grant's family?"

"Not that I know of. I told you how horribly they treated him and forced him to travel to evangelical churches throughout the country to speak about his redemption. Sometimes they made him sing with his sister."

"Yeah, you mentioned the sister before."

"I never met her, but I believe her name was Rhonda. Yes, Rhonda Ridgeway."

"What can you tell me about her?"

"Very little, but she sang gospel songs at churches in Texas and some other border states. Austin told me she had a beautiful voice but was far too evangelical for him to want to be around her for more than a few minutes. He said she was so preachy that she gave him the creeps. From what I understand, she was a big star within her small circle."

"Do you know whatever became of her?"

"I have no idea. Probably some Texas housewife who home schools her kids and sings in the church choir, but I guess I'm stereotyping."

"Stereotypes exist for a reason," I said.

"I'm sorry, I wish I could tell you more."

"That's all right. I want to ask just a little more about Zach Pickering."

"Go ahead, but I can't imagine what I haven't told you."

"I want you to elabora—"

"Mitch?" Dominique's voice was barely audible, as if it echoed from a distance. "Mitch? Are you okay?"

Dominique continued to talk, but all I heard was gibberish. I was not okay. I was partially in Afghanistan ducked behind the pillar again. I was protecting some of the locals while the Taliban fired upon us. They were grabbing at me and pulling at me while begging for help. In my flashback, they were all dripping with blood.

On the steps lay Suze as he was picked off slowly one bullet at a time, but he looked different this time. While his head was down, a bullet exploded the back of it across the landing. He should have been dead, but he wasn't. Instead, he reached an arm toward me, slowly raised up. It wasn't Suze in my vision. It was my fiancé Jackson. He raised himself to his knees, arms stretched in my direction, and he mouthed "Help me" before his head exploded from a round of bullets.

"Mitch, can I help you?" Dominique said as she made the mistake of shaking me. I responded by brushing her aside with my arm and nearly knocked her to the floor.

"My god! Mitch! What's wrong?"

I yelled, "Where's your bathroom?"

She pointed the direction, and I ran across the living room. I made it to the toilet in the nick of time before puking. I don't know how long I had my head in the bowl, but it was enough that I was dry heaving. I started hearing shots firing again until I realized it was the sound of Dominique rapping on the door.

"Mitch, Mitch. Talk to me! Should I call an ambulance?"

"No, I'm fine," I muttered. "I think I had a sudden attack of the flu or food poisoning. I'll be out in a few."

"Okay, if you're sure."

I wasn't fine. There was no sound, no action, no incident at all that triggered the flashback. I was getting worse. For an additional ten minutes I leaned my back against the vanity and wrapped my arms around myself while involuntarily shaking. Toilet tissue stuck to my face as I continually wiped the sweat from my eyes.

Once I got my composure back, I apologized to Dominique, told her I was certain it was food poisoning and that I would stop by an emergency care clinic as soon as I left her place. The skepticism showed on her face.

I cried the whole way back to the hotel. Trent pointed out that we had an hour left before we had to check out and grabbed my crotch. His eyes widened and mouth gaped when I smacked his hand and told him to get the fuck away from me.

"Sorry, Trent. It didn't go well. I need to get home."

I was glad we took his Jeep to Palm Springs. I wouldn't have been able to drive safely during our silent trip back to Los Angeles.

The day my unit was attacked in Kabul wouldn't leave my mind. Because of the rumors of a Taliban attack, we were escorting a crowd of locals to where we thought they would be safe. It was during that escort that we were ambushed. By the time me, George Suzuki, and K.K. reached the protection of the public building, at least a dozen of the locals and nearly a dozen from my unit were dead. I wanted to help Suze who was on the steps being shot slow and methodically to make him suffer. Each attempt K.K. and I made to save him was met with rapid gunfire that forced us back behind the building's pillars. Being that our primary duty was to protect the locals, there was little we could do to help Suze. The one major attempt by K.K. led to a shot in his shoulder. All I could do was helplessly watch Suze slowly die as he was picked off by bullets one by one. The howls of the locals in my care were deafening. Had backup not arrived, we all would have been dead.

Trent tried to start conversations, but I shut him down each time. As the silence settled in, my mind drifted to some loose ends. I had research to do on a certain young lady named Rhonda Ridgeway. When I was able to concentrate, I used our trip back by googling her background on my phone.

Thirty

When I opened the store in the morning, I jumped right on the computer to find more on Jared's escort from the hotel. I searched Gretchen Overton's birth name—it took too long to dawn on me she might have been using an alias. Within thirty minutes I had my answer—Barbie Bloom. I knew Josie would get a kick out of that.

Friday is usually one of my busiest days, but it was slow that morning. It was mostly sunny. Temperatures were in the mid-70s. I wondered if people took the day off to head to the beach. Tourist season was over which freed up the locals to have some fun and frolic. Whatever was going on, it kept them away from my store. It was rare that I was relieved to have little business, but that day was one of them. I had been on the phone with Harold until 4:00 a.m. We discussed my nightmares, and the flashbacks. He convinced me I needed psychiatric help. A large part of our conversation was about me focusing more on recovery. That meant some things, and someone, were going to have to take a lesser priority in my life. It had been a week since my incident in Palm Springs.

I began texting Josie about Gretchen's real name when the bell on the doorknob jingled. Before I could push my office chair to the side to see who it was, Trent's voice boomed from the front area of the store. "Don't get up. Don't get up. It's just me." He was in a chipper mood. More chipper than usual. It wasn't good timing on his part to be so cheerful. It tightened knots in the pit of my stomach. He stopped in the door to my office and grinned. "I'm so stoked for tonight. Aren't you?"

"You mean the Greek Fest?" I mumbled. "I forgot."

"Of course, the Greek Fest. You know, Aunt Ada isn't one to give me a Friday night off for just anything. This is our biggest event of the year. We'll have to hit the gym tomorrow because tonight we'll be drinking and eating until we're ready to burst." He frowned. "I'm just sad we won't be able to act as a couple. Too many Greek Orthodox there to be safe dancing with you without creating a scene. We'll have lots of fun anyway."

I was silent as I gazed at the papers on my desk.

"Something is wrong," Trent said. "Why are you being such a sad sack?"

"You'll have to go to the festival alone."

His voice quivered. "Alone? What are you talking about? We've planned this for two months. It's my favorite weekend of the year, and I want you there. Would it be better to go Saturday or Sunday?"

"I'm not going at all, Trent. You just said we couldn't act as a couple, so you can go with Aunt Ada and have a good time without me."

He plopped himself on the couch, leaned forward and clasped his hands. "Something is seriously wrong. What's going on?"

I told him to hold on while I posted an *Out to Lunch* sign on the front door and locked it. I sat on the couch with him. Trent grabbed my hand and put his other on my back.

"Tell me what's wrong, baby."

"Last weekend at the motel. Remember I had night terrors?"

"Do I remember? Those things are awful. I can't even begin to imagine what it's like for you."

"I didn't tell you what happened at Dominique's house. I had flashbacks again. I had to lock myself in the bathroom until I calmed down. She must think I'm crazy."

"Well," he said while cracking a smile, "you are a little crazy."

Saying I'm crazy like that would normally make me laugh. I suffered from a debilitating mental illness. Of course, I was crazy. We joked about it from time to time, but that was back before the flashbacks got worse. Hearing him say it in that moment stung.

"I'm sorry." He pulled my head against his chest. For a moment it felt warm and safe, but that was part of the problem. "I see it's not the time for jokes," he continued.

I sat up and grabbed both his hands. "My friend, I need some space."

Trent grimaced and pulled his hands away. "You mean you're breaking up with me."

"I didn't say that. It's not what I mean." I hesitated. "I'm not even sure I'd know what I'm breaking up from. We've never talked about making a commitment."

"In the last four months have you seen anyone other than me?"

"No, but—"

"That's not the Mitch O'Reilly I first met who spent half his life cruising to get laid."

"Half my life is a gross exaggeration, Trent. I'm sorry if I hurt you, but—"

"Then explain it to me," he choked.

I stood and sat one ass cheek on the desktop. "I'm not breaking up with you, or whatever we have. All I'm saying is I need…a break."

"What's the difference between a 'break up' and 'a break'?"

"I'm overwhelmed. I'm dealing with nightmares, flashbacks, and a major murder case that I feel responsible for. I have little to offer you. Definitely not what you deserve."

Trent scoffed. "You're saying you're doing this for me, huh?"

"No, not at all. I'm doing this for me. I have no choice but to step back, look at my life and figure it out. I need help - professional help. The last thing I want right now is to push you away, but I don't know how to move forward without doing so. I must focus on me. Please, understand that."

He sat silently on the couch. One hand was on each knee, and his head was lowered. I could barely breathe during the long minutes he stayed that way.

He stood, walked over, and embraced me. "I'm sorry; I'm being selfish. I know how hard a new relationship can be, and you don't need that added stress. I want you to get all the help you need to overcome your demons. I can't get in the way of that."

"Thank you."

"You just need to know one thing, mister." He pounded a finger into my chest. "When you're ready, I'll be waiting for you."

"I don't know how long this will be."

"I said I'll be waiting for you...I'll miss you tonight."

Without saying goodbye, Trent unlocked the front door and slogged to his jeep. He nodded a goodbye before driving off.

The store remained slow throughout the day, which was for the best. It gave me time to breathe. It also gave me time to make some calls to the VA about mental health assistance. I had talked with them before but refused aid. The attendant on the line highly suggested I schedule an appointment with a therapist and a psychiatrist, but I said I'd call back. I was becoming more convinced that I needed the help but wasn't ready to make the leap. Somehow, I thought – actually, I don't know what I thought.

Harold Beavers called me mid-day more excited than I had heard from him before.

"You won't believe what I just got," he said. Before I could respond he continued, "I've got two tickets for the Dodgers' game tonight against Atlanta."

"How'd you get tickets to the playoffs?"

Harold looked smug. "From a client."

"That's great," I said. "It'll be a good game. I think the Dodgers could make it all the way this year."

"I'm sure of it, but you don't sound all that enthusiastic."

"Just tired from talking to you all night, plus it's been a big day between talking with the VA and with Trent."

"Whoa, you did a lot in a short amount of time. Why don't you tell me all about it in the car tonight?"

"The car?"

"Yes," he said. "You're going with me to the game." It sounded like he was jumping up and down.

"Would love to go, but there's no way. I canceled a major date with Trent for tonight. You can't expect me to turn around and go to the game even if it is for the series."

"It's exactly what I'd expect. What you need right now is to get out of your head. If you don't go with me tonight, you'll mope at home and play all the bullshit over and over again in your brain."

I sighed. "Maybe, but something about it doesn't seem right. Like, it's a slap in Trent's face."

"You asked him to give you some space?"

I stayed silent, unable to answer.

"You still there?"

"Yeah, I told him. I don't think I did a good job of it though. I wasn't as gentle as I imagined I would be."

"Probably because you were tense."

"Definitely because I was."

"Any chance you can close the store an hour-in-a-half early, so I can pick you up for the game? It starts at 6:30."

"I was already planning on closing at 5:00 to go to the Greek Fest with Trent."

"Great! I'll see you at 4:30, sharp."

"Let's get serious," Harold said just as I climbed in the car.

"I thought we were going to the game to get my mind off things,

"We are. This has nothing to do with PTSD, the VA or Trent. It has to do with that Stumpf guy. The accountant at Topaz."

"Wesley Stumpf? What is it?"

"Sorry it's taken so long, but I've been busy as hell—which is good. But that guy is definitely skimming."

"You can tell from the files I gave you?"

"Clear as day, and not even good at it. All he's doing is overpaying a couple of vendors, and I presume he's getting kickbacks."

"How is that so obvious?"

"He's paying vendors less than what it says on the books. The best way to make money from vendors is through kickbacks, which he may or may not be doing, but what I'm seeing on his files is that he's taking an easy, more risky way about it."

"That blows my mind because Luna Salcedo seems like a sharp businesswoman. She owns the club."

"She's not looking so sharp to me."

"She said they've worked together for years. The bastard must have gained too much of her trust."

"Trust and friendship are the primary reasons audits are necessary. The last thing you want is to suspect a friend."

"What about the skimming of employee tips?"

"Given what he's making by cooking the books, that would be small change. My guess is there's a technical glitch in the registers or it isn't really happening."

"It doesn't seem likely Stumpf would kill Austin Mooney if he was confronted about skimming tips then, unless Austin scared him."

"You think that's possible?"

"Not likely."

"You going to tell the owner that Stumpf is stealing from her?"

"Not yet. I want to get more on him."

Thirty-One

The similarities between the two singers was too coincidental, though if Rhonda Ridgeway changed her name to Rachel Roundtree, she wasn't very original. At the very least she could have changed her initials. As expected, I found the records of Rhonda changing her name to Rachel in 2014, the same year she founded the Titmice. That was quite the change for a former gospel singer.

I called the Primrose Inn where she had been staying and was told she had checked out the week before. Luna Salcedo confirmed her gig had been over at Topaz, and she had no idea where she was going next. Rachel's website showed she did a three-night show in Seattle, and then she was off for a month before playing in San Francisco.

I made a call to Zach Pickering.

He said, "How do I know where she is? Probably at her place in Tucson."

"She's based in Tucson?"

"Have you ever been there? It's a nice city, and she loves the desert. She's got a place there a few miles out of town."

"I'm sure it's lovely as hell. When will she be back in LA?"

"I don't know. She usually plays clubs here about every six months to a year. She lives on the road mostly. I'm not her agent. I don't keep her schedule."

"Do you keep up with her enough that she comes to visit you now and then?"

"Mitch, leave her alone. She had nothing to do with anything, and neither did I. Austin was our friend, and there's no reason why we'd hurt or kill him."

"Oh, I can think of a couple of reasons."

"I've had enough of you."

"Don't hang up. You know I'll track her down. You might as well make life easy and tell me where she'll be."

"She's coming to stay with me, starting next weekend. I'll make sure she talks with you again if it will make you happy."

"You're one helluva guy, Zach."

"Cut your crap, or I'll cancel our deal. I'm only doing this so you'll get out of our lives for good."

"That's going to be up to the two of you."

He hung up the phone.

I was twenty minutes late when I reached the Beverly Place Hotel where I was meeting Jared. He had asked to meet me to discuss the investigation. There was nothing I was willing to tell him, but it made for an opportunity to get something out of him.

The bar, named The Place Lounge, felt like I took the five-hour drive to Las Vegas. For an upscale stuffy hotel, the bar was brash and played on my anxiety filled nerves that day. Pink and bright blue were the scheme. Metal framed pink upholstered chairs lined the bar and each table throughout the large facility. The bar top and tables were bright pink as well. From the ceiling, above the bar and the lounge area, hung a mix of felt pink and sapphire tasseled lampshades. The jazz music playing should have soothed the atmosphere, except the horns and saxes were set at a level that made it hard to be heard. Jared had no complaints that I was late, being that he was on his third martini. I'm sure his flirting with the woman behind the bar didn't hurt either.

He said, "Mitch O'Reilly, how is the investigation coming? I hope you're closer to catching the killer."

"Getting closer every day."

I got no reaction from Jared as he sipped on his drink. "What can I order for you?"

"A Rolling Rock."

He ordered my drink, and the bartender poured my glass within seconds.

"Let's talk privately over in the corner there." He turned to the bartender. "We'll talk more before I leave."

We took our seats, and a server rushed over to ask if we'd like appetizers. Jared teased with her too, but ended their conversation by saying food would soak up too much of the alcohol. She chuckled as if she'd never heard that before.

I asked, "Why did you call me here?"

"As I said, I want to hear how things are going. Dominique and I aren't on the best speaking terms, and I'm sure you've given her updates."

"It may surprise you to know I've told her very little."

"Because you know very little?"

"Oh, I know a lot now." Again, he gave no response. "It's just that I prefer not to share information with my clients until things become more clear-cut. Besides, without Dominique's okay, there's little to nothing I can tell you."

"I thought we were friends."

"We're friendly, but not friends. Friendship isn't possible while the case is in progress."

"That's a shame. I was hoping to invite you to a party on Dad's yacht sometime."

"Your grief is astounding."

"You act as if I don't mourn for my brother. I do, greatly. I also know when to take advantage of an opportunity."

"I don't mean to be skeptical, but I am. You didn't invite me here to discuss a yacht party."

"You're right: I didn't. Tennis is over for me for the year, so I'm going to Ibiza for a couple of weeks before the party season ends. I want an update on my brother before I go."

"I wish I had more to tell, but all I can say is it looks like the case is coming to a close."

"I'm sure Dominique won't mind if you spill the beans, plus we're buds, right?"

"I think I made myself clear."

"Damn, man. You seemed so cool. What's gotten into you?"

"It's just a business for me Jared, nothing more. I did get a chance to speak with Gretchen."

"Yes, she told me. Get any big scoops out of her?"

"She corroborated everything you said."

"So, I'm off the hook then."

"Everyone is on the hook until the big fish is caught." I downed the last of my beer. "Is there anything more you want from me, Jared? If not, I'm going to get going."

"You don't want to hang out and have another drink with a friend?" He called the server over and ordered us each another drink. While doing so, I checked my texts. There was one from Josie reminding me we had plans that night to hang out at her place.

"I've got to get going," I told him. "I forgot I had somewhere to go tonight."

"I won't hold it against you. Between the bartender and the waitress, I'm getting laid tonight."

"You're a helluva sweet guy, Jared."

Thirty-Two

After meeting with Jared, I went to Josie's place. Stu was out of town, but he had his furniture moved there, and she wanted me to see her new set up.

I took the elevator up to the third floor and waited on the exterior landing after ringing her doorbell. Josie swung open the door when we heard a woman from another building in the complex scream. There was a gunshot, followed by another scream. A second gunshot and the screaming stopped. From the railing I could see a person, dressed in black running through the parking lot. I busted my ass getting down the stairs and ran into the lot, but there was no one around. Rather than running aimlessly looking for someone, I had a more urgent priority, to get to who was screaming and see if they were okay. Based on the direction of the shots and a hunch, I had a pretty good idea where to check.

I was huffing from the run and adrenaline rush to the building housing Gretchen Overton's first floor condominium. I banged on her door.

"Gretchen!" I screamed. "Gretchen open up!"

"Are you the police?" a shaky voice asked from behind. It was a teenage girl looking out the cracked door of the condo next door.

"I'm an investigator," I bellowed. "Do you know where the shots came from?"

"I think it was in there. Ms. Overton's place."

I threw my shoulder against her door and gave it several hard kicks. It's never as easy as it is in the movies. I considered shooting the doorknob but thought better of it and ran around to the side of her place. The sliding glass door, and screen, were open and the gold curtain was flapping in the breeze.

"Gretchen!" I called out again. There was no response.

I hurdled over the half wall with my gun in hand. Police sirens were coming closer.

Making the unwise assumption that the person running was the assailant, I stepped forward to enter Gretchen's home, but tripped over a crowbar, fell through the curtains draped across the open door and onto the carpeting inside. Next to me was what was left of a man's head and lifeless body. Five feet away, Gretchen had fallen against the couch when a bullet went cleanly through her forehead. It was clear there was no need to attempt resuscitation on either.

Feeling it was unwise to touch anything by going out the
front door, I walked back out to the patio.

"Stop!" yelled one of the two cops standing on the
exterior side of the half wall. Both had guns pointing at me.

Having been a military police officer, I instinctively
dropped my gun and placed my hands on my head.

I was held in the squad car for almost an hour. Despite
protests from Josie, the girl next door to Gretchen's condo,
and two other neighbors who saw me chase the likely
killer, it took a call to Detective Matias Castro of the
Hollywood Division before I was released. I was still held
for questioning, but as a witness to the crime rather than the
assailant.

"I'm Detective Wanda Thompkins, Westside Division,"
said the tall, slim dark complected woman standing next to
me as I leaned against the squad car. "I talked with
Detective Castro and hear you worked that bathhouse case
a few months back."

"That's me. Mitch O'Reilly, Ace Detective."

"You're real cute. Bodies seem to follow you
everywhere, Mr. O'Reilly."

"No," I replied. "Bodies seem to show up everywhere I go."

"What is this? How many bodies is this in less than six months?"

"I'm a private investigator who deals in murder. It comes with the territory."

"'A private investigator who deals in murder?' Are you a tag line for a TV show?"

"You got me there. Use it in your next pitch."

"I'm not in show business, sir. I'd appreciate your seriousness of this situation."

"I'm a bit punchy after having the barrel of two guns aimed at my chest."

"Trying to be a hero can come with consequences." She kicked one foot in the pavement. "That was brave of you to try to find the killer and save the victims."

"There wasn't much to save."

"You didn't know that. What can you tell me about Ms. Overton and the other victim, Mr. Kristoff?"

"I wasn't familiar with the Kristoff fellow. All I know of Ms. Overton is she was an escort. I'd have thought you'd know this."

"I'm sure vice has a file on her, but there are much bigger fish to fry. Were you a client?"

"Not likely. I'm gay."

"How do you know of her business dealings?"

"I can't say much because I don't know much. One of her clients is someone I'm investigating in the murder of Austin Mooney. His brother, Jared."

"The tennis pro?"

"Most people know him as the son of T.J. Mooney, but yes. That's him."

"I'm a tennis fanatic. Don't care much for movies. You think Jared killed his brother?"

"I don't know who killed his brother. If I did, you'd have known it by now. I said I'm investigating him. Is that all you need to know?"

"No, I need you to tell me step by step what happened here tonight."

"I told the officers three times already."

"Then I'll be kind and only make you tell me twice."

Thirty-Three

Hector Rojas, the ex, hadn't been seen or heard from since I bumped into him on the hill below the Hollywood Sign. For all I knew he wasn't in LA anymore, but I took the chance to hunt him down. I needed more answers from him, as well as seeing what he knew about some of the other suspects. Based on our initial conversation, I didn't expect to find him in West Hollywood Park or any of the main gay district along Santa Monica Boulevard. Since he said he slept near Plummer Park, that was where I focused.

It wasn't long ago that the area around the park was the heart of LA's Russian community, but that was changing. Along the boulevard, most of the shops with Cyrillic lettered signs were replaced by typical chain stores and fast food joints. Behind those shops, however, many Russian and Ukraine immigrants still lived, and Plummer Park was their gathering place for chess and talking politics. I didn't find many homeless looking folks in the park, but there were too many along the streets nearby. I stopped at Target on my way and bought several bags of cheap socks to hand out to as many as I could. A lot of those guys were veterans from the Iraq and Afghanistan wars. Some of their faces were so lifeless, and I wondered if I served next to any of them.

When the socks were gone, I got back in my car and slowly drove back and forth along Santa Monica and the side streets around the park. Occasionally, I'd drive the two miles down to the WeHo central and then back again. It was a lot of waste of time and gas, but I knew of no other way to find him. Each stop I made, most people knew who he was, but hadn't seen him in a while. At 10:00 p.m. I decided to try again the next day in the other popular areas for young homeless in Hollywood and Venice Beach, but that's when I spotted him. He was walking off the Boulevard on to Gardner Street.

When Hector saw me pull up to the curb next to him, he dropped his backpack and ran into the park. I left my car in a red zone and took after him. He was fast, and it looked like he was going to lose me until he rammed directly into a man coming out of one of the meeting centers. They both sprawled on the ground. I pounced and landed directly on Hector. He didn't fight back. The man who'd been knocked down, scrambled up, gave Hector the finger and called him a shithead before limping away.

Hector was on his back with me sitting on his hips and my elbow pressed against his neck. He looked terrified.

I asked, "Are you hungry?"

"Huh?"

"I asked if you were hungry."

"Uh, yeah. I kind of am."

"Stop being afraid of me, get up and I'll grab you a bite to eat. We need to get your stuff before someone steals it."

I found a nearby parking space, we put his bags in my trunk, and we walked to Astro Burger. Still having a model mentality, he got a turkey burger and a side salad while I had a pastrami sandwich with fries. He smelled like a laundry basket full of wet towels, so we sat outside. It was slower than normal, so we only got a few foul looks.

Hector had lost a lot of weight in a short time. His once pretty face had aged: dark circles under his eyes and dry, chapped lips. One knee bounced furiously.

"Why are you being so nice to me, man?" he asked in a rapid-fire delivery.

"I figure this is the only way to get you to talk. Are you still sleeping in the bushes?"

He filled his mouth with a fork-full of lettuce and nodded his head.

"Why don't I make some calls and see if I can get you in a shelter. I doubt I can get you in this late tonight, but maybe for tomorrow."

"I'm not going to no damn shelter to lay in a cot with dozens of men snoring around me. I haven't sunk that low."

I refrained from telling him that sleeping in bushes was about as low as it gets.

He said, "You chased me down for some reason. What do you want?"

"I want to talk more about the *Breakfast at Tiffany's* photo. Do you have it?"

"How many fucking times are people going to ask me that? I'm tired of it. No, I don't have it. I don't even know where Austin kept it."

"I'm asking because a large number of people are certain that you do have it. Why do they think that, other than you need the money?"

"Because Austin struggled for money, too." I couldn't help noticing the inability to keep his eyes focused and the grinding of his teeth. "I kept telling him that if he wasn't going to ask his dad for help that he should sell it. He had no reason to struggle all the time. Both of his parents are rich as fuck, and if he didn't want to ask them then he should have sold that pic."

"Any idea who has it?"

"I don't know. If I had to guess, I'd say Zach Pickering. He's one shady sonofabitch. He was Austin's best friend one minute and was then ready to stab him in the back the next. Even Austin saw it, but he still hung out with him. Their relationship was weird."

"Did you know that Zach's place had been broken into and ransacked?"

"No, but why would I give a damn?"

"You were seen in the area just days before?"

"I'm not allowed to go to Silver Lake? What areas of the goddamn city am I allowed to go to, huh? Besides, I've been spending most of my time on the Rattler Trail."

"The trail?"

"Where they found Austin. Despite everything, I loved him."

"Have you ever heard Austin and Zach talk about that picture?"

"Oh yeah. He tried to buy it from Austin several times. He kept asking for a ridiculous amount of money. Usually five hundred to a thousand, but that thing is worth many thousands of dollars. I'll bet you he has already pawned it off somewhere."

"How well do you know Rachel Roundtree or Jared Mooney?"

"I never met Rachel, but I did meet Jared once. He didn't have much to say to me and looked at me with contempt the whole time."

"Anything more you can tell me."

"Nothing other than Zach is a general asshole."

"How about you and me taking a ride?"

"Where?"

"I can make some calls and find out where the nearest A.A. or Narcotics Anonymous meeting is."

"Nah, I appreciate it, man. That's cool, but I already have plans to go."

"When?"

"Tomorrow." He finished his burger, balled up his wrapper. "Thanks for the eats, but I've got to go. Anything else?"

"That's it. I'll look for you if I need you, but don't run away next time."

Hector gave me a thumbs up, grabbed his pack out of my trunk and headed down Gardner Street. I gave him a good head start then hit the sidewalk to follow. He walked with his head down and at a slow pace. An excruciating slow pace that was hard for me to maintain. I kept having to stop out of fear of getting too close. He took a right on Lexington Avenue and continued the short block to where it ended on Vista Street. I traced him after he turned left and stayed at the intersection to eye where he was going. A few doors down he stopped, looked around him and slunk across a yard to a house.

I practically crawled down the street as to not draw his attention. When I reached the house next door to where he went, I spotted him sliding behind a thick bush. It was exactly as he said.

Thirty-Four

After closing the store promptly at 6:00 p.m. I speeded to the home on Vista Street where Hector Rojas kept his nest in the front shrubbery. Given the time of day, it was a risky venture. I didn't know what time the owners came home from work, and it would be another ninety minutes before sunset. Since Hector refused to take me there himself, I had no other choice.

I parked three doors down from the targeted spot. The neighborhood was an eclectic mix of single-story adobe and mid-century homes. Hector's choice was a yellow mid-century with a large front porch. The type of porch rarely used anymore since people tend to avoid their neighbors. The front lawn was small – just grass. No bushes, trees, or gardens of any kind. The only plants were small ones that ran along the front of the porch and a series of thick large shrubs directly under a front window to the side of the porch. I took a couple of nonchalant glances at the surrounding area before hustling across the yard and diving into what appeared to be Hector's little dug out.

He was right that it was a fine choice for a hideout. The spot was shielded from view from the yard, porch, and the front walk. I had to part the sharp leaves to get a glimpse of the houses across the street. The well shielded hideaway allowed me to relax and catch my breath from the stress of being a snoop.

There wasn't much to see other than an indentation in the ground where it appeared he slept, plus a couple of empty beef jerky bags. As I looked around, I wondered why I had bothered to check his hideout. Knowing he leaves every morning and was protective of his nest, I had no idea what to expect to see or find. I should have known he would leave nothing behind. I circled around on my knees a couple of more times before giving up, but as I was crawling out from the bushes a blue Hyundai pulled into the driveway. An auburn-haired woman in her thirties climbed out of the driver's side and a thin, short, brunette preteen girl came out the other.

"Give me your phone," the woman said.

The child protested, gave what seemed like a fake cry and stomped her feet.

"Helena, I told you if you didn't behave, you'd lose your phone rights for the day. Hand it over, and you can wait out here for Brenda."

The girl remained defiant until she was threatened with grounding. The mother went into the house while little Helena stumped up to the front porch and sat on a bench. I hoped whoever Brenda was that it wouldn't take her long to get there. With nowhere to go, I sat my ass in the dirt and leaned my back against the house. I waited over thirty minutes.

During my time in captivity, I sent my third apology text to Trent for ruining our past weekend together. For the third time he responded with *There's nothing to apologize for.* I thumbed the keys to respond with an *I love you* but thought better of it. No need to confuse the poor man any further. I'd been thinking about our relationship since we returned from our trip. He was either the best thing or the worst thing I needed in my life. It was past time for me to decide which.

It was while my brain was playing roulette that I noticed something strange against the house. Something that should have jumped out and been obvious before. The ground behind the bushes and against the house was nothing but dark black dirt except for a small pile of leaves against the foundation. I scooted my ass over until I was next to them and brushed them aside. Underneath lay a small pile of dirt filling an obvious hole in the ground. It only took a few brushes of my hand to move enough dirt to reveal a gray metal cash box. The kind with a black handle on top.

The box was locked, but those things were ridiculously easy to break open. In less than a minute I opened the lid to reveal—nothing. Whatever it was Hector kept in that box was likely on him at that time. It seemed unlikely the box would still be hidden if he had gotten rid of it. Before closing the lid, I noticed what looked like a tiny scrap of paper stuck in one of the hinges. It was too small for my hand, so I used a locksmith's pick to dig it out. It wasn't paper as I thought. Instead, I held a tiny corner of a photograph. It was solid white, but there was no denying what the material was.

I folded my find in paper and tucked it in my pants' pocket. Five minutes later Helena's friend arrived, and I was able to free myself and jog to my car.

Thirty-Five

My calls to Rachel Roundtree were fruitless. She wasn't answering her cell. I did reach Zach Pickering who said I could come join him at The Big Gay in WeHo. Luckily, he mentioned Rachel was sitting next to him.

The Big Gay is the nickname of the Starbucks that sits on Santa Monica Boulevard in the heart of WeHo. Being across from a 24-Hour Fitness and Trader Joe's made it one of the community's places to be seen, thus earning its moniker. Under normal circumstances, I would have thought its location would add to the 'Zach is gay' rumors but wasn't swayed since the shop is popular with screenwriters and actors. The inside is usually packed with long lines at the register, and the outdoor seating was just as busy, so I didn't think it'd be the best place to try and question two people about a murder. Experience had taught me interrogations are best not done in a coffee house. That concern eased as the two friends were leaving just as I approached.

"We'd given up on you," Zach said smugly. "Took you long enough to get here."

"I was in Silver Lake when I called. Traffic was heavy. Can we go somewhere to sit and talk privately?'

"Not much privacy around here."

"The lobby in the J Hotel down the block should be quiet this time of day. Can we check it out?"

"Do we really have to deal with this shit?" Rachel spoke for the first time. "I've gotten tired of you."

"I'm not too fond of you either, Rhonda."

The two of them stopped, and Rachel's jaw dropped as she clutched Zach's upper arm.

"I thought that'd get your attention. Let's go have a seat." I nodded my head toward the hotel.

The lobby was more upscale than I expected for a small inn. Clean lined, golden fabric chairs were perfectly arranged near long leather couches for easy conversation. The restaurant was busy, but the lobby was nearly empty. Rachel and Zach each grabbed a chair and dragged them closer to me on the couch.

"I'm not going to fuck around with you, Rachel, or Rhonda Ridgeway. You were devastated by your brother's suicide, weren't you?"

"What a shitty thing to ask. Yes, I was beyond devastated. Why is that your business?"

"Because I saw you, Rhonda Ridgeway, on national television. *The Zeb Pullman Bible Hour* to be exact. You did your little gospel thing to the joy of everyone there and at home and then Zeb asked you about your brother."

"So?"

"You blamed Satan for your brother's homosexual acts. You told everyone there he was not gay but had fallen for all the allure of sin and self-indulgence that Hollywood offers. You continued to add that Grant had been seduced and corrupted by a member of one of the elites in the film industry."

"I was young and stupid. My parents told me what to say, and I said it."

"You didn't name Austin, but you blamed him for influencing Grant to behave sinfully against God's law."

She clutched the sides of her chair. She grimaced, and her face flushed. "Stop it!" The front desk clerks and the other two people in the lobby jumped and looked in our direction.

"You think your brother's death is Austin's fault."

"Shut up!"

"Excuse me?" A woman behind the front desk called over.

Zach stood and held up a thumb. "It's all cool. We're getting some unhappy news is all. She's a little shook up." Zach sat. "Look, Mitch, what are you trying to do to her?

How the fuck can you be so cruel to taunt her like this? Why would she blame Austin?"

"He's the one Grant was kissing in those photos. Right near a group of tourists no less."

Rachel continued to clutch the chair. She gritted her teeth while rocking forward and back.

Zach said, "If you've been researching her background, you know what type of parents she has. My God, her mom founded Mothers for Morality, one of the most anti-gay groups in the country. Why is it a surprise that she would act the way she did and say the things she did? She was just a kid."

"Ah, that's where you're wrong," I replied. "Rachel, or Rhonda then, was very much an adult. She was twenty-one years old when Grant killed himself."

"If you're so smart," Rachel butted in, "what happened the next year? Huh? What did I do?"

"You renounced Christianity, founded the Titmice and amazingly had a top hit in your first year. It wasn't very nice of you to abandon them and go solo the next year, by the way. Maybe you'd still be filling auditoriums if you hadn't."

Rachel reached a fist and swung. Lucky for me, Zach caught it before it hit my face.

"Mitch, does any of this really matter? Even if she did blame Austin and wanted to kill him, how the hell would you expect her to get him up that hill?"

"That's where you come in Zach."

Rachel slammed her palms down on the arms of the chair. "I knew he'd get around to this."

"Get around to what?" I asked. "The fact that Zach is a young strapping man who could have carried Austin's body. It would have been a struggle, but you had over eight hours to get there and back. It can be done. It was done."

Zach's unflappable face was starting to crack. "You think I would kill my best friend?"

"I don't know who killed Austin. Maybe you were involved and maybe not, but I do know you're capable of taking care of matters afterword. When did the two of you start dating?"

"Huh?" Zach grumbled. "We started dating when I was a Junior in high school."

"Robbing the cradle, eh?"

"You're a sick man," she said. "Zach was seventeen and I was twenty. That's only a three year difference."

"Three years is a long time at that age, but that's not my point. The fact is, you two didn't hang out in high school like you told me. Rachel, who was Rhonda, came to visit

LA during the summer months too. That's where she met you."

"I lived in Palm Springs," Zach growled.

"You're saying you never came to visit Austin while he was in Bel Air? I seriously doubt that, and I'm sure asking around will easily validate my suspicions." I leaned closer. "Zach, you were furious that Austin got the dream job that you thought was yours. Rachel, your brother died because of being caught with Austin up the hill." I stood. "It seems to me leaving his body below The Hollywood Sign could have been a statement by either, or both of you."

"Fuck you, O'Reilly!" Zach hollered.

A shush and a glare came from the two front desk clerks.

"Listen you two. I don't know that either of you killed Austin. I do know that you both have strong motives. Let's leave it at that for now because without proof either of you were up there, I've got nothing. Let's hope for your sakes it stays that way." I nodded my head. "Goodbye, Zach. Goodbye, Rhonda."

"It's Rachel!" she screeched as I walked toward the exit door.

After what I had put the two of them through, I felt like I needed a shower.

Thirty-Six

I took the Rattler Trail to find Hector. I had driven around his WeHo haunts and had no luck finding him. Since he told me he comes to the trail nearly every day, it was my best bet. A bet that played out.

Hector Rojas was sitting on the hill alone on top of a small boulder. He was picking up pebbles and tossing them out into the ravine while wearing a mournful look on his face. His eyes widened and his hands shook when he saw me.

He stammered, "What are you doing here?"

"Looking for you. What gives?"

"I miss Austin. More than I did before. I've been sober eight days and have nowhere to go or anything to do. Why were you looking for me?"

"We have lots to talk about."

"What?"

"Let's start with me saying, 'fuck you.'"

"What the hell. Fuck you."

"I have a reason to say it. You're not the one who got knocked down the stairs by having a lamp smashed in his face."

"When did that happen to you?"

"You know as well as I do. You were there when it happened. You're the one who did it."

He shot up to his feet. His face was flushed, and his hands clenched. "Why would you accuse me of that?"

"Because I know you're the one who trashed my place. You also trashed Zach Pickering's, and searched Austin's old apartment."

"I did none of that. You're trying to get me arrested?"

"Sit back down. You're okay. I'm still pissed about the lamp in the face, but I'm not filing charges."

"Why the hell do you keep saying I put a lamp in your face?"

"You didn't put a lamp in my face: you smashed my face with it. It hurt like hell."

"But no—"

"You were scared, Hector. You were looking for Austin's Audrey Hepburn photo and you thought I might have taken it from the apartment in Koreatown."

"How would you know if I did?"

"I didn't know at first, but then you trashed Zach's place when you thought he had it. You know he used to hold it for collateral when he loaned Austin money."

"Yeah, I knew he did sometimes. It doesn't mean I thought he had it then. You're making guesses."

"Not guesses. Hunches."

"I'm not answering any questions. I'm going to get a lawyer."

"Relax. Relax. I'm not a cop. I can't arrest you, but I do have this."

I held out my palm with the ripped corner of a photograph.

His eyes looked side to side. "What's that?"

"It's the corner to the Audrey photo. It ripped when you took it out of that metal box. It was jammed in a corner seam."

"That could have been a picture of anything!"

"Sure, it could, but it's from the Audrey pic. Look, you're cool with me. You thought it was in Austin's old apartment and were wrong. You then thought maybe I had it, but you were wrong again."

"How would you know this? You're drawing at straws."

"You were right up to a point. It was a hunch until you broke into Zach's place. That's where you found the picture."

"If I found it there, how would you know?"

"Because Zach doesn't have the Audrey Hepburn picture. Now hand it over."

Hector's hands shook so violently he could barely grasp the zipper in his backpack. He sobbed while he dug around then pulled out a manila envelope with thin cardboard to stiffen each side. He placed it in my hand. The picture was exactly as described. There was Audrey Hepburn, George Peppard, and Blake Edwards having a grand time. The torn corner in my hand fit perfectly.

"I know how much you want to keep this, but it should go to Dominique. She did give it to him."

He pulled his legs tight against his body and wrapped his arms around his knees. He nodded.

"Does everyone think I killed Austin?"

"I don't think you did."

"Why are you so sure?"

"Because I have a good idea who did. I just have to prove it."

Hector and I sat in silence for thirty minutes while I enjoyed the view across the city. It was a windy day, which cleared the smog for a spectacular view.

"Hector," I said as I stood. "You need a ride anywhere?"

"No, I usually stay here until close to sundown. Thank you for believing me."

I proceeded to walk toward the road that led to the path.

"Oh, Hector."

"Yeah?"

"Good job on being eight-days sober."

I took the short hike back to my car. The phone rang as I
was climbing in. It was Harold Beavers.

"I think I'm an idiot," he said frantically.

"I could have told you that a long time ago," I teased.
"How did you make this discovery?"

"It's about that accountant at the nightclub."

"Wesley Stumpf? Don't tell me now he isn't stealing."

"No. He's stealing alright, but based on what you told
me, there may be a timing issue."

"What do you mean?"

"When did you say that kid left the club? When did he
disappear?"

"Wesley guessed it was around 8:00, but the singer
talked to Austin at 8:30."

"How long do you think it would take to kill a man and
hide the body somewhere? Where was the body hidden?"

"I can't answer either of those questions. The body
could have been stashed in a trunk, or a truck. It's an
unknown right now. He was killed by a major blow to the

head. That wouldn't take long if he was hit hard enough.
What are you getting at?"

"It looks like this Wesley guy was working on multiple
files at once. One file shows it was modified at 8:39,
another at 8:50, a third one at 8:56, and the last one at 9:07.
The last file he worked on that night was around 10:00 p.m.
Do those times coincide with any possibility he could have
been the killer?"

"I guess he could have killed Austin between 9:00 and
10:00, but then I'd have to explain a gap. Where Austin
was for over thirty minutes? The last we know of Austin
being alive was a phone conversation at 8:30."

"What do you think that means?"

"I think it means the odds that Wesley killed him are
slim to none. He could have killed Austin at 8:30 and left
the body in his office until after 9:00, but that doesn't seem
likely. The guy is a dork, but not dumb. I can't picture him
dragging the body out of the rear door and into his car
either."

"What does this mean?"

"I think it means I've eliminated one suspect which
leaves me open to notify the owner that he's been stealing."

"How are you going to do that without her knowing you
broke into her files?"

"I've got my thumb drive with the files and the U.S. postal service. All I've got to do is a few clicks on the computer, and I'll have her home address. Once that's done, it's all in her hands.

Thirty-Seven

A week passed since I had sent the accounting packet to Luna Salcedo, but I heard no news of Wesley Stumpf being arrested. Many times, proprietors prefer to handle such matters on their own. Or, perhaps she was looking for more evidence. Either way, my dislike for Wesley had me hope he'd pay for his thievery in some manner.

Josie sent me a text saying she was on the way to the store, but my first obligation was to the customer who just walked in to buy a police whistle.

As the man, dressed in corduroy slid into his Jaguar, Josie squealed up next to him in her Beetle. At her speed I was amazed she didn't drive right through the window, but the car stopped when it rammed the curb.

"Mitch, I got it! I got it!" She screamed as she ran in the door.

"Got what?"

"I was tired of making these damn car rental calls, but I figured I'd give one last try. I called a place in Van Nuys called VNY Rentals and I got it."

"Got what?"

"I told them I was Barbie Bloom, and I thought I'd left a broach that was a family keepsake in their car. I even pulled some sobbing in the act. They checked the date that Barbie rented the car and told me nothing was found. He was very sympathetic."

"And the date was the night of the murder?"

"You bet your ass it was."

"Holy shit, we've got him."

"Are you going to call Detective Castro?"

"No, we still can't prove he drove the car to drop off Austin Bouchard's body."

"How are you going to do that?"

"I'm going to confront him head on. I have more on him than that. Can you watch the store for me?"

"I told the office I'm taking an early lunch. I can't afford more time off."

"Help me close the place. With what Dominique is paying me, it doesn't matter. It's time for me to go on a Jared hunt."

Thirty-Eight

"Who's calling?" said the woman with the cockney accent. I was at the front gate of the Mooney mansion.

"It's Mitch O'Reilly. I'm here to see Jared if he's home."

"Is he expecting you?"

"No, I'm just popping in to see a friend."

"One moment."

Within three minutes the gates swung open, and I pulled my car next to a three-tiered fountain.

"Good afternoon, Mr. O'Reilly," Paul said at the door. "T.J. Mooney is waiting for you in the swimming pool."

"I'm not here to swim, Paul. I'm here to see Jared. Is he home?"

"Indeed, he is, but T.J. asked to speak with you when he heard you were here."

"I'd rather see Jared."

"And T.J. would rather see you first. You may guess where I'll be taking you."

"Let's go."

"He's in the south wing."

"That's where the family room is. The last time I was there things didn't go so well."

"You're in luck. We're going past that to the pool solarium. Before we get there, would you care for a greyhound?"

"No, not thirsty, Paul."

"You know T.J. will insist. I can't make you drink it, but he will ensure you have a drink with him."

"A greyhound will do."

At the end of the hall, in the corner, a pair of French doors led into the solarium. There was a pool, some tropical plants and a round white table for four surrounded by mini palms. It was lush, but small and unassuming compared to the rest of the museum like mansion. T.J. was sitting at the table with a martini in hand. He wore an aqua blue swimsuit and had a lemon green towel wrapped around the back of his neck. His hair was wet, and water dripped from his portly belly.

Paul said, "Mr. O'Reilly requested a drink, Mr. Mooney. I'll have it brought out to him."

"Pull up a seat, Mitch. We need to talk."

"I'm really here to see Jared."

"I said sit. Your visit is what I want to talk about."

To my right out of the glass wall, I could see Jared and another man in the lower yard playing tennis.

"That's Jared's trainer with him. I told him as long as he's living in my house all his training will be here. He's not going to be cavorting with the girls up at the Stone Canyon Tennis Club anymore. He's a natural athlete, and I expect him to take advantage of his gifts for a change. I cut back on his allowance, too. If he wants to live the way he expects then it's time he earned it himself."

"I'm sure he's not happy about that."

"Not happy? He's ecstatic that I'm showing him some interest.

An elderly woman, likely in her eighties walked up. She was hunched, and like the other female servant I'd seen on my last visit, her gray hair was pulled into what looked like an excruciating tight bun. She placed my greyhound on the table.

"Here you go, Mr. O'Reilly."

"I recognize that accent. You're the British woman who answers the front gate."

Without saying a word, she smiled, nodded her head to T.J. and went back into the hall.

"That was Gemma," T.J. said. "She's worked for me for years. I've practically begged her to retire, but she refuses, so I let her do simple things around the home. I believe it makes her feel needed."

"That's mighty nice of you, T.J.," I said sarcastically.

"You say that like it's out of character. I always take care of those who take care of me. I believe I made that clear the first time we met."

"You mentioned it."

"That's why I have you sitting in that chair. I want to know what you're up to?"

"What do you mean?"

"Dominique hired you to find the person who killed my son, and you're hanging out with Jared instead. He mentioned to me you two had drinks together not long ago."

"At his invitation."

"You may be working for Dominique, but I'm not an innocent bystander. Do you understand that?"

"I don't know what you're getting at."

"You questioned Erin, you questioned me, and you questioned Jared. I presume we've told you all we know. I don't want you befriending my son and taking part in his shenanigans."

I started to tell T.J. I was there for business, not pleasure, but I didn't think he'd take that well either.

"I hear you, T.J."

"I don't know why you'd hang out with him anyway. It's not like you're interested in any of those girls who chase him. What are you thinking? He'd buy you a trip on one of those gay cruises or something?"

I laughed. "It's nothing like that, T.J. He's rather charismatic and enjoyable to be around."

"You're saying you have a crush on him."

"No, I'm saying I like him, and that's all. One can't have too many friends."

"One can have too many friends when they're hanging out with them instead of doing the investigation they were hired to do."

"Point taken. Let me go have a few words with him, and then I'll step out of his life."

T.J. slammed his hand on the table causing me to jump. "If the point is taken, you'll leave the house and stop bothering my family unless it involves your case."

"What has you so upset, T.J.?"

He growled, "You've been on this case, and I see no success. I'm going to have a long conversation with Dominique later. I've had enough of you."

"This is a change of character from the last time we met."

"You're being thrown out of my home for a second time, O'Reilly. You need to leave now."

"I'm sorry it has to end this way, T.J."

"Take your sorry ass out of here."

I walked a slow pace out the door and past the glass where T.J. could see me, and then I bolted down the hall to the foyer. I was able to reach Detective Matias Castro. I told him to send some squad cars to the estate. After turning off my phone, I saw Paul was in the sitting room off the foyer where I first met with T.J.

"Don't they ever let you leave this lobby?"

"Mr. Mooney insists I remain stationed here whenever we have guests. He wants to ensure I open the door and bid them a farewell."

"Look, Paul, all hell is going to break lose around here."

"What on earth? What do you want?"

"Just stay here and out of my way."

Thirty-Nine

I didn't leave the estate. I walked out an arched doorway in the back of the foyer and followed a pathway down the steps to the lower yard. Jared was alone on the tennis court hitting balls being shot from a launcher. They were going fast, from all directions, and he didn't miss a one.

"Mitch, what are you doing here?" he asked.

"I just came by to chat."

"Not more questions about the investigation, I hope. You've got everything out of me."

"Where'd your trainer go?"

"We were done for the day. He ordered me to do this for at least another thirty-minutes. I'm exhausted."

Jared continued to play against the machine.

"Why don't you stop, and we'll talk?"

"If my dad sees that, he'd kick my ass. He's putting the screws on me these days."

"So, I've heard."

"Anything in particular you want to talk about?"

"Yes, I want to talk about Barbie."

He missed the next two balls.

"You mean the doll?" he asked. "You should talk with Erin. She had a collection of them."

"You know I mean Barbie Bloom."

He stopped and turned toward me. A ball hit him in the waist. "Shit! Let me turn that thing off.

Jared jumped across the net and turned the machine off. He wiped his brow with a towel and walked back to the net without crossing it, staying on the opposite side.

"Whose Barbie Bloom?" he asked.

"You know Barbie, but you called her Gretchen."

"Gretchen's name is Barbie? I guess it's no surprise she'd use an alias. Isn't it sad what happened to her? I think coming upon a dangerous trick is what makes that a risky profession."

"Awfully convenient that she was murdered while I knew you were sitting at a bar."

"You're implying?"

"How much did you pay her, Jared?"

"How much money exchanged between Gretchen and me is none of your business. Let's just say she was way out of your league."

"I don't mean how much you paid her for sex. How much did you pay her to rent a car for you? To cover your ass for the night?"

"Rented a car? I don't know anything about a car rental. This has nothing to do with me."

"It has everything to do with you because it's the car you used to drive Austin's body up to the Hollywood Hills."

He swatted his racket across the front of him, in my direction. "You're accusing me of killing my half-brother? My brother? You're crazy."

"Explain why Barbie, or Gretchen, would rent a car that afternoon and then you not being in the hotel cabana that night."

"I was in the cabana, you idiot."

"She rented a car that day but said you picked her up to take her to the hotel. That makes no sense."

"This whole car rental business is circumstantial at best. It's laughable. That and me being in the cabana makes your hypothesis absurd."

"But you weren't in the cabana. Gretchen signed for the room service bill."

"Because I was in the shower."

"Look, Jared, I know what happened that night. On Tuesday when you and Austin had dinner, he told you about his plan to sneak out the back door of the club to ditch me. That is when you saw your opportunity. You arranged for Gretchen to rent a car in an out of the way place. She met you at the cabana, and you snuck off in her car, which I'm guessing she parked on the street."

"See, you're guessing."

"That area behind the club near the rear entrance is small. There is an alleyway and a place to park four cars. It's where the accountant and the club owner park, and you were lucky that only one of the two was there. You surprised Austin when you showed up out of the blue."

He flushed and bounced his racket off his knee. "And I killed him?"

"That's exactly what you did. You took an object. Probably a tire iron and beat him in the head. Probably only took one or two strokes."

"Now you're getting gross."

"While you were busy doing that, Gretchen was stuffing herself with two servings of lobster. Or, to keep her figure she may have stuffed some down the toilet. Your mistake was not telling her what to order for you while you pretended to be in the shower."

"What do you mean?"

"Seafood. At the tennis club you said you didn't want seafood. You said you're allergic to it."

"O'Reilly! What the hell are you doing here?" T.J. yelled from behind.

I turned and caught T.J. coming from the house when a sharp blow hit the back of my shoulder. Jared had thrown a tennis racket at me. I turned, drawing my gun in the process.

Smack! A ball hit me in the forehead forcing me to step back several feet. I pulled the gun higher.

Smack! A stinging pain caused me to gag as a ball hit straight into my Adam's apple. I released my gun as I grasped at my neck.

Still clutching my throat, I bent down to grab my gun.

"Jared!" I heard T.J. yell from behind.

Jared had jumped the net and hit me square in the forehead with his racket, knocking me backwards to the ground. Jared ran up, knelt, put one knee on my chest, and pushed his racket down on my neck. I grabbed the edges of it to keep it from breaking my windpipe. Just as I was about to lose my grip, I heard T.J. holler one last time.

"Jared, stop it, now! It's over. Get up."

T.J.'s son got up as he was told, but not before swiping his racket into my face again. I felt my nose crush.

"I got a call," T.J. said. "The police are on their way. What do you think if they found Mitch lying dead on the court?"

Jared turned and threw his racket into the garden like a child throwing a temper tantrum.

"It's over, son. I'll make sure you get out of this. It will be okay."

"What about Gretchen," Jared said. "I'm not taking the fall for that. If I'm going down, then you're going down."

T.J.'s eyes darted toward me. "I don't know what you mean, son." He grabbed Jared's arm and pulled him away from earshot. Despite them shouting, I couldn't make out anything being said.

I was so focused on T.J. and Jared that I didn't hear Paul walk up from behind. He helped me to my feet. "Would you care to finish your greyhound before things get busy around here…Mitch?"

"You brought me two?"

"No, I made one for myself. I need one now that I'm out of a job."

We clicked glasses.

"I best get back to the house," Paul said. "Gemma may be too startled to open the gates. I'd hate for the police to have to climb the walls.

"Paul," I said before he turned around. "At least we know the butler didn't do it."

He chuckled and headed up the steps to the house. The sound of sirens came up the block.

Forty

Dominique had spent an hour at Eye Spy Supplies to discuss the case with me. Her eyes darted from the black and blue marks on my face and neck to my bandaged nose. She gave a sorrowful look but didn't speak up until she was ready to leave.

"Mitch, you look terrible." She put a hand to her lips. "I'm sorry. That was rude."

"No offense taken. You're right."

"I wanted to bring your check personally and offer my gratitude. I never expected this to be the tangled mess it is. I never knew Jared had such contempt for Austin, though I understand his bitterness toward T.J. The man always favored what he couldn't have, and that's why Austin could do no wrong in his eyes."

"Kind of a Cain and Able situation, I guess."

"More like the Prodigal Son."

"I'm sure I'd agree if I knew what you meant."

"Just another Bible story," she said.

"It appears T.J. trying to get Austin to move into the Bel Air estate, while insisting Jared move out was too much for Jared. It was his last straw."

"My son was killed in a jealous rage." She grabbed a tissue to wipe her tears. "I'm sorry, but I can't stay. LA feels dirty to me now, and I want to go home to Palm Springs. I respect you, Mitch, and I wish you the best. It was important for me to let you know. You'll see there's a substantial bonus on the check to show my gratitude."

I had to fight to keep from opening the check, but I held back as I escorted Dominique to her car. We talked briefly about Hector, and she handed me an envelope to give him. When I was back in the store, I opened the pay envelope and yelled "Hot damn!" to no one there. My exhilaration only lasted a moment. Trent pulled his Jeep up to the curb. He strolled in wistfully.

"Hey, Mitch," Trent said before giving me a kiss on the cheek. "I know I'm supposed to meet you at your place tonight, but Ada asked me to work at the restaurant."

"Bad timing," I replied. "I want to have a talk, but not here."

He reached behind the counter and grabbed my *Out to Lunch* sign, placed it on the window, and locked the door.

"It's okay. I understand. I've given you your space, but now you want to make it official. We're going to break up."

"Don't put it like that…"

He grabbed each of my shoulders and looked me in the eyes. He whispered, "It's okay."

"Can I explain?"

"Of course, if it makes it easier for you."

"I've done the things I needed to do. I went back to my support group Saturday morning, I have an appointment with a psychiatrist tomorrow, and with a therapist next week. You can't know how hard that is for me."

"I do know, and I can't express how proud of you I am. I'm also proud that you've decided we should go our separate ways."

"Excuse me?"

"You see, I had a buddy in college named Joel. Joel was the type of guy who struggled a lot expressing his feelings, but—"

"Does Joel's story have anything to do with what's happening here between us?"

"It kind of does, but it's not important. What's important is that I let you know, despite the words coming out of my mouth, this isn't easy. It hurts like hell, and it will for some time, but that doesn't mean I don't think you're doing the right thing. There's nothing I want more than for you to get well. I love you, and that's the best way I know to show it."

"I do wish things could be different. I wish I could live a normal life."

"I don't know what normal is, but I'm sure the things you do will make it better. That's what's important. Perhaps down the road we can try it again sometime."

"Are you suggesting we'll still stay on a break? I don't think that's a good idea."

"That's not what you want. It needs to be a clean break, so you have nothing to focus on but getting better. I'm simply suggesting that you never know what's going to happen in the future."

"You're right. You never do."

Trent and I wrapped our arms around each other for over a minute. I rested my head on his shoulder and loved how warm and comfortable it made me feel. After too long of an embrace, we gave each other a quick peck on the lips.

"Thank you for understanding. I'm going to miss you."

"LA is a small town. We'll see each other around."

"You're probably right, and I look forward to it. I love the way you make me laugh."

We gave each other one last quick hug, and Trent walked out the door. I felt empty. I had learned from Harold that the best way to overcome that emptiness is to help someone else. I knew someone who needed help and I planned to see them the next day.

Forty-One

I was in good spirits the next morning after receiving a call from Detective Matias Castro. He came across as bitter that I solved the case on my own but was kind enough to tell me Luna Salcedo filed charges against her friend Wesley Stumpf.

"The auditors say he's been stealing from her for years," the detective said. "It doesn't look good. He'll be serving some time."

That was most of what Castro told me. It was a short conversation while I was driving to the hills. I was on a mission.

As expected, I found Hector Rojas sitting below the Hollywood sign. There were dark circles under his bloodshot eyes. He was picking at the skin on his arm.

"You started using again," I said as I approached. I sat on a rock next to the one he was on. "How long ago was your last hit?"

"I got strung out yesterday."

"Sorry to hear it, but you'll end up okay."

"What makes you so sure?"

"Because despite how fucked up your life is, you're a fighter."

"What makes you say that?"

"Because deep down everyone is. Look how low you've gone, and you're still here."

"I think that's supposed to be a compliment."

"As good as you'll get."

"Everything is pretty fucked up with the Mooney's, huh?"

"The tabloids are all over it. Nothing they love more than reporting on fallen icons."

"What do you think is going to happen to Jared Mooney…and T.J.?"

"I think there's enough to convict Jared. He'll likely get sentenced fifteen years to life, which means he'll be out on parole in seven or eight years."

"Seven or eight years?"

"As for T.J., I doubt he pulled the trigger, and they may never find the person he hired to kill that escort. He may not even go to trial."

"Holy shit. That's really fucked up."

"Welcome to the life of the rich and famous."

"And white."

"Yeah, that too."

We stared out to the valley below us. It was a clear day and the sun reflected off the buildings in Hollywood.

"I have a gift for you." I held out Austin Bouchard's picture of Audrey Hepburn and friends.

"I thought you were giving that to Dominique."

"Dominique says it yours, but with a stipulation."

"What do you mean?"

"She wants me to give it to you when you think you're ready for it."

"When is that? It was so important to Austin that I'd die to have it."

"You don't have to die, but I figure getting one year of sobriety is a good start."

"You're going to bribe me to get clean?"

"Not a bribe. It's about me, not you. It's about when I think you're ready. It may take more than a year."

"I'll start going tomorrow."

"Nope. Right now, you're going down the hill with me, so I can take you to an A.A. meeting. I have a psychiatrist appointment, and I'm going to drop you somewhere along the way." I gritted my teeth for letting the word slip out of my mouth.

"A psychiatrist?"

"I got my own problems. After I drop you off, you're on your own. Once you take a one-year chip, we talk."

"I don't think I can make it a year, Mitch."

"You don't have to. You've been clean for twenty-four hours. Now you only have to worry about the next twenty-four."

"Yeah, yeah, one day at a time."

We rose and dusted ourselves off.

"Oh, there's one more thing."

"What's that?"

"The photo will be in a safe deposit box, so there's no reason for you to smash me in the face with a lamp again.

While it's fresh on your mind, please take a

moment to leave a review for A Body on the Hill.

It'd be greatly appreciated.

Review on Amazon

https://www.amazon.com/author/bradshreve

Review on Goodreads

https://www.goodreads.com/bradshreve

Also by Brad Shreve:

A Body in a Bathhouse

For news and releases, sign up for
Brad's Monthly Newsletter at

https://www.bradshreve.com/signup

About the Author

After growing up in Michigan and North Carolina, Brad crisscrossed the country working in the hotel industry. In addition to working as a bellman, front desk clerk, and reservation call center director, he managed coffee houses, waited tables, sold potato chips off a truck, and even hawked pre-burial funeral plans.

He credits *Where the Wild Things Are* by Maurice Sendak for developing his interest in art and storytelling. He'd spend hours on the floor sketching and painting and writing stories. *My Side of the Mountain* by Jean Craighead George gave him his first inkling that he'd like to be a novelist someday.

He developed his love of mysteries from Lawrence Block and Sue Grafton.

He's a proud dad, beach bum, and coffee house squatter.

He currently lives in the South Bay of Los Angeles with his husband, Maurice.

https://www.bradshreve.com

WWW.STUDS4STUDS.COM